Didn't Expect You

USA TODAY BESTSELLING AUTHOR
CLAUDIA BURGOA

Sign up for my newsletter *to receive updates about upcoming books and exclusive excerpts.*

www.claudiayburgoa.com

Also By Claudia Burgoa

The Baker's Creek Billionaire Brothers Series

The Baker's Creek Billionaire Brothers Series

Loved You Once

A Moment Like You

Defying Our Forever

Call You Mine

As We Are

Yours to Keep

Against All Odds Series

Wrong Text, Right Love

Didn't Expect You

Second Chance Sinners

Pieces of Us

Somehow Finding Us

Standalones

Us After You

Almost Perfect

Once Upon a Holiday

Someday, Somehow

Chasing Fireflies

Something Like Hate

Then He Happened

Maybe Later

My One Despair

My One Regret

Found

Fervent

Flawed

Until I Fall

Finding My Reason

Christmas in Kentbury

Chaotic Love Duet

Begin with You

Back to You

Unexpected Series

Uncharted

Uncut

Undefeated

Unlike Any Other

Decker the Halls

To Patricia, thank you for all your support and love.

"Love is like a beautiful flower which I may not touch, but whose fragrance makes the garden a place of delight just the same." —Helen Keller

ONE

Nyx

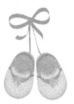

ALL MY ADULT life I've been fighting to be somewhat normal. To be the most conventional one in the family—or the only one for that matter.

My parents are...different. My three siblings... Well, they aren't like our parents, but they stand out easily in any crowd. Not me. Or at least I try to stay away from people's radars, unlike them.

While we were growing up, my parents believed we could learn more from the world than in a classroom. Were they right?

The jury is still out deliberating.

One thing I can say is that my dad is one of the wisest, most clueless men in the world. I understand how ambiguous that sounds, but my father isn't like any conventional sixty-three-year-old guy. Octavio Brassard is unique among any men. He lives by his own rules and has a license to teach young adults about ancient civilizations.

According to Dad, we're here to learn how to love, how to live, and how to preserve this world. Not that we, the human race, are doing a great job at any of those things. He insists that the most important moments in our life happen unexpectedly. That's why we have to stop and smell the roses. Maybe one of those special moments is the one that transforms our lives.

In that split second, we could find our destiny.

He's a philosopher, a poet, and one of the most loving people I know. He pushes us, his children and students, to believe in ourselves and always pursue our dreams. Take life by the balls. And no, my father doesn't believe in censoring our language.

Something else I learned from my parents is that family comes before anything and everyone.

This is why I'm spending my weekend working with my oldest brother, Eros, who like my father, is a dreamer. He doesn't like to think much about the bottom line, rather what he can do to change the world.

"I could be with Persy drinking margaritas," I protest, as I go through the partnership proposal he received from LNC Investments.

I could spend my time with my sister, who I haven't seen that much during the past couple of months.

"Persy is actually drinking some strawberry lager Dad made," he corrects me. "It tastes like fruity shit."

I glare at him. "I like fruity shit."

"Fruity doesn't mean refined," he informs me. "You two need to learn to drink better brands and less sugar."

Sighing, I finish reading the contract. We're never going to agree on the subject. He thinks spending a thousand dollars on a bottle of single malt is better than drinking margaritas. We'll have to agree to disagree.

"Listen, you shouldn't be signing this," I suggest. "Persy and I will amend her book deal and—"

"It's going to take me years to recover her investment," he interrupts me. "These guys don't need the money right away. She does."

He is right. Our sister lent him her savings. The amount included the advance she received from Blackstone and Morgan Press, the publishing company that bought the rights to her next book. A book she doesn't want to write because it's off-brand and forcing her to divulge more about her life on social media than she usually does. I'm trying to fix her current contract so she can change the title and the subject. But if we can't come to an agreement, she'll have to give the money back so I can terminate the contract.

I sigh.

"Thirty-five percent is a lot," I say, changing the argument as I continue reading through the partnership proposal. "We need to negotiate the terms before you sign anything. I understand that they are practically financing the entire operation, but..."

I pull out a calculator and run some numbers. "You're not earning any money for at least five years. Where are you supposed to live and what are you going to eat?"

"Funny that you mention this," he says, giving me his boyish grin. "You have an extra room in your house."

"No!" I answer with determination.

I have two guest rooms. I love my siblings, but I can only stand living with them for so long. Just earlier this year, Persy stayed with me for almost six months and even when we had fun, we both concur that we needed our own place. We're too old to have roommates. I can't imagine what it'd be like to live with Eros for five years—or until he gets his shit together. I'm going to become his maid, parent, and... No, thank you.

"Nyx, at least let me explain my plan to you." His pleading voice doesn't change my mind. In fact, I cross my arms. "I sell my place—"

"You have two mortgages on that house. You owe more than you'll get for it. You have to be sensible about your finances," I remind him, shaking my head. "Why do I always have to sound like the oldest one in this family?"

He shrugs. "You always liked to boss me around while we were growing up. Show that you were responsible. It's your thing. Just like Persy likes to analyze people. I watch over you three."

He's right. That's been our dynamic since we were kids. It might have to do with the way we were raised. Our baby sister, Calliope, doesn't fit in this dynamic, and maybe that's why she doesn't like us so much.

"No, we're going to go back to these Chadwick brothers and we're going to cut you a deal that will be beneficial for everyone," I state. "Do we have an understanding?"

He salutes me. "You're the boss."

THERE'S this idea that the person we become is partly defined by the order in which we come into our family. It's part of the sibling hierarchy. The oldest becomes the teacher to the rest of the siblings. Whoever established that theory didn't know the Brassard siblings. We are four, one brother and three sisters. Eros is the oldest. I'm the second out of four. Then comes my sister, Persy, and Calliope is the baby.

In theory, Eros should be our teacher. The one who takes care of us. Most days I'm the one who is rescuing everyone and saving them from not fucking up their lives. Maybe it has to do with my parents' philosophy. They believe that making mistakes is what forges our character. I keep telling them that there are mistakes, and then there are times when people should avoid failing. Letting others commit errors so you can learn isn't always smart. What if it's something that can bankrupt us, get us thrown in jail, or kill us?

Earlier today it was my brother. Thankfully, I was able to change the original partnership he was about to sign, and he got to save his home.

More like, I won't be having him as a roommate, and we won't end up killing each other because he's a slob.

Now, I'm on my way to talk some sense into Calliope. Most days I'm thankful for Persy. She's not only the most down to earth of my siblings, but she's also my best friend. Maybe the whole theory about birth order has some truth to it. She's only ten months younger than me. We have a connection like not many do. We understand each other, and sometimes we even guess how the other one is feeling.

As I'm about to ring the doorbell to the apartment complex where Callie lives, there's a person coming out who lets me in and even smiles. I blink a couple of times and shrug. What happened to security? I climb the stairs to the fourth story and knock on the door.

A male voice answers, "In a minute."

Not sure if the guy understands how long a minute is because only two seconds later the door opens. It's a tallish guy. By tallish I mean under six feet, lanky, and in a dire need of a trim. No, I don't have anything against guys who have long hair. There are some that look hotter with a mane. This guy though, he needs...a shower, a brush, and clean clothes.

"We didn't order take out," he says.

"I'm here to see Calliope, my sister," I inform him.

"Cal?" he asks and studies me. "You kind of look like her, but uptight."

"Is she here?"

"No, she moved out a week ago," he states.

"Who are you?"

"Ron," he answers. "I'm subleasing this place."

Subleasing the place? I'm blown away by those three words. She's not allowed to do that. Did he even sign a contract? Because I don't remember signing one where I agreed to let this man live in this apartment. I take a deep breath and ask calmly, "Did she leave you a forwarding address?"

He shakes his head. "No. You should talk to your sister, not me."

I hate to agree with him, but there's nothing I can say to him that'll make this right. Other than kicking him out of the place because technically he is living here without my consent.

"Thank you, I appreciate your time," I say and leave.

On my way to the car, I dial Callie's number. She sends me to voicemail, so I try again, again, and again until she finally answers, "What do you want?"

"Where are you?"

"Far away from you," she states.

Why do you always have to answer like a petulant fifteen-year-old? I want to protest, but I don't. Instead, I say, "I take it you made the decision to move out of the state. Did it occur to you to tell us about it?"

"As I said the last time we spoke, I'm done with your meddling," she comments. "In fact, I'm done with you. Lose my number."

"Well then, when will you be sending me the money I loaned you to buy your car and the deposit to rent the apartment where this Ron character lives?" I question. "Furthermore, this apartment is under my name too, and I didn't sign any agreement to sublease the place to him. My name is on that leasing contract."

"If I were Persy, you would've helped me move. Instead, you're demanding money that I don't have," she argues. "It's a verbal contract which should be binding. He is good for it. Don't worry about what can happen to your precious name."

I sigh. "That argument is so old it doesn't have the same effect. Calliope, our parents are going to be heartbroken and worried if you don't tell them where you are. At least give them a courtesy call."

"They are the reason I'm running away from this family. Have you realized that they aren't normal? They embarrass us. While growing up, I could never bring friends to the house because I never knew what they would do," she explains. "Please, don't tell me you aren't ashamed of them. How many times have you brought a boyfriend to the house? None, because you know it's horrifying to introduce them to Octavio and Edna Brassard. And then, there's Persephone. *She's a famous sexologist.*"

Our parents are unique. Yes, they can be a handful and we have to control their narrative sometimes. However, I'll take those two above many other parents who are abusive, neglectful, or plain. Persy is an influencer, a therapist, and yes, she markets herself as a sexologist. There's nothing wrong with her career. I'd be concerned if she was a criminal.

"We never had normal," she continues, and I laugh. "Stop laughing at me!"

I clear my throat and say, "I laugh because you're not making sense. You sound like a petulant child having a tantrum because you're not getting your way."

"You never take me seriously, Nyx. You think you are the smartest one of us. Just because you have a fancy office, a nice house, and a luxury car, you think that you are better than us. You are not!"

"Callie, stop while you're ahead," I warn her.

"You're upset because I'm telling you the truth. And the truth always hurts. You're pathetic, Nyx. Your life is fucking sad. Just boring and plain like you."

She's not wrong about being boring or having a life. I'm nothing like Persy or her. One thing I hate about my baby sister is that when she strikes, she hits where it hurts the most.

"Listen, Callie, we love you even when you're rude to us because you are our little sister. I stopped liking you a long time ago. You became this entitled woman that I can't stand, and you know what... I'm done being the one trying to keep this family together," I say. "Not only that, I'm done with you. If you want to play martyr and tell the world that you escaped your crazy family, that's up to you. Just don't come back groveling for money."

I hang up and fire up a text to Persy.

Nyx: *What are you up to?*

Persy: *I'm hanging out with Ford. Need me?*

Nyx: *No, I wanted to gossip about your hot grumpy neighbor. I guess we'll have to do it another time.*

Persy: *Liar. What's happening?*

I smile because she knows me too well.

Nyx: *Nothing important, I swear. Talk to you soon.*

Persy: *Love you, Nyx.*
Nyx: *Love you, Pers.*

As much as I would love to tell her what is happening with Callie, I don't do it. One of these days, I'll give her the Spark Notes. I just wish I had someone in my life who was there for me when I feel like the weight on my shoulders is too heavy to carry. Maybe I just have to dump it in some abandoned alley and be done with everyone.

I drive back to my house where I place my leftovers in the refrigerator and put on my pajamas. Instead of turning on the television to find some numbing tv show to watch, I pull out my tablet from my messenger bag and start working on my next case.

Callie isn't wrong. I don't have a life. Boring... I don't think I'm boring. I just don't have time to let my hair loose and just live for pleasure. I should add that to my to-do list. Maybe at the bottom of it. One day I'll get to it.

TWO

Nate

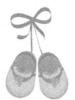

THE PRINCIPAL of my high school always said, "In every situation at least ask five questions. What, when, who, where, and why." He insisted that we have to ask at least a hundred questions a day to show that we're indeed thinking. I don't think I do that, but I never settle with what I'm told. I'm an inquisitive man.

If anyone has a complaint about it, they should take it to Mr. Richardson—may he rest in peace. He was smart and funny sometimes. We had a cool relationship. I guess we grew closer since I visited his office at least once a day, if not twice, until I graduated. I learned a lot about life from him. A lot more than I did from my own father.

Mr. Richardson always had something wise to say.

My favorites, and the ones I still follow are: Never be afraid to try. This is life and there are no do-overs. Honor your word and always be kind. But my mantra is, don't worry about what others think of you, but be responsible for your actions. Many think I take my life for granted, that I'm the irresponsible, adrenaline junky playboy, Nathaniel Chadwick.

I don't deny that I have fun racing cars, skydiving, or ziplining, among other fun activities. There's the occasional rafting through wild rivers. Everything I do, I do it as responsibly as it can be.

Am I a playboy? I'm sure there's an ample definition in the dictionary describing me or any man like me as a rich manwhore. A few years back I partied a lot and slept my way through every woman who crossed my path when I was horny. Which happened to be often. Not anymore though. I'm a few days shy of thirty-five, and these days I'm more selective of who I invite to play with me.

Make no mistake, I still have playmates, but they are fewer, and I hookup less frequently than I used to. Pretty faces aren't my requirement. I need a woman who challenges me physically and intellectually. Those women are like hidden gems. They are so hard to find that these days I don't have time to bother.

Maybe that's why I have more time to worry about my brother's personal life. He's a few seconds from fucking up his life. Since I'm the one who cleans up his messes, I'm trying to be proactive and avoid any mishaps. That's why I had to jump on a plane from Seattle to New York. He met a woman who has turned his life upside down and lately he's not using his brain.

Love is making him act like a fool.

One of us is usually the voice of reason, and when it comes to relationships it always has to be me. He's too...detached. Learning that some hottie who is the total opposite of him has unthawed his frozen heart is surprising. What's more surprising is that he willingly jumped on a plane to New York because she needs to fix her life. My brother avoids big cities, journalists, and influencers.

She's a fucking influencer.

These days he's behaving like a moth towards the bright light. Persephone Brassard is the blaze blinding his common sense. If I don't stop him, she's going to hurt him, probably kill him, but he doesn't give a shit. I should make him pay for fucking with my schedule.

Why do I have to be the one behaving like a responsible adult? Maybe because we didn't have a good role model growing up.

I wish my father had a few wise tokens to share with us. Langford, my twin brother, and I could have used a little more guidance about life and fewer golf lessons from him. At my age, I understand Dad is clueless. My grandparents sheltered him from the world and he's not in touch with reality. It might've not affected him directly, but that fucked us, his children.

Well, we're not just fucked because of the way my grandparents raised him, but also because of his divorce. That was a nasty affair. Mom hated that everyone knew her as Mrs. Chadwick or the mother of the terror twins. She lost her identity, and when she came to her senses, she walked out on us. I'm not sure if she hated us too, but maybe she did and that's why she left without saying goodbye. Even if Ford and I are twins, I tried to shelter him from what was happening. He's always been the more apprehensive of the two of us.

Needless to say, I've had a big attitude since I was six. Teachers hated it, and my peers feared me. I take no shit from others. I did learn how to channel it and use it to my advantage though.

Mr. Richardson used to say, "Mr. Chadwick, I'm not asking you to change. I want you to learn when and where to push those boundaries. You know why your twin brother is in college and you're not?"

Ford skipped a couple of grades. I love my brother. He's my best friend. However, we're very different and I hated it when they compared us. Our IQs are similar, but my attention span when I don't give a shit about a subject is microscopic, unlike his.

Ford can sit in one place for hours to solve a problem. I, on the other hand, find someone to do it for me. Usually him, while I move onto something that's a lot more fun. No, I didn't mooch from him. We have different strengths and interests. We always help each other with what the other needs. That's why at almost thirty-five we are still a fucking great A team.

He might've been ahead in school, but I caught up and we started our own company, LNCWare. I'm the president of the company and handle all the deals, but he's the brains. Without his products, I wouldn't be in the tech business. We'd probably just be doing something else, but we'd be the number one at it.

He doesn't do well with people which is why he chooses to lay low. His current hiding spot is in Denver, Colorado. I live between Seattle and New York, overseeing LNCWare and its subsidiaries. Trying to drag him to either office is almost impossible. He shows his face once in a blue moon. I'm still surprised he traveled to New York, and that he agreed to stick around at least until Friday.

This is what love does to people. We stop thinking and do crazy, stupid things. Which is why I have to be the one asking the questions, what, who, why, when, and how for him. Because I could bet my left nut that he's thinking with his dick—or worse, with his heart.

I could stay in Seattle and just let him handle himself in Manhattan, but I have to make sure this woman is not using him.

When I arrive at the penthouse, Demetri, my house manager, greets me as the elevator doors open at the foyer. "Mr. Chadwick, it's good to see you."

"Hey, D," I greet him. "Where is he?"

"Your brother is in the library, sir. Everything you ordered arrived a couple of hours ago. The guest rooms are ready too," he answers and looks at Brock, my Wheaten Terrier. "Do you require me to walk him?"

Brock barks and I laugh because this guy understands more than people want to believe. "You said the *w* word." Handing Demetri the leash, I reply, "Of course he wants you to take him along the park. I'll be in the office. Is he alone?"

"Yes," he replies.

"Thank you, D," I say, walking down the hall to the library where I spot the one and only Langford Chadwick sitting at my desk.

He is wearing one of my favorite suits. The fucker couldn't bother to bring his own clothes. At least he shaved.

"Look at you, showered and looking like a respectable man. You even look like me," I joke as I enter the library.

He grins, standing up and saying, "I wonder why that is, asshole."

He hugs me and I pat his back. Even though we're identical twins, there are a few differences between us. I'm an inch taller, my skin is a shade darker, and my eyes have a hint of gray with the sunlight.

"Where's your mutt?" he asks, his eyes grow slightly wide. "You just came for a day, didn't you? You're going to leave me here to fend for myself until Friday."

I shake my head. "He went on a walk with Dimitri," I inform him.

"I'm glad Persy didn't bring Simon," he states, and I growl at him on behalf of Brock who's not a fan of the feline.

The last time we went to visit Ford, he let the cat into the house and that creature kept taunting my poor guy.

"Where is she?" I ask.

"She's with her publisher," he answers, checking his watch and then glancing at me. "Look, I know you want me to go to the office, but would you mind if we do it tomorrow? I need to know what happened with her book deal."

His request annoys the fuck out of me. Sighing, I walk to my computer, switch the username to mine, and pull up the NDA contract so I can print it.

"I wish we had planned this visit," I confess, turning to the printer and grabbing the papers. "Listen, before we discuss the next three days at the office, let's go through the NDA. It'll be nice if she could sign it today before things go any further."

Ford and I tell each other everything. I know he hasn't professed his love to her, but I also know he will be doing so within the next hour or whenever she comes back to the house. If I can get ahead of the game, I'll be able to sleep peacefully tonight.

"No," he barks.

"Ford, I get it you're in love but—"

"Stop, Nate." He lifts a hand, showing me his palm as if he's stopping traffic. "What Persy and I have is special, and I don't want to treat it like some kind of business transaction. I understand your hesitation and I appreciate your concern."

"She's a fucking influencer, Ford," I remind him as my pulse elevates and my throat dries from the rush of breathing. "You can't possibly believe that your picture won't be on her social media feed the moment you kiss her. This will help you prevent it."

"I trust her blindly," he declares, and I feel like he punched me in the gut. Which is when he amends, "You're my twin, but she's my soulmate. I understand why you're asking me to do this, but she needs to know that I trust her with my life."

Is she taking my place?

This is it. We're still brothers, but he has someone who'll come before me. And I know him well enough to understand that no matter what I say, he won't make her sign shit. He's never been like this—in love.

What am I supposed to do now?

I could remind him that being in love doesn't guarantee happiness. Having someone to trust doesn't mean that she's trustworthy. Feelings have an expiration date. We lived it with our parents' marriage. I lived it with... It's not worth the trouble to even remember my past.

Should I just let this one play out on its own?

This kind of flight doesn't include a parachute and it should always include a partner. We jump and hope that the other person will hold onto us. That we'll glide together until the end of time, or forever, if that exists.

More times than not, that's not what happens. One person always leaves or doesn't even jump, and we don't realize it until it's too late. I'll have to wait close by then. When he falls to the ground, I'll be there to pick him up and salvage what's left of his life from the wreckage.

Poor Langford Chadwick, he's about to smash his head against the concrete. I wonder if his heart will survive. In most cases, hearts shatter and it's impossible to put them back together. I speak from experience.

This is almost like looking at a teenager about to crash his first motorcycle against a parked car. We can't take our eyes away from the disaster. We can't prevent it. Most of all, we know the damage is going to cause internal bleeding. However, the only way to learn how to drive or in this case, have a relationship, is by getting fucked for the first time.

"You don't approve," he confirms, his eyes stare at me pleadingly. He needs me to drop the subject and just support him.

"I'll be here," I offer.

"Thank you, though you don't sound thrilled about it," he answers. "I thought your motto is, 'Don't hesitate to explore.'"

"This isn't exploring. This is diving into a ditch. You should learn from my experience. Been there, done that. I have the freaking T-shirt, the fucking pictures, and the shards from the wreckage as a souvenir," I remind him.

"Try therapy, it might be worth it. Persy has a book on how to cope with a loss and renew your faith in life," he argues, not sure if he's upset that I'm fucking jaded for the rest of my life or because I'm trying to convince him to stay away from what will be the most catastrophic chapter in his life. "It's been a long time since it happened."

"Five years, but who's counting?" I answer with a shrug. "Since you're a stubborn son of a bitch, let's get to work before I get fucking mad. We're having a conference call instead of a meeting at the office. I anticipated that you'd be with *her*. Afterward, I have a few meetings at headquarters. We can discuss the rest tomorrow morning and make plans for what's to come for the rest of the week."

I dial the number and forget the memories about my shitty love story. He can have his happy bliss for now. We'll drown his sorrows with alcohol in a couple of years, or maybe months.

THREE

Nyx

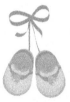

SOMETIMES I WONDER what would've happened if my parents were normal. Not that I regret my life the way Callie does. It's just... every time I have personal time off, I wonder if the path I'm following is the right one.

Then I go down the rabbit hole wondering if I would have chosen a different career and what that would be?

Did they fuck my future because I was trying not to be them?

I love them dearly. They are two of the smartest, quirkiest, most loving people I've ever known. It's ironic that they've studied society, its structure, and behavior throughout their lives. They dug, analyzed, and wrote books about civilizations. Yet, they don't follow social etiquette.

Their work is important, and I respect it, but would it be too hard for them to be a little more conventional?

During my college years, I panicked that I'd end up like them while we were growing up. Homeless, poor, and with four kids traveling around the world. At least, that's the way I saw it back when I was younger. Perception is the key.

We didn't own a house. Our belongings fit inside our luggage. We had a few things stored at our grandparents' home in Los Angeles. Mostly pictures and a few memories. Poor Persy. She always got my hand-me-downs when I grew out of my clothes. We never had money to go to Disneyland, buy a car, or buy the latest toys they advertised on the television.

The reality was different. We weren't poor. We had enough money to live. It was easier to give my sister my hand-me-downs rather than purchasing something we already owned and she'd outgrow soon. There wasn't a point to owning a car, a house, or furniture if we were always going from one archeological site to another.

My parents were practical. They tried to teach us that material things aren't as important as our family. Most of all, they taught us to pursue our dreams.

That's not the way I saw it while growing up though. I swore I wouldn't be like them. While in college, I worked my ass off to get straight A's and also to earn enough money to buy a car, a home, and have whatever my heart desired. Once I became a lawyer, I saved enough money for a down payment to buy a house. Since then I've upgraded my car three times and I bought a bigger house because it's a great investment.

My sisters and I go on vacation at least twice a year. In hindsight, I have everything I wanted while growing up.

However, it's while Eros and Persy are making deals and really reaching for what they want that everything hits me at once. I'm in somewhat of a rut. Again, everyone who sees my life from the outside might think, *Nyx has her shit together. Look at her kicking ass in court, owning the latest luxury car, and wearing the trendiest clothes.*

For years, I've neglected my dreams. Actually, I don't even know what it is that I want out of life. I've been taking care of everyone around me. Eros, who is the oldest of us, needs a full-time babysitter. That's me. I adore my big brother, but he's a man child. I have to get him out of the contracts he signs, and he's always looking for the next big thing that'll get him his first million dollars while he's helping others.

Then, there's Persy. She's only ten months younger than me. We're like twins, and even though she's pretty self-sufficient, I still look out for her. She trusts easily, and even when I'm watching her like a hawk, shit happens. Like her stupid agent stealing millions of dollars from her.

My baby sister, Callie... Well, I tried to be a good role model for her but I'm not sure when I'll speak to her again. I'm still fucking mad at her.

It is when Persy is signing her new book deal, *The Last Swipe: A Guide to Find Yourself,* that I realize I don't know where or who I am anymore.

Ironic, I have a sister who has a blog, a podcast, and books about self-help, and I am lost. Even though I'm smiling, nodding, and paying attention to this meeting, I'm lost. My goals seem insignificant now. Maybe Callie was right when she said I was fucking boring. I only allow myself to have certain moments of fun.

When was the last time I had fun on my own?

I'm not talking about going out with Persy and having a few drinks or too many where I end up puking. When I go out on dates, things never go past the one-night stand—if they go anywhere. Being a kick-ass lawyer isn't fulfilling anymore. Am I happy?

Where do I swipe right for myself?

I should make a list of the things I need to do for myself. Do I even have time to do anything about my current situation? I have student loans, a mortgage, and the option to become a junior partner within the next couple of years. I can't throw away my hard work because I feel unfulfilled. Can I?

We adjourn the meeting and though I grin at my sister and celebrate our big win, I'm depressed as fuck. I'm lucky my sister is too busy thinking about Langford Chadwick, her love interest. She sees me as someone who breezes through life effortlessly. She swears I always have a plan and my to-do list is full of checks because it's all done. But everything I do focuses on work, financial goals, or my family. What about my personal life?

When was the last time I let my hair loose and just lived for the moment?

Never.

Persy and I have been silent for most of the drive. My heart sinks when we stop right in front of an old, tall building that sits across from Central Park. This is it. The moment when she finds her future and I'm kind of left behind. There's no doubt in my mind she's going to find her happiness. What's going to happen to me afterward?

I might stay stuck in my current life because there won't be anyone to reach out to when I need help. I want to tell her, "Yo, I'm drowning. Is there any way that you can throw me a life jacket before you set sail and leave me behind?"

That's not what older sisters do. We smile reassuringly and squeeze our little sister's hand as she's about to embark on a new adventure.

The building is gorgeous. The interior exudes an air of elegance. The doorman walks us to the elevator and even pushes the top floor for us. When the doors open I almost gasp at the breathtaking view of New York. I want to run toward the floor to ceiling windows so I can see the entire city from the top.

A man in his mid-fifties wearing a dark suit looks at us and nods politely. "Ms. Persephone, Mr. Chadwick is waiting for you in the library. If you follow the hallway to your left, you'll see the French doors immediately. Ms. Nyx, if you want to follow me, I'll take you to your room."

"I have a room." I glance at Persy and give her a mischievous smile. "Something tells me *you* are going to share a room."

"Doubtful," she disagrees.

"I'm Demetri," the guy introduces himself as we walk toward the staircase. "I manage the household for Mr. Chadwick. If you need anything, please let me know. Do you have any preferences on food, intolerances, or...? I need the information so I can order."

"No, I'm not allergic to anything, and I will eat pretty much everything," I state. "Except insects. Crickets are crunchy but the aftertaste is...not my favorite."

He arches an eyebrow and shakes his head, "I'm sure we can accommodate your preferences, Ms. Nyx. This is your room. The bathroom is to your left and the closet to your right. Your luggage is already on top of the bench. If you require a personal shopper, let me know and I'll have someone from Nordstrom or Neiman Marcus come over to measure you and show you a few options."

I blink a couple of times, startled by his offer. This is better than a trip to Disney World and I bet more expensive. The last time I went to those stores I left half of my savings in the hands of the evil personal shopper who kept handing me beautiful clothing.

"After you freshen up, come downstairs so I can show you the house," he states. "Mr. Chadwick will be busy with Ms. Persephone for the remainder of the day. He wants you to be comfortable."

"Thank you," I state and stare at him as he leaves, closing the door behind him.

I change into a pair of jeans and my black halter top. I brush my hair, wash my face, and put my hair back into a bun. When I reach the main floor, a honey color, fluffy dog runs my way rubbing his head against my leg. I pet him behind his ears.

"Well, hello there," I greet him.

"Brock, don't upset our guests," Demetri orders and gives me an apologetic smile. "He's rambunctious, and his owner doesn't believe in training him properly. No matter how much time I spend teaching him proper decorum, when Mr. Nathaniel is around, he lets him do as he wants."

"He's not upsetting me. On the contrary, I love animals," I explain. "You're just a happy pup, aren't you?"

"Woof!"

Demetri rolls his eyes but doesn't say a word. He shows me the terrace, teaches me how to turn on the fire pit in case I need it later in the evening. He gives me a tour of the kitchen and the library, which is now empty. I wonder where my sister is, but I'm pretty sure I know what she's doing.

When I spot Brock's leash I ask, "Is it okay if I walk him?"

Brock wags his tail and jumps around me.

"We prefer not to say that word in front of him. He takes his walks seriously," he warns me. "If you wish to take him out, you might want to stay on this side of the park. The bags to clean after him are attached to the leash handle. We'll have dinner ready for you around six," he states.

"Don't worry about dinner," I say. "This is New York. I'm pretty sure there are plenty of places where I can find something to eat while we stroll around the city."

With that, I make my way toward the elevator. When we step inside, I say, "Maybe you're what I need, a dog. Do you think Mr. Stuffy will mind if I kidnap you?"

He barks at me and wags his tail, and I wonder if he's just as tired as I am of following rules and being just good enough for everyone.

FOUR

Note

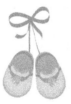

AROUND NINE O'CLOCK AT NIGHT, I arrive at the penthouse. This is why I hate traveling from the west coast to the east coast on weekdays. I lose about six hours and it leaves me restless. If my brother wasn't preoccupied with his new girlfriend, I would persuade him to go out with me. We could have dinner or just hang out on the terrace with a couple of beers.

My other option is to head to a bar and just pick up a chick, but it's Tuesday and I'm sure the selection of women is slim. Also, I'm over having one-night stands. As I said before, I'm too old for that nonsense. What I need is a fuck buddy. Someone who understands and shares my goals. All fun, zero emotions, and no messy endings.

"Mr. Chadwick," Demetri greets me. "I was about to leave for the day. Is there anything else I can do for you?"

"No, I'm just going to prepare a sandwich and go to the library to work. Where is Brock?"

"He's on the terrace with Ms. Nyx," he announces.

"Ms. Nyx?" I ask and smirk.

I forgot the guest Ford brought along with his girlfriend. I saw her briefly and from afar a few weeks ago at the Children's Hospital in Denver while my brother and I were dropping off a donation. From what I saw, she's gorgeous in an elegant, conservative, yet sexy way.

"Your brother is in his room with Ms. Persy. However, he left you an important message," he states. He pulls out a cue card and sighs. "Stay the fuck away from her."

"He made you write it?" I can't contain the laughter.

"No. He wrote it himself, in case I wanted to change the wording," he asserts.

"Of course, he did. I'll make sure to give zero fucks about it," I respond almost snicker. "Have a good night."

"But sir, Mr. Chadwick—"

"Should know better than to try to forbid me from making acquaintances," I state and make my way to the kitchen where I prepare a platter with cheeses, antipasto, and some grapes. I grab a bottle of wine and two glasses.

Once I place everything on a tray, I make my way to the terrace. Nyx Brassard sits on one of the patio couches across from the fire pit, watching the horizon. She's a beauty. I've seen her picture a few times. Most of them are of her next to her sister, Persy. My least favorite is her mug shot posted on the website of Bryant, LLC, the firm she's worked for since she graduated from college.

Fuck, I sound like a stalker, but it's not her I've been investigating; it's her sister. She just happens to be around every time I pull information about Persephone Brassard. By now, I can tell them apart. Nyx's nose is slimmer, her eyes bigger, and her eyelashes longer and thicker. She doesn't smile as often. Her hair is almost always pulled into an elegant knot. Don't get me wrong, she looks beautiful, but she looks way hotter when her wavy hair is down, gracing her bare shoulders.

Never have I thought I'd have the chance to be close to her. Not that I've been fantasizing about her. That'd be creepy, wouldn't it?

You know what would be creepier? If you make a move and she ends up being part of the family.

That's a true fact, just like the fact that if I do it, it'll piss the fuck out of Ford, and we live to prank one another. Would this be going too far?

Explore the possibilities, I advise myself. *There's nothing wrong with trying, is there?*

When I step closer, I notice Brock is on her lap. The asshole is already cozying up to her. There's no doubt that he's my dog.

"Brock, are you familiar enough with the lady to be sharing this lovely night with her?"

The damn mutt doesn't care. He stays where he's at and even makes that whiny noise he does when I'm petting him at night.

She turns around and smiles at me. "You must be Nate. I'm Nyx. We've spoken a few times over the phone."

"Indeed, you are. I could never forget such a lovely voice," I state, placing the platter I hold on the coffee table and reaching out to grab her hand. "It's nice to finally meet you."

I lift her delicate hand guiding it to my mouth so I can kiss it.

"Enchanté," I whisper.

The moment my lips touch her skin, there's an electrical surge that zaps me, stopping my heart, even my breathing.

"Pleasure," she whispers, and her raspy, sweet like honey voice restarts my entire body.

Fuck if this isn't frightening and exhilarating. I think that cue card should be set on fire because *we* are about to get to know each other on so many levels she won't be able to walk by tomorrow night.

"Would you like some wine, cheese, or we can get a table for two at Atla?" I offer. "I believe we could make this evening a lot more...interesting."

She laughs pulling her hand away from my grasp. "Smooth. Demetri warned me about you."

"Of course, he did," I groan.

Showing her a bottle of Cabernet Sauvignon I brought from my last trip to Paris I ask, "Wine?"

"Wine would be lovely, thank you."

"I'd like to point out that not everything D says is true."

"Well, he mentioned that you spoil your dog. Which is bad when he's trying to educate him to be a civilized dog," she states. "I'm pretty sure he'd send him to the equivalent of dog boarding school and away from you if that was a choice. You're obviously a terrible influence on this honorable canine."

I laugh as I uncork the bottle of wine. She tries not to join me and ends up coughing.

"And you said that with a straight face. I'm impressed," I declare, pouring us some wine and handing her a glass. "You must be great at playing poker."

"It's part of my character. When you're in the courtroom you have to look the part. If the jury, the opposition, or the judge get ahold of your emotions, you could lose the case. It's almost like showing your hand during poker."

"I assume you always win."

"My law firm makes sure to pair newer lawyers with seasoned partners, so we can learn but also avoid any losses at all cost," she answers. "When the senior partners think one of us is about to lose a case, they 'add' an extra lawyer with more experience to the team in charge. They only like winners and don't take losses too well."

"Time to open your own firm," I suggest, not because she might lose a case, but because she sounds apathetic toward her employer.

It's only a brief conversation. I don't know her at all. However, I read people easily, and I get more information from their body language than the words that come out of their mouths.

She sighs and nods.

"You have a lovely view," she changes the subject. Case closed. I'm not one of her people, and this isn't up for discussion. "Demetri told me that you split your time between this place and the one in Seattle. Do you have a penthouse in some swanky neighborhood in the Pacific Northwest?"

This woman is good. I bet she's great at getting a confession out of anyone. Even outside the courtroom, I'm sure she always gets people to talk. After all, she made Demetri spill information he's not allowed to say. I wonder what else she got out of him.

"Nah, actually it is a house in Hunts Point, right by Lake Washington," I inform her, not because I like people to know about my business, but because I want her to reciprocate my trust with information of her own. "Some days, I take a boat to work."

She nods, "I'm impressed. You're not exactly what I expected."

I stare at her slightly shocked. This wasn't something I anticipated.

"You had expectations?" I take off my jacket, lose my tie, and roll up my sleeves after taking off my cufflinks and placing them on the table. "Please, tell me more about them. I wouldn't want to disappoint you."

She laughs, staring at my forearms. Most likely trying to read my tattoos.

"Your brother is quiet. I thought you'd be less—"

"Forward?" I ask, reaching out for the bottle of wine, topping her glass, and then taking a seat next to her.

"Well, yeah. Plus, every time we're on the phone, you're an—"

Her long pause and the sparkle in her eyes tell me she wants to say, *asshole*, but she stops abruptly because that's not her style. I don't know her at all, but I bet she doesn't cuss in front of strangers.

"Nothing personal, beautiful. This past Sunday, it was a business transaction. It was never against you, and it's always about protecting my brother, our assets, or making a better deal than the one we are offered," I explain. "I recall you being pretty cutthroat during our negotiations."

She laughs, "It was pretty personal. You were trying to get a big chunk of the pie on a business my brother has been trying to build from the ground that will bring revenue but also give a lot to those in need."

"I hate to lose. I'm sure you understand the concept." I bow my head in reverence and drink some of the wine before conceding my defeat. "Which in this case you won. Maybe we should celebrate your triumph. As I just mentioned, we can get a table at any restaurant in the city. Just say the word."

"Thank you, but I already ate," she says with a smile that barely touches her eyes. "You should eat something."

I take a grape and pop it in my mouth. "Nah, I'm good with this tray. I just want to make sure you are being taken care of."

She studies me for several beats and then asks, "What's your story, Nathaniel Chadwick?"

"Story?"

"Grump Next Door is a loner. What are you?"

"A wicked adrenaline junky. Businessman during the day, playboy at night, a kid with expensive toys during the weekends," I respond the way I do with almost everyone.

That was me a year or two ago. Now, I skip the playboy shit and play harder in the finance field.

"Would you like to join my playground?" I tempt her, because with that body, that mouth, and that wit, I'd like to have a good time with her.

"Isn't it a little early to place your cards on the table?" She waves her glass of wine, drinking it all and then asking for more. "We're just getting to know each other."

"You don't seem like the kind of person who likes mind games," I answer, pouring more wine. "All I have to offer you is unlimited dates with extreme outdoor activities, exotic locations, and out of this world sex."

She licks her lips. "Direct. And here I thought you were a smooth operator with a lot of lip and too little game."

"I might have been ten years ago," I respond, stretching my hand and touching her knee. "Life is too short to pretend that I'm not attracted to you."

She laughs and I stare at her seriously.

"Oh God, you're serious." She straightens herself, touching her collar bone. Those dark, beautiful eyes open wide.

"I never joke about my intentions, Nyx. There are three things you need to know about me. I never lie, I'm loyal to my friends and family, and I don't change for anyone."

"You forgot the part that you're arrogant as fuck," she states and yawns. "It's been an informative night, but I guess it's time for me to leave."

"Too afraid to handle me?" I taunt her, and I can see she's teetering on the other side of the line. One push and I can make her fall into my net. "I could go easy on you."

"And he's funny too, huh." She glances at me. "The man isn't just a pretty face. He can make women laugh."

"But my favorite is making them scream," I add, winking at her.

"Is that so?" her voice has a flirty tone to it. "So, it's not all bark. You know how to bite."

"I know my way, and I can make you reach places you can't imagine," I say, caressing her forearm with the back of my finger. "Unless you can't take a man like me," I challenge her.

"I eat guys like you for breakfast...after I make them eat me until I'm satisfied," she states.

And now there's no doubt this is the woman who should become my next playmate. I just have to find a way to convince her that we could be perfect.

FIVE

Nyx

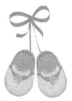

WOW, I'm a great liar. Even I believed what I just said. In truth, I don't eat guys like him for breakfast or have sex that often. The last guy I hooked up with was a few weeks ago. He was average at best. He wasn't that memorable... my *God, did I seriously sleep with Edward Bryant?*

Nyx, forget about that oopsie moment and focus on the big bad wolf in front of you.

I'm no Little Red Riding Hood scared of his sharp teeth and big blue eyes, so of course I won't back down. This guy can think that I have an active sex life just like him. I'm one of the best bullshitters in the legal business. I've never lost a case, and I'm not planning on losing this standoff with Nathaniel Chadwick. Best known as the hottest, most wanted, and unreachable playboy in the country.

His *so fucking-sure-of-himself* grin takes over his handsome face. "So, you want to eat me?" he asks with a deep, calm voice.

Well, yes, Nathaniel, I'd love it if we could eat each other. I could think of the many ways it could happen, including a perfect sixty-nine. I'd be happy to be the six to your nine—or to your ten if the rumors are correct.

His dark blue eyes lined with long, thick lashes stare at me, trying to command me to just submit. With any other guy I might be willing. Not with him. My sister is somewhere in this penthouse having passionate, delicious, hot sex with his brother.

Being with Nate seems a little depraved. But is it really?

This is what happens when you change your routine, Nyx. You should be back home, in Colorado.

Actually, more like at the office, working on my next case. Instead, I'm still in New York enjoying the company of a snuggly dog, his wicked owner, and a delicious glass of wine.

I'm in the presence of the infamous Nathaniel Chadwick. The playboy everyone loves—and desires. The pictures of him on the internet don't do him any justice. Tousled dark brown hair that I bet he combed with his hand after a shower. Handsome is a weak word to describe this man. He has the kind of face that stops everyone in their tracks. The olive color of his skin makes his blue eyes pop. Those piercing eyes could make anyone weak at the knees. Broad shoulders, slim waist, and I bet under that suit there're a lot of defined muscles that I'd love to touch.

It comes as no surprise that every woman in the world desires him. His proposal is tantalizing, but I have to pass. What would it be like to be touched by his big, strong hands? I can't help but blush when I imagine his lips running down my body. I shiver as I think of his deep voice whispering dirty words as he thrusts himself inside me.

In my experience, men fall into three categories, though there are plenty of subcategories. The one you fuck, the one you marry, and the one you friend zone. No, it's not fuck, marry, or kill. But let's be realistic. Friend-zoning a guy literally kills any chance to have sex with him—ever.

Mr. Billionaire Playboy falls into the fuck category. I'd love to say, "Where is your playground and will you be providing the condoms?"

The problem lies in my sister being madly in love with his brother. If I accept his open invitation and my sister ends up marrying Ford...this will become pretty awkward when our tryst is over.

Seriously, what if he turns out to be a major asshole? He could be lousy in bed. There's a saying about too much bark and no bite. Does that apply to him?

"You're overthinking," he states. "My gut was right. You're a good girl. You never skipped class, always obeyed your parents, and followed the rules. No, you actually enforce them, which is why you are a lawyer."

"Are you about to crack lawyer-y jokes?"

He arches an eyebrow and crosses his corded arms. "Is that even a word? That's a transgression against George and Charles Merriam. Is that allowed?"

"Look at you, throwing some useless knowledge my way to impress me," I retort. "Why would you think I'm a good girl? Maybe I like to dress classy and underneath I'm wearing a lace bodysuit, a bustier, and maybe a garter belt."

"That'd be a sweet treat. I'd love to unwrap you. I like my women naughty," he says with a husky tone.

"No doubt you do. Shouldn't you be at a bar fetching a woman for the night?"

He snickers "I'm more than what my bio says on Wikipedia or any other website you've been clicking through, sweetheart."

I gasp, narrow my gaze, and ask, "What? Were you spying on me?"

He smirks "That'd be odd. No, that's what I expect from... Let's just say you're predictable. You're beautiful, but definitely not my type, and I apologize for coming on so strong."

"Reverse psychology, nice," I say and sigh. "Does it work?"

He blinks a couple of times and laughs. "Not today. I'm running out of lines. Cut the guy some slack."

"A few years back this could've been the beginning of a beautiful train wreck, but I'm too old for this."

He frowns. "I'd say you look twenty-five, but if you're older than Persephone you should be around twenty-nine?"

"I turn thirty this December," I announce. "Why do you know Persy's age?"

"I have the bad habit of running a background check on everyone who gets too close to my brother," he confides. "It's nothing personal. Just a way to keep him safe."

"But not you?"

He shakes his head. "Nope. I'm not some nerdy recluse. I'm more street smart, if that makes any sense. Which is why everyone who gets close to Ford has to sign an NDA."

"Like I'd let my sister sign an NDA," I laugh.

"Well, if it makes you feel any better, he's not going to ask her to sign one—or any of you for that matter. Apparently, this is fucking serious." He presses his lips together and looks out to the horizon. His voice comes out so harsh that Brock moves away from my lap and onto his.

"Irritating, isn't it?" I joke. "People finding love and trusting each other."

"Listen, I'm happy for him," he states, standing up and pacing around the terrace. "I know from experience that relationships fuck you for life."

I arch an eyebrow giving him my best inquisitive look and say, "Now we're getting somewhere. What can you say about this dark past that makes you hate love?"

He makes a huff or maybe a snicker sound and shakes his head. "What's your story, Nyx? Any particular reason why you don't have a significant other?"

"Why are you assuming I'm single?"

"The predictability factor," he continues nitpicking me. "If you were in a relationship, you'd be on the phone with your boyfriend, or girlfriend, talking about how much you miss them and describing the breathtaking view. During the conversation, they'd promise you to take you to New York during the fall."

I tilt my head, raising an eyebrow. "Fall?"

"The view from here is even better. The orange and red foliage is unique. If those two love birds are still together, you should come over," he invites me. "Unless...your boyfriend is the one who brings you."

"You're just generalizing and watching my reactions." His mischievous eyes stare at me, waiting for my next move or my next statement. "I'm single because I spend most of my time working, and I'm an avid subscriber to Worst-Dates-R-Us."

He laughs, "What is that?"

I'm sure a guy like him wouldn't understand my life. He can pick and choose who he goes out with, and I bet none of the women he dates disappoint him. He has unlimited amounts of sex—good sex. The only way I've been getting off is with the help of the sex toys my sister recommends. Another perk of having Persy as a sister, she's a sexologist and knows the best and latest available gadgets for couples, and for us spinsters.

Not that I am one, but sometimes I feel like I'm going to die alone, and I don't even have a cat. I don't have time for a pet.

"It's an imaginary place that provides *me* with the worst dates that a human being can experience," I say, sighing.

"How bad can they be?"

"Let me count the ways, Skippy," I answer, showing him one finger. "There's the one with the guy who brought me to his parents' home and our dinner was leftovers. His father is now a client of mine."

He laughs. "Was he fifteen?"

"No, almost forty. He lives in his parents' basement," I answer and then show him a second finger.

"You get your dates at losers-are-us," he concludes before I can tell him about my latest loser adventure.

"Most likely," I agree. "At least my sisters can say that they have steady relationships that don't work out. Mine don't go past the second or third date if I'm lucky."

"Nothing against your sisters, but maybe you're the smartest of the three," he says reassuringly.

"Flattery won't get you anywhere, Mr. Chadwick."

"I don't know you or your sisters, but here's what I'm thinking," he says with a serious voice. "Persy is a psychologist. She probably has to stay in the relationship at least until she can prove that she couldn't salvage it. Call it determination, resolve, or plain stubbornness. I only know your younger sister by picture. Without more information I can't guess why she has more long-lasting relationships than you. You are different. If you don't see potential, you walk away because you don't have time for nonsense."

"I..." I want to fight him, but he's right, so I nod in agreement.

"You know what you need?"

"A loser radar," I guess.

"No, a guy like me," he says haughtily. "You have a busy schedule, but I bet you can get away for a weekend. Guys like me know how to have a good time in and outside the bedroom. Just think about it. I can fly you wherever and whenever you want."

"Give it a rest," I hear a male voice, and when I turn toward the penthouse, I spot Ford and Persy walking toward us. "What part of 'stay the fuck away' didn't you understand?"

"Oh great, two men about to show who has the bigger dick," I mumble, standing up from the couch and stretching. "Such an innovative concept. If you guys don't mind, I'm heading to my room."

"You okay?" Persy asks as I walk by her.

"Not as great as you. That dreamy face tells me that you've been having a lot of naughty fun. Though, I have to ask, is everything okay with...?" I trail my gaze to Ford who is now talking in hushed voices with Nate.

"Perfect," she answers. "He just told me that if you need to leave for Denver earlier, he can fly you."

"I might take that invitation if you're certain that you are okay," I question, expecting her to blink if he's keeping her hostage.

"More than okay," she reassures me. "Though, I'd rather you stay. There's nothing better than having my favorite sister around. If you want, we can go around the city, do some touristy things. Ford is going to be working all week. We haven't had sister time in forever."

"Sounds like we can be Thelma & Louise in the City," I joke, giving her a hug. "I'm heading to bed, but let's kick off the day tomorrow morning with a walk around the park. We can take Brock. He's a great dog."

She scrunches her nose. "I'm not a dog person."

"You are. You just don't know it," I argue. "Just because one bit you as a kid... Time to move on and appreciate the puppies of the world."

"Goodnight, Nyxie."

"Don't let the bedbugs bite," I answer, and she glances at her man saying, "I'm sure he'll be doing the...biting."

I sigh and wave at her. What would it be like to have those hazed eyes, hot boyfriend, and a promising future?

SIX

Nate

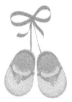

I CAN'T RECALL the last time I was in the same room with Ford working, and not just hanging out. For the past few years, we handle most of the business via text, phone calls, or video conferences. A month or so ago when he visited me in Seattle, he stayed home brooding and refused to work.

This Persy affair might be beneficial not only to him, but the company. Time will tell though.

"I miss this," I tell him while I take a piece of nigiri, dip it in soy sauce, and put it in my mouth.

"Don't you eat sushi often?" he asks, arching an eyebrow. "You order it with almost every meal."

"No, idiot. Working like this," I clarify. "We've gotten more done today than in the past couple of months."

He glances at me unamused. "No."

"I haven't said anything," I argue. "But you know we could launch the new software by January if we meet more often. I'm willing to fly to Denver too, if that's what it takes to work with you in person. It'll make my life easier. I understand that without you, LNCWare wouldn't exist but..."

He looks at me and lets out a loud breath. "Give me time to get used to it, okay?"

"That's all I am asking, that you open your horizons and start doing more for the company."

It's on the tip of my tongue to also ask him for a break with his someday-to-be-sister-in-law. Fuck, I can't believe that I'm saying that and accepting it. It's pretty obvious that he's in a serious relationship. I witnessed it last night. They are clearly a match made in... I'm not sure heaven is the right word.

They are total opposites. I doubt they have anything in common, and yet, they fit perfectly together. In all thirty some years of my life I've never seen my brother in love. Am I still afraid that this will end up in tragedy? Of course. Just because I understand this is the real deal, it doesn't mean that it'll stay like this forever.

Cynical? No, I like to call myself practical.

Now his love story is blocking my chances to have Nyx A. Brassard. If Ford hadn't interrupted last night, I could've convinced her to give me at least this weekend. What a fucking joke. I have a hot, smart, available woman sleeping under my roof, and I can't have her. The obstacles are making her more desirable.

"So...the sister?"

"...is off limits," he responds with a warning voice. "Who you want to hook up with is none of my business, but stay away from *her*. Listen, I'm not judging you. It'd be hypocritical of me. I was there a few months ago. Except, this is Persy's sister who we are talking about. They are close, like you and me. It'll be fucking awkward if you make a move and things go wrong. You could even break up my own relationship."

"You're exaggerating," I debate. "You'll probably have a fight or some disagreement, but if she loves you..."

He points at me, "I swear Nate, if you do something stupid..."

I glare at him, waiting for him to threaten me. He's been pissing me off since yesterday with his attitude.

He exhales and says, "Please, I never ask you for anything."

"Really?" I give him a challenging glance. "I've been running this fucking company by myself because you can't stand to deal with people. Not just in the company, but in your life. I won't pursue her, but if it happens, it's between Nyx and me. She seems old enough to take care of herself."

He shakes his head. "Let's get back to work. You just pissed me off."

"Because it's so hard, isn't it sunshine?" I tease him, gathering the trash and tossing it in the can.

"Why her? When you can have any other woman?" he asks.

I freeze for a moment as I replay his unexpected question. *Why her?* Taking a deep breath, I step closer to the floor-to-ceiling window overlooking Park Avenue. There's an inexplicable attraction between us. I want to get to know her—not only her body. She's a challenge.

None of those answers seem to be like something I want to share with my brother. At least, not yet.

"She's smart. She's a career woman. And she's gorgeous," I explain. "She's perfect."

"Perfect how?" His voice lost the edge and has a curious tone. "You can find one just like her here in New York."

I turn around. He's still seated on the leather couch grimacing at me with a pinched expression.

"Which is convenient because with her busy schedule and my busy life we can see each other once a month. No feelings, messy entanglements, or regrets," I explain. "If either one of us doesn't want to see the other again, no one will lose any sleep."

That's a perfectly great explanation. It sounds like something I would do, but as I say the words I'm wondering if I mean them. Do I only want something superficial with her or...? The *or* kept me awake last night, and I've been thinking of her all day long. The breathless moments I shared with her weren't enough. I want to spend more time with her. At the same time, I know there's no point in pursuing this...

This attraction that has my heart throbbing just with the memory of her raspy voice and her sweet scent.

He shakes his head. "And I thought I was fucked up," he states.

"I'm also practical," I state, but really, deep down, not even I believe that Nyx and I could keep things casual.

Taking a breath, he raises from his seat and says, "We have a meeting in the conference room. Do whatever the fuck you want. I hope Nyx is smart enough to stay away."

FORD LEAVES the office around six. I stay until eight, and when I arrive home, Nyx is on the terrace with Brock.

"Good evening, Nyx," I greet her. "Why are you here and not bar hopping?"

She turns around and smiles at me when she sees me. Her dark wavy hair is down, framing her gorgeous face. She tucks a strand behind her ear before saying, "You're confusing me with someone else."

"No, that's called sarcasm," I state, taking off my suit jacket. "Would you like some wine tonight?"

"I'm not supposed to fraternize with you," she answers.

I smirk, pull a chair from the dining table I have on the terrace, and drag it close to where she sits. I set it down, the back of it facing her and mount the chair. "This has to be good. What did Ford say about me?"

"It was my sister," she corrects me. "She's concerned that you're too emotionally immature to sustain a romantic relationship, and if you hurt me it'll be awkward."

I nod. "Seems like our siblings don't trust our maturity, do they?" I text Demetri, asking to bring some wine to the terrace. "I find it refreshing that they're both sure about their future."

"We discussed it yesterday. Persy likes long-lasting relationships. As disgusting as it sounds, it seems like they love each other enough to believe that they'll have to split holidays between us if we...do something stupid and can't stand to be in the same room."

"Because we wouldn't last? They have so little faith in us."

She tosses her head back and laughs at me.

I wish I could say something but that's when Demetri arrives with a bottle of wine, and the two glasses on the tray are already filled. He hands one glass to Nyx and another one to me. He sets the tray on the coffee table.

"Thank you, D," I say as he leaves the room.

She sips from her glass, then licks her full lips. Her warm, dark eyes stare at me. My skin hums with need for some human touch—her touch to be exact.

"We could have something amazing," I bring back the conversation.

Her face hardens. She tilts her head to the side. Her inquisitive eyes stare at me. "Have you ever had a long-lasting relationship?"

"Have you?" I retort.

"You first." She narrows her eyes further.

"Her name was Bronwyn. We met when I was twenty-eight. The offices of LNCWare used to be in the financial district. It was before we started branching into other sectors," I explain, remembering the first time I saw her. She was tall, caramel-honey hair with warm amber eyes that sometimes turned a yellow tone in the sun.

I pinch the bridge of my nose because it's been a long while since the last time I thought about our first encounter. The memories that remain in my heart are too painful to remember the good times we shared. We were at a coffee shop. I was picking up my order when she tripped on something and almost fell. I reached out to catch her and instead of helping, I dumped my coffee on her.

We laughed, exchanged information so I could pay for the dry-cleaning of her dress and a new pair of shoes. That was the beginning of what I thought was my forever. She's the love of my life. I wasn't hers though.

"We dated for two years," I continue and swallow hard. "She was it for me. I wasn't sure when I'd be proposing to her, but—"

"Wait, we're talking about l-o-v-e word here, aren't we?"

I nod a couple of times, as I rub my chest.

She hugs her legs and asks, "What happened to her?"

"Back then, I traveled a lot," I say and pause for a second. Maybe I'm still traveling a lot, and if there was a lesson to learn from that time I...well, I didn't learn much. "I believed that quality was better than quantity. So even when we didn't see each other every day, we had a deep, meaningful relationship."

That's how I remember it, but now I wonder if it was that way, or if I made all that up inside my head. I shake my head and continue. "We didn't see each other as much as we did at the beginning, but we were happy. One day she said, 'I'm pregnant.'"

"Please tell me your kid is fine," she begs, and it feels like she's about to cry.

I nod. "I did the most logical thing and proposed to her. She said yes. However, she suggested we waited until the baby was born. He arrived in this world five years ago. Ten fingers, ten toes, and I fell in love with the most beautiful boy in the world. We named him Wyatt Callum Davis-Chadwick. Seven pounds two ounces and twenty inches. I should have known something was wrong, but I adored him and there wasn't anything I wouldn't do for him. Why would I doubt his mother's behavior?"

"What happened, and where is he?"

I close my eyes and let out a breath, "Four months later, during the wedding, my world collapsed. She said the wrong name during our vow exchange. Instead of saying 'I take thee, Nathaniel,' she said, 'I take thee, Callum.' He was her boss. The guy happened to be among the guests. One moment we were supposed to exchange rings and the next I'm punching the guy, she's crying because she doesn't know who she loves, and my brother is hauling me out of the place."

Counting from one to ten, I open my eyes and smile at her. "She wasn't sure who she loved. There were too many uncertainties to continue with the ceremony."

"What about Wyatt?" Nyx asks, and I'm sure she knows what is coming up next.

"Later, we sat down to talk. She confessed that she had been going out with both of us. Not only that, but she wasn't sure who Wyatt's father was. When I asked why she stayed with me she said that I was the better choice."

"Nate..." Nyx whispers my name and touches my hand lightly.

"With me, Wyatt would have everything he desired. It was my bank account, and not because she loved me," I say, looking at the dark sky and feeling just as dark as I felt during those months. "I was angry, hurt, and heartbroken. I loved her, and I adored my boy. Except..."

"He wasn't yours," she finishes what I can't say.

"There's nothing left in me to give," I confess after a long silence. "She shattered me the moment I learned he wasn't mine. She snatched my little boy away from me. He's now Wyatt Callum Davis-Mattis. It hurt to lose her, but him... I could've forgiven her for cheating and forged a friendship with her while we parented our son. She wiped me from his life. It's like I never existed. That's why my brother wants me to stay away. Because if you get attached and want more..."

She squeezes my hand. "Thank God I'm not one of those women who tries to fix men, or we'd be a lethal combination."

I smile, nodding in agreement.

"What about you?"

"As I mentioned last night, my track record is terrible," she confesses. "I had a couple of boyfriends during college and law school. They were too busy to entertain something serious."

"So, casual dates," I conclude.

She snickers humorlessly. "Well, I thought we were heading somewhere until they set me straight. I guess they taught me to not trust my heart to anyone."

"Where does this leave us?"

"That's the beauty about who we are," she says. "We're mature enough to speak what we feel and talk about our limits. We're without a doubt heading to the famous friend zone."

"Ouch." I wince

"It'll be fun," she assures me. "We could be each other's wing-person since my wing woman is now otherwise occupied and happy with your brother."

"But you see, with your busy schedule and my life I think we could make a deal that'll benefit us both," I propose. "Unlimited sex, no entanglements, and trips around the world when we find the time. It'll be mutually exclusive."

She gives me a sad, yet tender look that stirs something inside my chest. "Call me when you're ready to be real and have a relationship that lasts more than twelve hours—or a weekend. I can find you someone who'll be perfect for you then."

"Not you?"

"No, because if I find the guy who's buried under the pain your ex left, I'm afraid I'll do something stupid like fall in love and end up with a broken heart," she confesses, rises from her seat, and kisses my cheek. "I wish I could tell you it gets easier, but what you lost is bigger than just the love of your life. I'm sorry that happened."

I want to know what she'd do if she found him, the guy Bronwyn destroyed. I've been looking for that asshole for five years and I can't find him. What makes her think that she can reach out to him?

Actually, I believe that Bronwyn Davis killed him. Sadly, I couldn't avenge his death because I can't do anything to hurt Wyatt's mother. He might not be mine by blood, but I'll always love that kid more than anything in the world.

SEVEN

Nyx

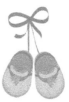

NEW YORK WAS INFORMATIVE, uneventful, and somehow relaxing. Most of all, I learned that I need a dog in my life. Brock is a sweetheart. If it wasn't because Nate seems to adore him, I'd have tried to bring him home as a souvenir. Also, I had time to reconnect with my sister. For the last couple of months, I've been in and out of town. Other than texts and the daily phone call, we've barely had our sister time.

While Persy and I were around town visiting museums, shopping, and having fun, she didn't post much on her social media the way she usually does. Her last three posts were called 'hiatus.' She's recharging for her next chapter.

Having a boyfriend who hates being in the spotlight could be a deal breaker for an influencer, but not for my sister. She's always known how to handle her social media presence and she already has a plan. I wasn't sure about this relationship before, but after spending time with them, I know they'll be together forever.

I'm not jealous of my sister, but the loneliness I've been feeling increases when I board the plane to fly back to Denver. Ford has work to do and Persy can stay with him for as long as she needs to. When I arrive home, I call Eros to check on him and Simon. Persy left him in charge of her feline child. He suggests I take the cat with me, but I remind him that Simon hates to be alone and I spend too much time at the office. He's the best choice since he works from home.

As predicted, I spend the entire week at the office working on two different cases and helping one of the partners while he's out of town. Sarah Bryant, my boss, hates when I ask for personal time off. When I do, she finds me crappy cases and assigns me extra work. Maybe Nate is right. It's time to open my own firm or... There's no other option. I'm too seasoned to start in a new firm and try to climb my way to the top.

It's past seven at night, the sun is still shining, and I am ready to put in at least three more hours of work when the landline rings. I should let it go to voicemail, but what if it's something important that can't wait until Monday?

"Nyx Brassard's office."

"Predictable," the husky male voice on the other side of the line says. "You should be home or partying. After all, it's Friday evening."

I stare at the New York number and guess, "Nathaniel Chadwick?"

"You like to say my name, don't you?" he says with his flirty voice.

"How did you get this number?" I ask as I turn off my computer.

"Internet," he answers with a simple word.

"Are you cyberstalking me?"

"Not exactly," he states. "When we were drawing the contract to lease the penthouse to your sister, I checked the Bryant, LLC's website where your direct line is listed. Since I don't have your number it was easy to look this one up. We need to exchange information."

I groan. "How can I help you, Nate?"

"Eros and I were planning our trip to Costa Rica," he answers. "As his lawyer, we thought it would be wise to bring you along."

"Have I mentioned that you are hilarious?" I ask and even laugh. "Hey, I need to leave, but it was great hearing from you. Bye."

This should be a sign that I need to head home and stop practicing law on the side for my siblings—for free. While I gather my stuff, the phone rings. When I spot Nate's number, I ignore it. We shouldn't fraternize. He's tempting, fun, and delicious. Just like cookies. If I'm strong enough to keep away from cookies, I'm strong enough to stay away from him.

When I get in my car, my cell rings. It's my brother, Eros. This guy and I have to discuss boundaries. And talk about his future too. Like getting a new lawyer to help him with his business and keeping Nate away from me.

"What's happening, big brother?"

"Are you joining us then?" he asks.

"Sorry, I feel like I missed half of the conversation. Give me a second," I say, turning on the engine of the car and waiting for the phone to connect to the Bluetooth. "Okay, let's try this again, but add context."

"I'm organizing the trip to Costa Rica. Since you're my lawyer I was hoping you'll join us. Nate tried to call you about it, but he said you weren't answering your phone."

"Hmm, I don't have any missed calls from him. Maybe he has the wrong number," I say casually. "I don't recall giving him my information"

"Not to worry, I just shared the contact info I have on my phone with him," he answers proudly.

If I wasn't driving, I'd smash my head against the wheel. Clearly, I have to have a word with Eros about Nate. Not today though.

"I'm swamped with work," I announce wiggling my way out of this deal. I should call Pierce. He quit the practice a few months ago and moved to Oregon. He's dealing with his family, but he might have time to deal with my brother and his new partner.

"Are we looking for an excuse, Nyxie?"

"No, I've been in and out of town for almost two months," I remind him. "I have so much on my plate right now—"

"We could make it work. Before you try to dump me with one of your buddies, let me remind you that I only trust you."

I sigh and say, "You're going to have to text me or email me any details about your trip. We could connect through video conference while you're down there. I'm going to be swamped at least until the second week of September. After that I might be able to go but… it's unlikely."

"It's scheduled for the beginning of October. There's a lot we have to set in place before we can fly out there," he warns me. "I'll be sending you some of the documentation as I receive it. Do you think we can have lunch tomorrow?"

"Tomorrow?" I ask, as I arrive home.

"Listen, according to Nate, Persy isn't coming back for another week," he announces. "It's not like you have your bestie to find a good excuse to avoid me."

I grunt because I know that lunch is going to include talking about his new company and Nate. I wanted to hang out with him this weekend, not work for him.

"I'm open all day, but I might go to check on our parents," I state. If I drag Mom and Dad with us, I might avoid working for him all day.

"Perfect. I was thinking that we can go down to Conifer," he suggests. "Ziplining is part of your bucket list."

"Sounds—" On one hand, I've been meaning to do it, but on the other I'm not one to be daring, and that's several feet above ground.

"Like torture, but I swear you'll have fun," Eros promises.

Unlike Persy who likes adventure, I prefer to stay as close to the ground as possible. I mean, what if the equipment fails and I get stuck? Or worse, what if I fall and die smashed onto the ground?

"We'll pick you up at eight so we can have breakfast before heading to Conifer. See you tomorrow, Nyxie!"

Once I'm out of the car, I look at my phone's screen and there's a text.

212-xxx-xxxx: *I can't believe you hung up on me. You're scared of me, aren't you?*

It's the same number that called my office. Eros is going to pay for this.

Nyx: *No, I'm busy.*

I add Nate's number to my contacts.

Nate: *:eye roll emoji:*

Nyx: *Some of us work on Fridays.*

Nate: *I never lie, and I also hate when people lie to me.*

Nyx: *The truth is I don't have time to text. I need to find something for dinner, and I need to call my mom.*

Nate: *What kind of food are you in the mood for?*

Nyx: *I need to check the menus I have in my drawer.*

Nate: *You don't cook?*

Nyx: *I do when I have time. My fridge is empty, and I'm starving. Not everyone has a Demetri to manage our household.*

Nate: *He does more than manage my house. I can let you borrow him if you need him. He gets bored sometimes.*

Nyx: *I'm not sure if you're joking or you're seriously offering to lend him out.*

Nate: *It's a joke. He'd quit if I did something like that. Anything special that you don't like to eat?*

Nyx: *I eat pretty much everything.*

Nate: *Any allergies that I should know about?*

Nyx: *You are weird, and none.*

Nate: *Okay, we'll see what I can find you.*

I stare at the phone suspiciously, but I don't reply. What is he trying to find? I choose not to fixate on him and go on with my night. When in doubt, stay away from the playboy.

EIGHT

Nyx

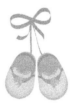

INSTEAD OF ORDERING FOOD, I take a shower, blow dry my hair, and put on my pajamas. Nothing says I'm home better than a pair of lounge pants and a tank top. What would make this evening perfect would be a bottle of wine and something delicious for take-out. I skipped lunch, and the bagel I ate for breakfast is a fading memory.

Mom is right. I have to eat better and stop skipping meals. It's just so hard to concentrate on work and keep track of what my body needs. I can only multitask so much. I walk toward the kitchen to search for the menus when my doorbell rings. Grabbing my phone, I check if Nate sent a text announcing that he ordered me food. There are no notifications. When I check who is at the door through the doorbell app, I see none other than Nathaniel Chadwick holding two brown paper bags. Also, he has my favorite guy with him.

Swinging the door open, I squat and greet him, "I missed you, Brocky!"

"He missed you too, and his name is *Brock*. As in Eddie Brock from Venom. Not Brocky," Nate answers annoyed at my pet name for this handsome dog. "Though I have to say that we're here because his new favorite word is Nyx and not w-a-l-k."

"We're best friends, aren't we, *Brock*?" I scratch his belly. "You're such a happy pup."

"Lucky bastard," Nate says and laughs. "He gets a greeting and a lot more attention than I do, and I'm the one who brought you food."

"Thank you, Nate, for being so thoughtful. Not to sound rude, but why are you here?" I question, as Brock licks my hand playfully.

"I have a few things to discuss with Eros and the two love birds didn't need a third wheel to keep them company. I decided to escape them and visit the Brassard siblings instead," he explains.

"Is the new couple being disgustingly sweet?" I lift my gaze to take a good look at Nate.

Today he's wearing a short sleeve navy blue t-shirt, a pair of washed jeans, and his tousled hair looks shorter than it was last week. He looks irresistible. It's such a shame that I have to ignore him. It's like staring at the most decadent dessert in the world, but he's off limits.

"Ford and your sister are too...irritating," he agrees, showing me the gifts he's bearing. "Can I come in?"

"Yeah," I say, standing up and leading Brock into the house.

"Nice place," Nate says, as he follows me. "Cozy."

"Why do I get the feeling that you're calling my house small?"

"It's the right size for you," he counteracts. "I like the decorations. They are elegant and yet, you have a few antiques and artifacts around. You have a classy style."

"Whenever you decide to redecorate your places let me know, I charge by the hour though," I joke.

He smirks and shakes his head. "Don't tempt me. I might use that as an excuse to spend more time with you. I have several places, including a villa in Portugal."

Does he even enjoy everything he owns?

"You could've told me you were in town," I say, changing the subject.

"And wait for you to find an excuse not to invite me for dinner?" He shakes his head and starts picking up the frames I have on top of the fireplace. "So, you and Persy look like your mom and Eros and the youngest Brassard look like your father. Interesting," he states.

While he's studying each picture I have, I set the bags on the counter and start taking the food containers out from one and the wine from the second.

"Do you have a bowl I can use for water?" he asks, pointing at Brock.

"Yes, they are in the top cupboard. Check the one next to the refrigerator," I suggest while searching for the wine opener. "Do you need me to order some food from the pet store for him? They might be able to deliver it tomorrow morning."

"He has plenty at Ford's place, but thank you for offering," he answers while filling the bowl with tap water.

"Is that where you're staying?" I ask, opening the take-out containers with sushi, fried rice, and a variety of Chinese food he brought. "Are you planning on feeding an entire army?"

"No, Eros mentioned your favorites while I was ordering and I chose a few from them," he replies, giving me that sly grin of his that threatens to melt my panties. "You might think my offer is off the table, but it's there for you to grab it and...enjoy it."

I laugh and shake my head. "You're cute."

He stares at me with disbelief and points at Brock. "He's cute. I'm manly."

"You can be whatever you want, Nate." I stand on my tiptoes to reach for the wine glasses. I feel his hand searing my skin as he touches my waist. My stomach twists and a lustful heat spreads from my head all the way down to my toes.

When I move my gaze to where Nate towers over me, I meet his bright blue eyes looking down at me filled with desire. His mouth is open as he moves his gaze down to my body. The energy between us is palpable. My heart beats faster and harder. I want to throw caution to the wind and touch him, taste him, take what he's offering.

That's not me though.

Without saying a word, I break our connection. Taking a step back, I walk away from what could've been a big mistake.

"I'll get that for you," he stares at me intently. His eyes moving slowly from my face and down my chest. "You might want to change if you want me to behave. The tiny see-through top you're wearing is giving me a lot of ideas that you might enjoy but...we can't because I need you to be sure of what I'm offering."

I look down and my face is on fire because of the embarrassment. He's getting a good look at my bare chest.

"Damn it. I wasn't expecting company," I complain, heading to my room to grab a bra. I also put on a sweatshirt for the lack of chastity belts. Not that I need one. I can control my hormones.

"Well, this is a little extreme, isn't it? Afraid I'll take advantage of you?" he jokes, winking at me as I walk into the kitchen.

He has everything set up on the table. He even poured wine in the glasses.

"It's taking me a lot of restraint not to make a pass. I promised myself not to pressure you," he says as we take our seats.

"The answer is still no. We won't become *a thing*," I insist, wanting to cover my chest because he keeps looking at it even though I'm wearing a bulky sweatshirt. "Plus, I'm sure you like someone with bigger boobs."

"I'm not planning on engaging in this conversation. That has trouble written all over it," he concludes, splitting his wooden chopsticks and reaching for a piece of sushi. "What is it that you do on Fridays when you're not with Persephone?"

"Work?" I answer, but it comes out more like a question. "I should still be at the office. Honestly, I left because you called, but I have a ton of things to do."

"Tell me more about what you do," he says.

As we eat, I tell him about my boss and what she usually does when I ask for personal time off. He listens and asks me about my current cases. I brief him on what I can say.

"Why law school and not something different?"

"I'm good at arguing with others, finding loopholes, and it pays well," I reply, hoping I don't sound shallow. He wouldn't understand what it was like for me to not have a home or stability while I was growing up.

Yes, we lived in a big adventure, but I worried most days that we wouldn't have a place to live or food on the table. That's the perception my parents gave me while we were growing up.

"What would you be doing if your brother wasn't a genius?" I question, not wanting to tell him about the traumas I carried during my childhood. They don't seem valid anymore, but for a child, it was different.

He looks at me and smiles. "I've always been good at numbers and convincing people to do things. Probably marketing or something in finance. I could've accepted being part of a reality show."

"Like *Survivor* or any of those contest shows?" I ask, intrigued.

"No, like *Man vs. Wild*. When I was seventeen, one of my late grandfather's friends who was still a producer back then, wanted to do a show with a young adult who could go around the world living in extreme conditions. They ended up signing an ex-military with more skills than I had—he looked young and they never mentioned his background or age while the show aired. I was bummed when I realized I was out of the running. I was so excited about living in places like the Amazon with nothing but a knife and a bottle of water...and, well, the camera crew."

I stare at him with wide eyes, speechless.

"I know what you're thinking, 'This guy is crazy.'" He shakes his head. "Even though my father has money, Ford and I had to be resourceful while growing up. When I broke the rules, he punished us by sending us to work with a landscaping crew. There were times when he sent me to a farm down in San Diego where I had to help with the crops or the animals. Other times I joined a construction company where I helped remodel and build new houses. It's as if he had us do community service for fucking up."

"So, you thought you had the elements to survive in the wilderness," I ask, shaking my head.

"Hey, I was seventeen. Boys think they are invincible at that age," he concludes. "I do like my extreme sports. By the way, Eros told me you were joining us tomorrow."

Oh boy, my brother just found himself a best friend. We're not losing Persy, we're gaining two guys who are just as annoying as my brother.

Shaking my head, I say, "I'd rather not do it. What if something happens to the equipment?"

"Trust me, I'll make sure everything is secure," he says. "I'm sure you don't want me to say it, but you need a little adventure in your life."

"And you're here to provide it?" I chuckle, taking a piece of California roll to have an excuse to eat the ginger. I love pickled ginger, though I'm not a fan of raw fish.

"If you allow it, I'll teach you how to live a little. Maybe I can learn how to... What is it that you do?" He snaps his fingers, pretending he's thinking.

"Don't call me boring or you'll be wearing these chopsticks up your ass," I warn him.

"Hmm, we found your hard limit. The word boring. Would you like to tell us more about it?" he asks, and I shake my head. "Hey, if we're going to be friends, the least you could do is tell me what I said wrong."

I explain to him about Calliope. My baby sister and the bane of my existence. How our parents let her get away with everything. They didn't discipline her, and she's a brat. The way she refers to me and our last fight.

"So, you don't know where she's at?" he concludes when I finish.

I shake my head, reaching for one of the several fortune cookies he brought.

"If you want, I have someone who could find her. At least you'll know if she's safe," he offers. "It's just so you can have some peace of mind," he explains, pouring more wine for both of us.

Tonight turns out to be more relaxing than I thought. I reach for my glass of wine, take a sip and wonder if I should accept his offer. My parents are worried about Callie too.

"You think we're a lot different, but we're not. I understand you. Family comes first, and we protect our own," he continues. "Even when you're upset because she treated you like shit, there's this need to protect her ingrained in your brain. We can at least figure out what she's up to so you can have one less thing to worry about."

"I don't want to like you," I warn him.

He laughs and takes my fortune, reading it out loud, "A lifetime of happiness lies ahead of you."

Nate waves the small paper and says, "This could be us."

I smirk and put a cookie in front of him. "Let's see what the cookie has to say about your future."

He rolls his eyes, unwraps it and breaks it, handing me the small paper while he takes a bite of the crispy cookie.

"Love is like sweet medicine, good to the last drop."

I read it out loud, and he says, "Do you know that fortune cookies are not a tradition in China? There was a big debate back in the eighties about where and who served them first. Rumor has it that it was in fact a Japanese immigrant in the early nineteenth century. They baked them without the fortunes. That came a few years later somewhere in San Francisco."

"Subtle change of subject," I state. "Also, a pretty random fact."

"That's me, I store useless information," he concludes and checks his watch. "It's time for me to leave. I'll pick you up tomorrow so we can go for breakfast."

"Eros told me he'll—"

"Before you protest, remember that Ford's place is close by," he interrupts me as he starts gathering the trash while I put away the leftovers. "It makes sense that I'm the one picking you up. Your brother mentioned that we could leave Brock with your parents. As you already know, he likes company."

As much as I want to disagree with his suggestion, he's right. Driving in separate cars doesn't make sense, and this is for Brock's gain, not mine.

"Okay," I agree and remind him, "We're only friends."

"Are you saying that for your benefit or mine?" He throws a charming grin my way. "Kidding. I think this is the beginning of a beautiful friendship."

I narrow my gaze, not knowing if he quoted a movie or said that casually so I answer with, "You talking to me?"

He winks at me. "You're my people, Nyx. Other than Ford, no one answers me with another movie quote. I hate to leave, but I'll see you tomorrow."

After his departure, I feel like the end of my day wasn't as bad as I thought. It actually changed my perception of the daunting week and my mood.

NINE

Nate

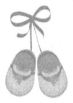

AROUND SEVEN IN THE MORNING, I arrive at Nyx's house.

"Stay. I'm just going to get Nyx," I order Brock.

He pants and wags his tail excitedly. I've yet to understand how it is that he connected with Nyx in less than a week. He's a friendly guy with everyone who crosses his path. With her...he simply adores her. If I allowed it, he'd pack his toys, bowl, and blanket and move in with Nyx on a whim.

As I'm about to ring the doorbell, a voice comes from the camera, "I'll be out in a moment," Nyx says.

I don't answer back, unsure if she can hear me, but I stay by the door. A couple of minutes later, she steps outside her house, wearing a sweatshirt from Duke University, light washed skinny jeans, and a pair of hiking boots. Instead of having her hair up in her trademark bun, she's wearing it in a ponytail. I like it better when it's down past her shoulders and her shoulders are bare.

"Morning, sunshine," she greets me, handing me one of the traveling mugs she's holding before shutting the door and locking it. "Coffee, black like your soul, but with a few drops of rose syrup."

"Hey, you look great," I observe, taking a sip of my coffee which tastes good but has a sweet after taste. "You tainted my coffee."

"No, I added some TLC," she corrects me, kissing my cheek. "Thank you for picking me up."

My gaze trails behind her as I touch my cheek which burns after the contact from her lips. It's a friendly kiss. A soft caress. And it leaves me breathless.

What is it about this woman that pulls me toward her?

Don't get me wrong. She's stunning, smart, and witty, but what I feel for her is more than the simple attraction I could have for a woman. It's a lot more than just liking her pretty face. I want to figure it out, but also run away fast. Things will never go beyond the allure. All I can offer her is my company and good sex. I don't have anything to give, and I bet she deserves the world.

I glance at her again and I feel it, the magic swirling between us. It'd be a crime letting it go to waste. I can just feel the sparks flying between us just with one kiss. Her and me in bed...we'd ignite like two supernovas colliding.

Should I let it go to waste?

Magic is meaningless. It doesn't last long, and you can ruin the best thing that's happened to Ford.

Stop wondering how she looks naked and think of something unsexy, like—

"Is everything okay?" she asks, cocking her head to the side and biting her lip. "You seemed concerned or maybe... Trouble at work? I could help if you like."

And now I want to suck on her bottom lip. Kiss her, running my mouth all over her perfect body.

Stop fucking around, Nathaniel!

I simply smile at her and say, "We're in a good mood today."

I open the passenger door for her, letting every emotion that's awakening inside of me go back to hibernation. Reciting the alphabet, thinking about my appointments for next week, and...everything I think of still makes me want her.

"Maybe I'm drunk since we're going ziplining," she jokes, turning her body to pet Brock. "He has a car seat?"

"Yes, it helps him stay in place. It's hard to drive with him when he's jumping from one seat to the other," I explain as I enter the address Eros sent me last night in the navigation app.

"I could tell you how to get to my parents' place without that thing," she says with annoyance.

"Sure, but can you warn me about accidents, roadblocks, or police vehicles?" I question making sure my phone is connected to the car.

She grunts, "You are one of those people who drives above the speed limit, aren't you?"

"I obey to the best of my ability," I answer innocently, and she laughs. When I reach a stoplight, I turn my attention to her, and I notice her eyes are scanning me and then Brock. "Are you trying to find any similarities between us?"

"No, just wondering why you have a Wheaten Terrier, and not a Rottweiler, German Shepherd, or Golden Retriever. He seems...I don't know, like a family dog," she explains, switching her attention toward her phone.

"He is part of my family," I inform her.

As the light turns green, I push the gas pedal and tell her a little about how Brock came to become part of my family. "The breed wasn't a choice. It's more like we were introduced while I was visiting a friend, and we hit it off."

She laughs. "Like a puppy blind date?"

"It's a complicated story that I can sum up with, I know someone who fosters dogs. They introduced me to this guy. He was a ten-month-old pup. We hit it off. I needed a roommate, and he was looking for a place to stay. We just agreed to live together. You can't say no to that face."

"That's an adorable way to put it. You can try to deny it as much as you want, but you're cute," she says with a mocking voice.

"Hear that, boy? You are cute."

She laughs. "So how old is he?"

"Three, why?"

"He makes me want to have a dog," she answers. "I researched dogs last night, and it's not that simple to just go and get one. According to the tests I took online, I need a dog who doesn't need much exercise because I don't have time for him."

"Start your own law firm. You'll be able to bring your dog to work and lower your stress levels," I insist, and I'm tempted to offer her a contract with me. She could become one of my legal consultants. There are so many things she could do with her degree, her experience, and her determination. The few times I've dealt with her during legal negotiations, she's left me impressed.

"It takes a lot of money to set up a firm. Where am I supposed to find clients?" she asks, a tad flustered. "I'm still paying for my student loans, there's the house, the car... You wouldn't understand."

"You might be surprised," I argue. "Did I live a comfortable childhood? Yes, but I also worked my ass off because I always got in trouble. Dad made us pay for everything we broke."

I don't add that when we started LNCWare, we didn't have much money. Once we became successful, I had to bail my father out of the stupid investments he had been making. He almost lost his father's fortune and was about to sell the rights to every movie Grandpa had made. Not even Ford knows about it. That's when LNC Investments was born.

"You're right, I don't know anything about your current situation," I yield. "You might want to start charging Persy and Eros for your services. I understand they are family, but they could be your first clients and referrals too. What happens if tomorrow your boss decides to retire, sell the practice, and the new owners only wanted the clients but not the lawyers? You'll be out and—"

"Though you have a point, I can't contemplate my future career at this precise moment," she interrupts me. "It's stressful. Don't you think I spend enough time considering what can happen if they kick me out tomorrow? I do often, but for now, I'm tied to them. If you don't mind, I'm trying to have a relaxed weekend."

"My apologies. I get caught up on finding solutions."

"Thank you for the advice," she answers, her voice is now soft and relaxed. "Sorry for being defensive. It's just scary. I...my parents traveled a lot while we were growing up."

She tells me how her archeologist parents dragged the family from one archeological site to the next. They switched schools, addresses, and friends often. Which is why Persy and Eros are her best friends. Callie lived with her grandparents for the first three years of her life. Her parents retired before she started high school.

Nyx had a taste of normalcy during the holidays when she visited her grandparents, who used to live next door to Sheila, Persy's agent and the wife of my stepbrother.

"Wait, your grandparents are Bertha and Teodoro Casanova?" I ask, surprised.

"Yes, they are Mom's parents. How do you know them?"

"They lived a few houses down from ours. Dad and his wife moved out after we left the house," I respond. "Your grandma makes the best cookies in the world."

"I'd like to defer, but they are tasty," she argues playfully while sipping her coffee. "When you have traveled around the world, you learn where to find the best of almost everything."

"Where was your favorite place to live?"

"That's a hard question," she answers. "All the countries in Latin America were fun. England is gorgeous. Mostly the countryside. I liked Ireland too, but I'm not sure if I'd like to live in Europe. Visiting yes, but I'd rather be in a more tropical place close to the ocean. I might want to retire to Costa Rica or Peru. I think that's why Eros wants to set up the business there. He loved it there too."

"You'd love my place in Seattle. Except it's cold during the winter," I state as we arrive at her parents' house, which I'm not surprised to see that it is in the middle of a woodsy area and their next neighbor seems to be at least a mile away from their home. "Why did you move to Colorado?"

"My parents," she answers. "When they decided to stop digging and start teaching, CU hired them. Eros was in Ithaca, New York. Persy and I were in North Carolina. She was studying at NCU, and I went to Duke. We were close enough to watch out for each other but had our own space because...hello, college. It's the time when you want to find your own path. Once we were ready to work, we both agreed to move close to the parents."

When I kill the engine, I reach out for my mug to drink more of my coffee. Nyx glances at me giving me a mischievous smile. I arch an eyebrow and wonder if she poisoned my coffee.

"What is it?" I ask, checking myself in the mirror and finishing the cup of TLC she shared with me. I won't tell her it tastes better than black coffee though.

"Okay, I'm ready to meet *the parents*," I state.

"Cross your fingers that they're not naked or having sex by the entrance."

I almost choke and start coughing loudly. She watches me with amusement and adds, "I'm warning you. You might regret meeting the Brassards."

With that, she unbuckles her seatbelt and leaves me staring at her swaying ass while I'm trying to recover from what she just said.

"Woof!" Brock barks and I shake my head, wiping the horrifying picture of her parents... I hope she's joking.

I swallow hard and get down from the car, unbuckling Brock and getting him down after hooking the leash onto his collar. He's pretty well trained, but I don't know if the Brassards have a dog or if there's an animal around that might be close by. I march towards the path Nyx followed and find her right by the door.

"Ready to meet them? They are probably having breakfast. Let's hope they aren't on each other's menu," she laughs, moving the handle.

"Shouldn't we call or something," I suggest as she pushes the door open.

"And miss their show?"

"Which is why I'm on the edge of my seat," I joke, walking behind her. "Nothing says happy Saturday better than catching your parents having sex."

She laughs walking away from me.

"Cool, you arrived on time," Eros says from the kitchen.

"Where are they?" Nyx asks.

"Dad went out for a run and Mom's in the backyard tending her plants," he says and looks at me. "Who scared you, bro?"

"Your sister played a fucked-up joke," I answer, glaring at Nyx.

She takes Brock's leash away from me and marches toward the back door. "Yes, think that it's a joke. That's what it was...just don't come crying when it happens."

Her maniacal laugh makes me chuckle.

"She's in a good mood. A little insane, but in a better mood than yesterday," I tell him.

"Only Saturdays and Sundays and only when she's not working," Eros answers. "Don't get me wrong, I adore my sister, but she is too responsible to let her guard down."

I stare at him and shake my head. "Then we'll talk about the company on Monday," I say, pulling out my phone.

"You're leaving tomorrow," he reminds me.

"My assistant can move everything around. Unless you plan on paying her, I'm not going to bother her during the weekend."

He frowns, narrows his gaze, and asks, "Do you have a thing for my sister?"

"Not at all," I lie.

Do I want to have sex with her? Definitely. Am I going to act on it?

Never say never, Nate.

"Okay. Just remember, hands off Nyx. Of my three sisters, she's the most vulnerable, and I'd hate to kill you. I'm still not sure if Ford is good for Persy, but if I say anything, she'll cut off my balls, and I like them where they are," he states. "Now that I delivered my big bro warning, let me introduce you to our mother before we leave."

I hate when people tell me what to do, and now that Eros delivered his brief and lame speech, I get it. The reason I want her is because everyone is against us being together. Now that I see the logic in my actions, I can let it go. Let her go.

Right?

TEN

Nyx

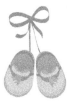

"I LOVE YOU," Eros says after the crazy ride through the zipline. "But you're going to pay for my hearing aid. I think I'm deaf."

Nate grins and shakes his head. "Thank fuck I went first. I barely heard her screamfest."

"It was..." I'm trying to speak, but I'm still recovering from the ride. My heart beats fast against my ribcage. Blood pumps through my veins. My stomach churns, but I ignore it.

This wasn't just exhilarating. I felt free in a way I haven't felt in so long. Sometimes I forget how wonderful it is to let everything go and just enjoy the moment.

"This is what you need," Eros says. "Let yourself loose. You were like that, until you started college. Consider this my most brilliant advice, get off the fast track. Find a good balance between work and life. Get out and enjoy the world. You encourage us to do what we love and follow our dreams. What about you?"

His advice isn't helpful while I'm feeling slightly lightheaded. As I'm about to speak, a wave of nausea hits me, and my stomach is turning upside down violently. One powerful contraction and the little breakfast I had splatters all over the floor. I squat, putting my head between my legs and breathing slowly.

"Nyx, are you okay?" Eros asks while Nate is requesting tissues or napkins.

Someone hands me a roll of paper towels. I clean my mouth and straighten up, taking a long inhale of air.

"Here, drink some water. Just little sips, and don't finish it." Nate offers me the bottle of water he had strapped to his belt. This should serve me right, for mocking him. He has a utility belt with a first aid kit, water, a pocketknife, and other things that I thought were useless.

"Thank you," I say, handing it back to him after I take a few sips. "This is a sign that I shouldn't be ziplining or doing crazy things."

"As long as you didn't catch some flu during your last trip," Eros says. "Every time you catch a bug, I get sick too."

"My last trip was to New York with Persy. In a private jet. If I get sick, she's the one who would get it. Not you. Also, it's summer. Flu season is months away."

"You've been traveling for the past couple of months. Your defenses are low, and you probably caught a bug," he insists.

"Time to find a new career," Nate suggests, bringing the conversation back to the plate. "You might be working so hard you're getting sick."

"It was the ziplining," I argue. "I'm doing what I love. I always wanted to be a lawyer."

"To save the Rainforest, push laws that will save the environment, and...you wanted to be an activist," Eros recalls and stares at me. I'm not sure if he's challenging me to fight him or just telling me how disappointed he is about my life. "Instead, you work for a greedy bitch, you live off of takeout, and you completely forgot how to have a good time. Look, now you're sick because your body is asking for a break."

I stare at him dumbfounded. Yes, things didn't turn out the way I wanted. I became a career-oriented woman who wants stability. If I lose my job tomorrow, my savings will last me for about six months. I have a cushion, and he doesn't.

Perhaps I should remind him who bails him out every time his bank account is overdrawn? Me. Well, other times it is Persy. But if it wasn't for us, he'd be living under a bridge.

Wouldn't he?

"You chose to be like our parents, I refuse to do the same," I state, then bite my lower lip regretting my comment.

"What does that mean?" He glares at me, his nostrils flaring.

Nate watches us, puts himself in between us and then says, "Let me take you home. You don't look well."

"We have business to talk about," I remind him.

"No, that can wait till Monday," Nate says, worry sketched in his blue eyes.

"I have work on Monday. Unlike you two, I have a boss who expects me to be there on time."

"We can do a conference call," Nate suggests.

"How about tomorrow?" I ask.

He frowns and lets out a loud breath. "I... Fuck, Ford is in New York."

Eros and I look at each other and then at him puzzled by his reaction.

"What does that mean?" I ask.

"Nothing. I don't have plans, but I'd rather not work tomorrow. It's a part of balancing my life. I can teach you a trick or two if you want." He winks at me.

"Dude," Eros says.

"Just giving her options since you seem to be worried about her," Nate jokes, but I think his mischievous eyes say we could do a lot more than hang out tomorrow.

"I can try to be off by seven on Monday," I offer, not engaging with my brother or Nate's flirtatious advances.

"Works for me. If we're not working today, I rather go home. I have to talk to Misty," Eros announces. "Are you sure you're okay driving her to her house?"

"You're not going to profess your love for her, are you?" I ask.

"No. We're still friends. She asked me to help her today since her fiancé is out of town," he explains.

Somehow, I don't believe him.

"Please, don't do anything stupid," I beg.

"I won't, *Mom*. You two behave," he gives Nate a warning glare.

"Who is Misty?" Nate asks on our way to his car.

"One of his closest friends. She's getting married, and he's now wondering if maybe she's the love of his life—or the one who got away."

"Is she?" he asks.

I shrug. "Persy and I think he's just missing the attention Misty used to give him. I just hope he doesn't do something he regrets later. Sometimes he doesn't think about the consequences of his actions."

"In contrast, you overthink them too much," Nate argues, and he's right.

I always weigh the pros and cons of every action, but that's the key to my success.

"One of us has to be the sensible one in this family," I say. "If all of us were like my parents, we'd be a disaster."

"Balance," is all Nate says after he opens the passenger door for me.

When he gets in the driver's seat I say, "You're an adrenaline junky."

"I can balance work with my weekends at the race car track, at a lake, on a plane...you name it. I might be doing it while I take a break," he defends himself, reaching for the glove compartment where he takes out a container and hands me a piece of dry fruit. "Here, ginger candy. It's good for nausea. Your brother worries about you. He might've been fucking around for the past four years, but before that he was just like you."

"How do you know?" I ask him as I take a bite of the piece of ginger.

"About your brother or the ginger?" He hands me his water bottle. "Drink it slowly."

"Both? Why would you have ginger with you?" I ask, staring at him.

"As you mentioned, I'm an adrenaline junky," he answers. "I carry everything in case of an emergency. Some people get sick after ziplining. Brought it with me in case you needed it. You seem to be a homebody."

"Not sure if I should say thank you for being prepared or be upset for labeling me as boring," I argue. "Now, how do you know about Eros?"

Before he quit his job, he used to work as a financial consultant in Manhattan. He made a lot of money but, like me, he lived to work.

"Do you think I'm going to partner with just anyone? I talked with him for about a week or two before we even considered the partnership. We're a few steps ahead of you. You don't need to follow his advice but think about what you want long term," Nate responds.

"Well, I'll probably continue what I'm doing for another five years," I say, drinking a little more water and closing my eyes. I feel so tired. As if all of a sudden someone sucked all the energy out of me.

Are five years enough to slow down and plan on having a family? Maybe by then, I'll fall in love. Having a child or two might be in my future. Is that even possible? I have a career, and with a kid, I will have to shift my life to accommodate not only the kid but my... Will I ever meet someone?

I internally grunt because my personal life is pathetic and just trying to think of the possibilities depresses me.

"I love my career." I break the silence and hush my thoughts away.

"That's respectable," Nate answers.

The car stops and I shiver when his finger caresses the inside of my arm. "Do you need me to take you to the doctor?"

"No, I'll be fine. It's just...I'm not used to flying up in the air outside of an airplane. I respect gravity," I joke, drinking more water.

After a pause I say, "It was good, you know. It's been a while since I let myself just run wild, even if it was just for a few moments."

I don't even know why I confide in him. This is a discussion I usually have with Persy. My chest tightens because even though I'm happy for her newfound love, I feel we're not as close as we used to be. Maybe it's the loneliness speaking.

"If I say, 'It's time to rethink your priorities,' I'll just sound like a broken record. Just...think about it," he says.

He's not wrong, but I still have a lot to do before I can leave the firm. Maybe I should start a dream board with what I want to accomplish and create a timeline.

"What do you want from life?" I ask him curiously.

"I already have it. This is my life," he answers.

For some reason, I want to tell him that it seems just as lonely and mechanical as mine. Except he has Brock. Just because he has plenty of hobbies to keep him occupied, it doesn't mean it's a fully lived life.

"Don't forget we have to pick up the pup at my parents'," I remind him, and the sentence sounds too domestic.

"On it," he answers. "We'll pick up the kid before heading home."

His words feel weird and wonderful. It's hard to explain, but there's that strange yearning inside my chest again. Wanting a man in my life and maybe a child or two. Him telling me let's pick up our babies from my parents—or his. Wanting more than what I currently have. Something money can't buy...company.

A partner.

I'm not one to want a man in her life or children, but for the past couple of weeks it's crossed my mind several times.

What if...?

Once we arrive at my parents', he parks and asks, "How are you feeling?"

"Better?" The word comes out like a question. "Not sure if I have the energy to see my parents."

"Don't worry. I'll just go and get Brock. You stay here, okay?"

I think it takes less than a couple of minutes for him to rush back inside the car and say, "Fuck, that was... They...they were having sex in front of my dog."

I open my eyes and laugh when I get a look at his horrified face.

"Told you to be careful," I say laughing, but the laughter upsets my stomach and I barely have time to open the door and throw up the little I had left in my stomach.

"Nyxie," I hear mom's voice. "Are you okay? Octavio, bring something to clean her, a wet washcloth, and a slice of lemon."

"Ziplining isn't for the weak of...stomach? I bet it's the adrenaline. I might be allergic to it," I keep saying nonsense while Mom rubs my back.

"It's going to be okay," she whispers.

"I'm fine," I assure her, but really, I'm not. My stomach isn't upset, it's actually raging. I can't even straighten up because I feel super lightheaded.

"You have an ulcer," she states, she continues drawing circles on my back and then places a wet washcloth on my neck. "How many times do I have to tell you that not eating is going to make you sick."

Mom and Dad are like a real life WebMD. With only a couple of symptoms, they are already diagnosing me with some obscure or incurable disease.

"Promise me that if you continue like this, you'll go to the doctor on Monday," she says, handing me a napkin and a lemon. "Suck on that after you wipe your mouth. It should help you. If not, we should give you a teaspoon of baking soda with ginger and honey."

Great, home remedies for my ulcer.

"What happened?" Dad asks.

"She went ziplining with Eros and Ford's brother," Mom answers. "I think she has something in the stomach."

"His name is Nate, and I can't believe you two were having sex. You could've stopped when he rang the bell," I argue.

"I didn't think he'd be opening the door when I said it was unlocked," Mom claims, and I shake my head. "Right now, let's worry about your health. You work too much."

"With the junk she eats, it can be stomach cancer," Dad offers his wise knowledge.

"Please, don't start diagnosing me. I swear I'll go to the doctor on Monday, but stop throwing out names of the latest diseases you read about," I beg them while slowly rising from my crouching position. "See, I'm fine. It's just the movement while sliding or...maybe I have altitude sickness."

"Now who is making up nonsense," Dad says, shaking his head.

Mom stares at me, holds my face and sighs, "You're pregnant."

I laugh loudly and say, "When you show me your medical diploma, I'll believe you."

She rolls her eyes. "Go home, drink water, and eat slowly and in small portions."

"I'm not pregnant, Mom," I correct her.

"Ready to go?" Nate offers. "Thank you again for keeping an eye on Brock."

"You should stay," Mom insists. "I'll take care of you."

"Mom, I'm fine, and Nate needs to leave."

"I promise to keep an eye on her," Nate assures them. "Again, thank you for..."

"Anytime. Call us if she needs us," Dad says as he helps me get inside the car. "Call me if you feel worse. I know you like to show us that you're independent and strong, but let us take care of you."

"Love you, Dad."

"They are something," Nate says, as we head to my house. "I can see Persy as their child, but you..."

"Why not me?" I wonder.

"Your sister has zero inhibitions and you are too reserved," he explains and then snaps his fingers. "Which makes sense because you've lived secondhand embarrassment all your life."

"Spot on," I say.

"Do you mind if we go to Ford's place instead of your house?" he asks.

"Why?"

"Because he has groceries and you don't. I'd rather cook for you," he offers. "If it's a bug, hopefully, it'll be gone by tomorrow."

I nod in agreement. I'd be lying if I say I want to go home and be alone. I'll take Nate over my parents and my empty house.

"Thank you," I say and close my eyes. "I should be better in a few hours. It was the ziplining or maybe a bug." Anything but stomach cancer or...a baby.

ELEVEN

Nyx

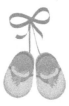

NATE DRIVES us to Ford's house. When we arrive, I regret not asking him to take me home where I could shower and change clothes. Thankfully, Persy lives right next door, so I go to her place to take a shower, change clothes, and brush my teeth a million times until the foul taste in my mouth is gone. Once I'm ready, I go back to Ford's place. It would be easier to ask Nate to take me home, but I feel too sick to be alone. If Persy was in town, I'd be with her.

"You should take a nap," he says as I make my way into Ford's penthouse. "Follow me."

I do as he says, and he shows me his room. "I'll be downstairs if you need anything. Brock is staying with you."

"Thank you," is all I can say because I feel too tired to have a conversation with him—or anyone. I don't wake up until my phone rings. Persy's picture appears on the screen along with the time, seven o'clock. Well, this bug really hit me hard. I've never slept during the day and for this long.

"And she's out to take some air, finally," I joke when I answer the call.

Brock grunts and that's when I realize he is snuggled right next to me. I pet his head and he goes back to sleep.

Persy laughs, "You're not funny. Did I wake you up?"

"Yeah, I got sick earlier today," I explain to her.

"That's what Nate told Ford," she counteracts. "Do you need me to fly back?"

"No, I'm pretty sure it was just the ziplining. I feel much better," I assure her. "You deserve this. A break. And I assume that you are having safe and crazy *fun*."

"Yep, we are...having a lot of fun and also sex," she answers, and I bet she's staring at her dreamy boyfriend longingly.

"When are you coming back?"

"I don't know. Apparently, Nate is staying in Colorado until Tuesday," she responds. "Not that I'm in a hurry. I've finished ten chapters of my book. At this pace, I might finish writing the first draft by the end of the month or early September."

She tells me what she's been writing and how easy everything is coming to her. I tell her about my stupid boss and her childish way to punish me for taking time off.

"Hey, I wanted to give you a heads up," she says once we're caught up with each other's lives.

"Tomorrow is Ford and Nate's birthday."

My early conversation with Nate makes so much sense now. He didn't want to be working during his birthday.

"Ford wants to spend it just with me but then he's worried that Nate is alone."

"He's with us. We'll make it fun for him," I promise, but then I think about my parents. They can be a handful.

"Are you sure?"

"On second thought, I'm not sure if he wants to see Edna and Octavio ever again," I say and sigh.

"Oh no," she sighs louder than I did. "What did they do now?"

When I tell her she laughs and groans. "There goes the family bonding. He's never going to want to spend holidays with us. It was Nate's fault, after all. You warned him."

She catches Ford up with what happened, and I hear him guffawing.

"He thought I was joking," I tell her, and I think she puts me on speaker because I can hear them both laughing loudly.

"Well, he had the special Brassard welcome," Persy continues. "If he doesn't want to visit our parents, you can make him pancakes and maybe go for a hike, please. I owe you."

"You won't owe me anything. I'll make sure he has a good day. I'll call Mom so she can prepare him something for dinner. I'd be happy to cook, but my fridge only has takeout containers and a few veggies that might work best as compost for Mom's plants."

She snorts. "You need a life, Nyxie."

"Not you too." I groan.

"Me too?"

I tell her about my conversation with Nate and Eros, and I hate when she says, "They are right. The past couple of months we barely saw each other. You were traveling a lot and the days you were in town, you were at the office. Quit. I'll hire you as my agent."

"We might kill each other," I warn her.

"Please, give someone else that excuse," she says exasperated. "You and I work perfectly together. I'd rather give you twenty percent of my earnings than give it to some scumbag bitch that... Deep breaths, Persy."

"Good, you're at the anger stage. What changed?" I ask.

The last time we discussed Sheila, her former agent, she was sad. It wasn't because of the money Sheila stole but because she came to the realization that her oldest friend betrayed her. With a childhood like ours, we didn't get to have many friends. Losing one of the few we had stings.

"Clyde asked Ford to loan him the exact amount of money that we're demanding from Sheila," she responds angrily.

"No way!" My anger rises and so does the nausea.

I jump off the bed and run toward the bathroom barely making it on time.

"Sorry about that," I apologize after rinsing my mouth.

"Are you okay?" Persy's voice has the same concern Mom's had earlier.

"Yes?" I lie because I don't want to discuss what's happening to me, so I go back to her scumbag agent. "I'm guessing Sheila wants to settle. Is Ford going to lend them the money?"

"No, he doesn't want to do it, which is good. I don't want to get into a fight because of them," she answers and then asks, "What is happening with you? That bug sounds lethal."

"I'm feeling like shit," I mention and give in to the conversation because Persy is my best friend and who else but her to listen to what can be a tragedy. "You know what Mom told me
today when she saw me?"

"I'm afraid to guess. Did they pull an internet browser, added your symptoms and tell you, 'You are dying tomorrow?'" She laughs, but I don't join her. It'd be funny if it wasn't hitting too close to home.

"Dad said stomach cancer. Mom said, 'You're pregnant!'"

"What?" she squeaks.

"They need to stop playing doctor."

"I keep telling them that, but they don't listen," I agree with her and leave the bathroom.

Nate is outside looking at me. "Are you okay?"

I nod, "Yeah. Was I so loud that you heard?"

"No, Ford texted me. Persy is worried about you."

"I'm fine," I assure him. Not sure if it's to Nate, Persy, or for my benefit.

"Are you?" Persy asks.

"Yes, I am fine," I repeat. Giving Nate a reassuring smile.

"No, are you pregnant?"

"No. Oh God, no. I'm not expecting anything. Not a shipment or a baby," I swear and let out a long breath. "No, it's impossible."

"Have you...had sex in the past few weeks?" Persy asks, I look up at Nate who is still in the room.

Well, isn't this an awkward conversation to have. Thankfully, he can only hear one side of it.

I bite my lip and nod. "Just once, a couple of weeks ago," I whisper, remembering the night I ended up having sex with Edward Bryant.

He's one of the nephews of my boss, Sarah. My heart stops just thinking of what could happen if I am. *Oh please, don't even think about it, Nyx. Stop that train of thought.*

I start counting the weeks since that trip.

"It was three weeks ago," I mumble. "While I was out of town, but we used protection."

"What if..." she trails her voice.

"Shut up!"

Just the thought of having a kid, and with *him,* makes me shiver and not in a good way. This is a great example of why I should focus on my goals and not let my guard down. I was lonely, bored, and horny. He was available, kind of funny, and we said what happens outside of Colorado doesn't come home. It'd be ironic or some kind of punishment to get pregnant after a year of not having sex.

"I'm sure Mom's wrong," Persy comforts me, but why don't I feel better with those words? "But what if he used an old condom?"

"It was new. I bought them that week...a girl could hope. It had been a year, Persy."

I begin pacing around the room. What if my mother is right? Am I having a baby? No. This can't be happening. I...nope.

"Calm down, I'm sure it's a bug, Nyx. You'll be fine by Monday," she reassures me.

"But condoms are only ninety-eight percent effective," I almost stammer, setting her on speaker and pulling the information on Google.

"Leave it to you to know the statistics of a condom's effectiveness," Persy hisses. "Don't fixate on that and just enjoy the weekend. I should ask Nate to take you out and distract you. Go to The Hideout sports bar. That should keep your mind occupied."

"I've been trying not to worry, but what if Mom's right. This will ruin...everything," I protest feeling selfish, but how am I supposed to react.

"Nyx Andromeda Brassard, stop this insanity," she orders. "You're not a neurotic mess. You're the sensible one of all of us. Now, go have dinner with Nate and remember that you'll be fine."

Easy for her to say. If she got pregnant, her dreamy boyfriend would step in. If I end up knocked up... What am I supposed to do?

Do I want to raise a child with Edward Bryant? I don't think so. I should've thought about the consequences before we slept together. I mean, working with him after what happened has been easy. Neither one of us has acted awkward because we're two mature adults. But a kid will change everything.

"Repeat after me," Persy says. "My parents aren't doctors, and I'll be fine."

"Miss you."

"See you soon, okay. Nate, if you're there, take care of my sister, please."

"I will," he assures her before I hang up.

He stares at me tenderly and suggests, "Why don't we take Brock for a walk and then we can come back and have dinner? I made some chicken soup."

"That sounds good." Much better than going home and worrying myself sick about what is happening to me.

It's just a twenty-four-hour bug. Nothing major, Nyx. Chill. Maybe everyone is right, and you need to slow down. You're stressing yourself for nothing.

TWELVE

Nate

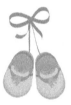

THESE PAST COUPLE of days haven't worked out the way I planned. When I boarded the plane from New York to Denver I thought to myself, *maybe you can get lucky this weekend.*

We'll be away from Ford and Persy. No one will be there to play third wheel. Nyx seems like a woman who knows what she wants and likes to have fun—when she allows herself to have it.

On Friday night while we had dinner at her place, I planned my next move. By Saturday night I'd have her in bed. It's just a matter of loosening her up a little.

It was foolish to predict what would happen between us when it seems like everything is working against us.

She spent most of the day in my bed, but not in the way I had in mind.

Whatever bug she has not only had her puking, but she spent all day napping after we came back from her parents' house. I spent the rest of my afternoon and part of the evening working and watching over her.

When I realized that my dinner plans had changed from a fancy table for two at Frasca to Ford's kitchen, I started making chicken noodle soup. That's one thing I remember about my mother. When we were sick, she'd prepare soup for us.

Before dinner, we walked Brock who had stayed with her almost all day, and then ate dinner. I'm positive that she doesn't feel well since she didn't hesitate to stay with me. She went to her sister's house to grab a pair of pajamas and we stayed in my bed watching old movies.

Well, that was the intention. We picked out five movies for the evening. It hadn't been ten minutes after the first movie started when she was already asleep. I stayed until the movie ended before I turned off the television. I should've moved to Ford's bedroom, but Nyx's head rested on top of my chest, and I didn't have the heart to move her away from me.

As planned, I slept with Nyx Brassard. There wasn't any sex involved, but one of the goals was achieved, right?

It's kind of ironic to wake up to my thirty-fifth birthday next to a beautiful woman with whom I haven't shared anything but stolen caresses and a few scenes I'd love to erase from my mind.

She might be gorgeous, but no one looks good while vomiting.

I should be running away. More like drop her at home and fly to Seattle without looking back—ever. If she has the flu or a bug, I'll get sick. If she's pregnant...God bless her heart. It sounds like the father is a loser. The thought of being around an expectant mother makes me angry. It reminds me of Wyatt, Bronwyn, and the family she snatched from me.

If he was mine, I'd be picking him up from his mother's place today and spending the day with my kid. Sometimes I wonder if he's okay, if the other guy is a good father to him. Not sure if it's my brain or my heart that can't understand that he's not mine to worry about. But how can I stop loving him when I haven't forgotten his mother either.

What a fucked up life I live!

Nobody, not even Ford knows that I'm still pining for my ex. Which is why I should just move from this bed, leave this state, and forget Nyx Brassard. Whatever it is that keeps pulling me to her isn't real.

I don't do anything. Instead, I stay still, waiting for her to wake up. It's been a long time since I've woken up next to a woman, and this time we didn't even have sex—or a fight to justify the lack of fucking between us.

Brock is the one who stirs first and gives me that, *we have to walk now* face. I push myself out of the bed, change, and we head outside for his morning walk.

When I come back, Nyx is in the kitchen, moving her luscious round ass to the rhythm of Oasis' "Champagne Supernova" while singing at the top of her lungs.

"Morning," I greet her.

She turns around and smiles. Her big brown eyes sparkle when she sees me and says, "Happy Birthday."

I had no idea she knew, but I bet Ford or Persy gave her a heads up. This is the moment when I should say, *"Thank you. I'm thinking about having those conference calls from Seattle if you don't mind. There are things I have to attend to personally."*

Instead, I ask, "How are you feeling?"

"Much better. I told you it was the ziplining and maybe bad sushi." Her voice is so mellow and relaxed. I like this Nyx. The one who isn't checking emails, worrying about work, or trying to make sure everyone around her is doing alright.

"I made you coffee. This time I didn't add anything to it."

"Thank you. You didn't touch the sushi," I remind her.

She glances at me, her eyebrow arched, and I'm judging myself too. Was I paying too much attention that I knew exactly what she ate? She mentioned not liking raw fish. I heard the story about living in Korea and getting sick after eating hoe at a restaurant. There's so much I want to ask her about her life while growing up, the places where she lived, the different cultures she experienced.

There's so much I want to know about her. This is why I don't leave. I'm around because she's interesting and not because I am attracted to her beyond her beauty, right?

"Observant," she declares and hands me a plate with pancakes and eggs. "What do you want us to do today?"

Leave you at home. Escape from you.

"We could go for a hike," I offer, hoping that she can do it without getting sick. "Unless you're not up for it. Then we could do something less—"

"I'm feeling great," she reassures me, smiling at me tenderly.

While drenching my pancakes with maple syrup, I ask, "You're not having breakfast?"

She sighs and shows me a cup of yogurt. "I'm going for something light. A bowl of blueberries, yogurt, and tea. Mom texted me earlier to remind me that I should eat more often and in small portions."

"Is she still thinking that you are..." I trail my voice, taking a bite of pancakes. "Mmm...these are delicious. They are like pieces of clouds. Your mom doesn't seem like a regular mother."

She grins.

"Everything I bake comes out fluffy, even pancakes," she states and then adds, "Mom is different. I'm impressed that she hasn't quit and moved to some remote town in South America."

"Would she do it?"

She nods, eating a spoonful of fresh blueberries.

"In a heartbeat. I'm sure my parents stay because we're tight." She looks at me and shrugs. "It'd be hard to live far away from them. Mom is going nuts because Callie moved—and we don't know where she's at."

"Say the word and I'll have that info for you," I offer again. "What do you usually do on Sundays?"

She looks at me and twists her lips a couple of times and sighs. "Work?"

Perhaps I connect with her because we're not so much different. Maybe I'm here to learn something from her. To teach each other that there's more to life than making deals. It's not like I have my shit together, but I can balance my life a lot better than she does.

"You are a workaholic. I should take you under my wing and teach you how to balance out life with work," I offer wondering if that's something we could do.

"Maybe in a couple of weeks. I'm working on two important cases and closing the third one this Monday," she informs me. "Once I close them and my boss is off my ass, I can take a weekend off."

I want to tell her that weekends are supposed to be always off, but it seems like a waste of energy. She's too focused, and maybe that's one of her best qualities.

"You're giving me today, right?" I ask, hopeful. "I promise to make it an unforgettable day."

She gives me a playful smile. "Isn't that supposed to be my line?"

"Probably, but I'm making this easy for you. Next year you can make it up to me," I wink at her, finishing the pancakes. "Thank you for breakfast."

While she finishes her food, I head upstairs to take a shower. Once I come back to the kitchen, I find her playing with Brock. She's dressed in a pair of jeans, her hiking boots and a white T-shirt.

"I grabbed some clothes from Persy. We can just head out instead of going home."

Whatever Nyx had could be a twenty-four hour bug, an ulcer, or maybe, as she insists it was, going on the zipline. Still, I suggest we prepare a picnic instead of taking her to eat at some restaurant. From what her parents said yesterday, she could use a homemade meal. Heating up some of the leftover chicken soup, I pour it into the thermos I have stored in Ford's house.

Nyx makes a couple of sandwiches, washes a couple of apples, and fills the water bottles before we put everything into my backpack.

As we're making our way out of the penthouse, I run back for crackers just in case she gets sick.

"You know why we wouldn't work out as a couple?" she asks.

"Please, enlighten me," I answer as we head toward the elevator.

"You're an outdoorsy guy, I'm not," she concludes. "But I have a few friends who would love to date you. As I said, when you're ready to let go of your past, you should give me a call."

I laugh. "So, you spend time convincing yourself that we're not possible, huh?"

"No, it just occurred to me," she states. "Clearly, you wouldn't understand my mind. The oddest thoughts come to me without warning."

Opening the passenger door for her I whisper close to her ear. "I'm just glad that you think about me."

She shivers and jumps into the truck to put some distance between us. I grin at her. I'll wear her down, even if it takes me years. But do I really want to?

THIRTEEN

Nate

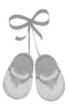

WHEN I COME to Colorado to visit Ford, we usually drive up to the mountains. There are plenty of things to do up there, including hiking. Since I'm still concerned about Nyx's health, we go to Roxborough Park instead. The place is a forty-five-minute drive south of the city. It reminds me of the Grand Canyon. There are a lot of big red rocks surrounding us. When I make the observation she says, "Duh, why do you think this state is called Colorado?"

"I guess there are a lot of places I haven't visited yet to come to such a conclusion," I say mockingly. "You should take me on a road trip around the state."

"It's not like I've lived in this place for long," she says instead. "Just moved here five years ago. Though, when I visited my parents during holidays or breaks, they'd take us to whatever part of the state they had discovered."

See, this is what I don't understand. She's lived a big adventure all her life and she chose to settle into a life that, even though fits her, doesn't seem to be what she loves. Is it fear?

"You're intriguing," I say, instead of hashing out her life.

I'm enthralled not only by her beauty and her personality, but her fascinating past. What I would've given to be traveling around the world with a loving family. Her parents might be quirky, but they seem like good people.

My father is clueless. Everything is black and white for him. Mom just packed and left. She traded us for a better family—or is it that she ran away to create a family she liked better?

She offers a forced smile and says, "Is that another way of calling me boring?"

"Stop beating yourself up about it," I protest. "The next time you call yourself that, you'll owe me something."

She comes to a halt and stares at me for a long beat as if trying to guess but then asks, "What would I possibly owe you?"

"A kiss," I joke.

She throws back her head and laughs. "They are that bad, huh? This is my first. No one has ever threatened me with kisses."

Her eyes are on my mouth, and I swear I can see her pulse thrumming in her throat. My heart hammers inside my chest. Something changes between us. A switch flips, or maybe it's not a change, but the walls that we've put up to avoid messy entanglements are disappearing with every minute we spend together.

"You'll be the judge," I pause, focused on her pouty lips. "Not sure if it's a good idea though."

She lets out a small, breathy laugh, and says, "It's terrible. Which is why I'll start calling myself the life of the party."

"Now you're just throwing fibs to miss what might be the best kiss of your life," I warn her, resuming our walk. "You are scared of me."

She rolls her eyes but doesn't argue. If she feels a little of what I do, she's craving more than just a simple kiss. That should be my birthday present. Shouldn't it?

We stop at some picnic tables that are outside the visitor center. She eats some soup, drinks water, and munches on a cracker while we talk about the archeological discoveries that have happened in the park.

"Do your parents keep any of the objects they find?"

She twists her lips and looks at the visitor center before answering, "No. That'd be illegal. They have plenty of pictures, papers, and have written books about it. I should start getting them better deals with their publishers."

"They write?"

She nods. "Teaching is their second passion, and if they can teach the world through books, they are happy."

"But you don't want to be like them?"

She squeezes her eyes and lets out some air before speaking. "I adore them, but it was nerve wracking to be their child. Imagine not having a place to call home and having to fit all your belongings in just a suitcase you share with your sister. That's something I never want to experience again or want my kids to undergo. It's not fun to live with uncertainty."

I reach for her hand and clasp it. Her eyes open and she smiles.

"It sounds selfish," she continues. "But the anxiety is still there, lurking underneath the fun experiences, the happy memories, and the adventures."

"Your feelings are valid. Parents never think about their actions and how they'll affect and shape the future of their children," I voice, wondering if I'm speaking from experience or just trying to validate her.

I let her hand go because the heat between us is beginning to burn me from the inside out.

Her brown eyes stare at me widely.

"Time to continue this hike and shake the past," she announces, and I want to ask her if it's worth fighting the attraction.

We're right on the edge of the cliff and one push can get us naked and ready to fuck the brains out of each other. It's easy to talk myself out of it when I receive a text from Ford wishing me a happy birthday. I wouldn't do anything to jeopardize his happiness.

For the rest of the way up and back to the car we're silent, but it's a peaceful calm that I enjoy just as much as her presence. When I ask her where to, she tells me her parents'. The traffic isn't bad, but the distances make up for the time I spend on I-5 or around New York fighting the congestion.

We arrive at her parents' home around four, and her Dad offers me a handcrafted beer. He gives a ginger seltzer to Nyx.

"It's good," she admits.

"I made enough to fill up a case. I left it by the door. Take it home," he instructs and glances at me. "It should help you with your condition."

"Thank you, Dad." Nyx kisses his cheek and hugs him. "But I don't have a condition."

He takes me to the room where he crafts his beer and whatever drinks his daughters request. I haven't seen them with the rest of his children, but I can see that he adores Nyx. He doesn't ask her how she feels, but he watches her closely. Before I do anything else, I put the case in the trunk.

When I come back, Nyx and Brock are on the couch. There's a book on top of her chest, but she's fast asleep. I grab the purple throw blanket from the top of the other couch and cover her. I head to the backyard where her father is in front of the grill.

"What is it that you do?" he asks me while he's grilling eggplants and other vegetables.

"Ford and I own a few companies," I answer.

"Do you program like him?"

"No. I manage, sell, and plan, while he produces," I explain, believing it's the easiest way to give him a glimpse of what we do.

I wonder if Ford explained his job as just being a programmer.

My brother doesn't talk much about what he does and keeps his identity as the famous Langford Chadwick private. So private, that Persy had no idea who he was until a week ago.

"You seem more relaxed than him," he speaks then looks at me. "You're not. You just know how to fake it better. You don't trust easily either. I understand that it is hard to let your guard down when you have so much money and you don't know who to trust. But I'm guessing there's more to that. Probably, one of your parents left when you were younger. Just know that here you're in a safe place."

"My mom," I answer. "How did you know?"

He shrugs, flipping some veggies and setting the ones that are done on a plate.

"I've been studying the past, trying to understand the present. Human behavior is...interesting," he explains. "I'm just not understanding why you are here, yet. Is it for Ford's benefit or Nyx's?"

His question makes me take a step back and not only physically. Am I here to check if these people are good enough for my brother?

"I'm Eros' business partner. I'm here—"

He laughs and shakes his head. "Don't bullshit me, son. I've been on this planet longer than you. If you feel alone, you're welcome to be a part of us. Just don't use my daughter, okay?"

What is it about Nyx that makes them so protective? She's strong enough to stand up for herself. However, I noticed yesterday when I spoke to Ford that Persy is no different from her father or her brother. Is it because she's always taking care of them and this is the way they reciprocate?

Maybe this is how a family works. They look after each other. Ford and I have been doing it, but not because we learned from our parents, but because we are all we have. Now he has this, and I...I hope he doesn't leave me hanging.

HAVING dinner with the Brassards is pleasant. Their conversation goes from the oddly cold weather expected for tomorrow, to trying the last position in the *Sixtysutra* book that Eros gave them for Christmas.

"That book is a godsend," Octavio states.

Edna explains to me that it's a Kama Sutra book where the poses are modified for couples over sixty. I almost choke on my beer.

"I'm sure you can skip that information. We don't need to hear about your sex life, Dad," Nyx protests as we clean up the table.

"Not many men my age are as lucky as I am," Octavio says. "Even with my hip replacement, I can still—"

"Oh God, please make them stop," Nyx complains covering her ears.

I want to hug her, tease her, and whisper that maybe we can be like that in thirty years. Thank fuck, I don't do anything stupid. I owe it to Edna who carries in a cake and begins to sing "Happy Birthday" to me.

"Make a wish," Edna prompts, and I'm not sure what to wish for.

I thought I had everything, and this weekend with Nyx and her parents is showing me the holes in my life. I'm not sure if I want to fill them and search for what I'm missing.

Is what I have enough? Looking around the room, I see more than three people smiling as they wait for me to blow out the candles. I see love, company, and support.

So, I think to myself, *to have this next year*. After I blow out the candles, I'm not sure what exactly it is that I want to have, and partly regret it. Then again, wishes are just childish desires that never come true.

"Thank you for everything," I say on our way out, because this day was even better than I thought it would be.

"It's our pleasure," Edna says and takes my hand, giving me a motherly look and hugging me once again. "This is your home. Don't wait for an invitation. Come and visit us soon, okay?"

"Your mom is a hugger," I say when we are driving back home.

"You could say that." Nyx's voice has a hint of annoyance and then she adds, "Actually she's a very affectionate person. That's one thing we love about her. Complaints aside, I adore my parents. Will I have to defend her in court for over hugging someone...maybe?"

I laugh and take her hand as I drive along the highway until I arrive at her house. Silence isn't something I enjoy but the serene atmosphere between us feels nice.

"Thank you for this weekend," she says as I walk her to the door. "Sorry about yesterday."

"Hey, I'm just glad you're feeling better."

I stare at her beautiful eyes. Unthinkingly, I lift my hand and caress her cheek with the back of my hand before I cup her chin.

"Happy birthday," she whispers.

"Thank you again for today," I mumble, my face closing up to hers slowly. "You still owe me my present."

"This is a bad idea," she mutters. Her uneven breath caresses my lips.

"Terrible," I agree, melting by the heat increasing as our bodies get closer together.

I bend my head and kiss her. Her lips freeze at first, but when I put my other arm around her, they soften. Her fingers push through my hair and entwine behind my head. For all the bad decisions I've made in my life, and I've made a lot of them since I could walk, this might be the most dangerous, lethal, and delicious one I've made.

She tastes of lavender, honey, and vanilla. Just like the cake we ate earlier. But there's also a sweetness that I'm sure is all Nyx. Placing a hand on her neck, I pull her closer to me and the slow, tantalizing kiss becomes eager, hungry. I want to devour her.

But this isn't just lips pressed together, tongues dancing, and hands exploring. It's like we're connecting, exchanging secrets, opening a door that should remain closed. Her hands push me, but her lips don't let go. It's as if she's willing to be consumed by the fire we've ignited but also wants to run far away from this situation.

"This is wrong," she mumbles against my lips. "I...I'm not in a good place, and you..."

"I know," I say, giving her one more longing kiss.

"For what is worth, if I had found you before, maybe we could've been perfect together."

She kisses my cheek and pats it, "Doubt it. Take care of yourself, Nathaniel."

FOURTEEN

Nyx

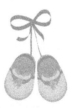

NOTHING SAYS professional better than reaching for a trash can during a mediation. The stupid bug is back. Yesterday I was fine. Maybe Mom is right, and I have an ulcer. This must be due to the stress. It has been a terrible day and it's only eleven in the morning. Earlier today, I lost a case. This day can't get any worse.

Can it?

Once I'm done heaving, I excuse myself and run to the bathroom to rinse, clean myself, and try to settle down before I go back to the conference room.

"Better?" my client asks, arms crossed, hateful glare, and foot tapping.

"Umm, yes. Sorry, I think I caught a bug while I was in New York."

She sighs. "Listen, you've been gone for a long time, and I need someone to be here for me. Your firm came highly recommended, and you're one of the best family law attorneys, but I think I'm going to hire someone else before my soon to be ex-husband ends up with everything we own."

Not my fault, sweetheart. You're the stupid one who met with him thinking he was going to ask for forgiveness and move you back into the house where he's now living with his mistress.

"I told you to wait until I was back," I argue, and this is why I try to avoid divorce cases, but Sarah, my boss, doesn't understand the meaning of the word, no. "You're the one who decided to sit down with your ex-husband and his lawyer without me. You can't blame me for not taking my advice."

She huffs. "So, you're telling me that they reduced the alimony because of me? That's rich. You made me lose that twenty percent."

"No, I told you to stay at home and wait for me. What did you do?"

"They tricked me," she defends herself.

I try not to give her a *do you think I'm stupid* lecture and instead I hit her with the facts, "They have a recording. I'm trying to fix what we—"

"You're fired," she interrupts me, turns around and leaves.

MY BOSS HAS NO BOUNDARIES. Sarah Bryant thinks that she not only owns the place but owns us all. When she wants to speak to us, she lets herself into our offices. It doesn't surprise me to find her waiting for me when I arrive at the firm. This is like the cherry on top to end my Monday of Hell.

She glares at me. Her eyes bore into mine, her jaw is clenched, and her finger is wagging at me, "I didn't hire you to drag the name of my firm through the mud. You lost the Bortner case."

No, I didn't lose it. More like I puked, had to run to the restroom, and the new counselor—your nephew—opened his mouth without me being in the room. He lost the case. Oh, by the way, you should stop hiring your family and start searching for good lawyers.

Of course, that's not what I tell her because I'd like to stay employed for a few more years.

"We were going to settle with the hours the ex-wife was offering us," I remind her. "This custody case was...delicate. He agreed to go to rehab and stop drinking. He didn't, and your nephew said, 'Dude, you smell like a distillery,' while I was taking a break. You should teach him to keep his mouth shut."

Yes, I lost the case, but if I'm being honest, I am happy that Joseph Bortner won't be seeing his children. He's a raging alcoholic—with money. The guy should stop paying lawyers to get him to see his kids. His wife divorced him because he was abusing her and his children. Get a hint, buddy. I should be defending people like his wife.

"Are you going to blame my nephew for Cathy Eigner's dismissal too?"

"I emailed you about her case," I respond, not adding that I was also puking when she decided to fire me.

"Well, we lost the client and she left us an ugly review."

"Against my advice, she sat down with her soon to be ex-husband and his lawyer to iron out some of the divorce details. I told her not to do it while I was out of town."

"You shouldn't be out of town," she growls.

"I agree, but you sent me to work a case with Edward." My response is laced with frustration.

I should remind her that his license was suspended a couple of months ago and I've been doing his job. We've yet to finish with that case.

"Well, you should've told me. We have plenty of lawyers who could have represented you while you were helping Eddy."

My God, the man is almost forty and they still call him Eddy.

I sigh and nod. "Look, Sarah, I'm not sure what you want me to tell you. Losing the Bortner case isn't the end of the world."

"You're on probation," she announces.

"What?" I ask, staring at her with horror. My stomach twists, and I barely reach the trash can.

I run to the bathroom to get cleaned. Looking at myself in the mirror I repeat. "You'll be fine. This is just a bug, and that woman is just being spiteful because she's bitter. You're going to walk into that office and show her that she can't intimidate you."

When I come back, she gives me a pitiful glare.

"This is what I'm talking about," she states. "You're unprofessional. Your behavior during the mediation was atrocious. Throwing up, not even going back to the room to apologize...then losing the client. You're lucky I don't make you pack your things."

Deep breaths, Nyx.

Once she's out I close the door and call my mentor, Pierce Aldridge. If he was still working for the firm, things would be so different.

"Need help killing Edward yet?" he answers instead of greeting me.

"No, but I'm about to quit. Remind me why I need to stay," I ask.

"You're next in line to become a junior partner, but... Maybe it's time to leave," he says, and I freeze.

"What?" I ask, staring at the phone astonished by his words. "You told me this is worth it. How can you change the speech all of a sudden? Is this you, Aldridge?"

He laughs. "Yes, it's me. Tell me what happened with my mother, Brassard."

I explain everything from the litigation to just now and he huffs. "Are you all right?"

"Yeah, I mean...what am I going to do if she fires me?"

"Not about the job, your health. It sounds like you're sick," he amends.

"Mom thinks it's an ulcer," I comment, not mentioning the other probable causes.

"Go to the doctor," he orders.

I sigh defeated because I should pack my things and just leave this hell hole. Then again, I need the job.

"As I said, she put me on probation. If I take an hour off, she's going to fire me."

"Document everything that's happening," he recommends. "If she fires you for any of this, we have a case against the firm."

"We're talking about your family."

"Which is why I'll represent you for free," he offers.

"Are you still being held against your will? Because if that's the case, you can't do it."

He laughs. "No, I'm living my best life. My advice to you is to stay until Mom fires you so we can take them down. I love my mother, but...the firm isn't what it used to be. We know how they win some of the cases."

By buying the judges, I don't say out loud.

"You think she's going to fire me?" I ask, scared.

"Honey, Ed is going to do something stupid and lose the case. You're the one leading it, so he'll blame you. I told you not to accept it. He's done that before," he announces, and I feel the entire weight of the world settling on my shoulders.

This phone call has the opposite effect of what I expected. What happened to work hard and fuck the opposition? Climb to the top... What am I supposed to do with his new advice?

"I can't lose my job."

"You can come and work for me," he suggests.

"In the middle of nowhere Oregon? I thought we were working on getting you out of there," I press, not understanding what is happening with him.

"It's not as bad as I thought. Listen, I'm working on a deal, and I need your advice. I'll email everything to your personal address. Bill me for that okay? Remind Mother that you're good, but you're better suited for corporate, estate law, and intellectual property. That's what you were doing for me."

"Like she's going to listen. Send that over. I'll go through it tonight and send you an invoice on Friday," I agree. Usually, I'd say no, I'll do it for free. However, if I'm going to be without a job soon, I might as well start gathering some seeds for the winter like a smart ant.

My conversation with Pierce doesn't make me feel any better. He knows his mother better than the rest of us. She's planning on firing me, and if she does, what am I supposed to do?

I don't have time to think because nausea hits me hard and I end up puking in my trash can—again. Talk about having a shitty Monday. This is probably the worst I've had in a long time.

FIFTEEN

Nyx

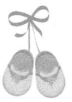

IT'S SAID that if an unfortunate event has already occurred twice, it will most likely happen a third time.

On Monday I lost a case and a client fired me. I'm not ready for the other shoe to drop, but I followed Pierce's advice. I spent all night preparing for the worst. Those two events were enough ammunition to put me on probation. On Tuesday, things don't get any better. I'm interviewing with a potential client. This IT company is growing, and they don't have a legal department. They are contemplating the possibilities of hiring a law firm or hiring lawyers to work just for their company. It's important for Bryant, LLC to land the account.

Since Pierce left, most of his corporate clients have left the firm too. He's not working with them, but he referred them to a different legal firm. Now that I'm looking at everything closely, I can see how he's screwing his family from afar. I have to sit down and talk to him to see what happened between them.

All morning I've been sick, and before I step into the conference room, I explain to Sarah that I'm not feeling well.

She doesn't care, and like the previous day I end up vomiting and dry heaving for five minutes in a row. The clients excuse themselves. When I have my assistant call them to reschedule, they respond saying they have decided to go in a different direction.

Sarah blames it on me.

To no one's surprise but Sarah's, Edward Bryant fucks up the case even before we have to go to trial. I'm on the phone with the client when Sarah barges into my office. Security is right behind her.

"Out!" She yells, making me jump.

"I'm on the line trying to salvage what your nephew did," I protest. "Pierce and I think that—"

"Wait, you discussed this case with someone outside our firm."

"Pierce is your son," I remind her.

"He could be the pope and you are still not allowed to discuss this case with him. He doesn't work for Bryant, LLC. This is a breach of the client confidentiality agreement. I'll be filing against your license."

I feel as if a cluster of spark plugs ignites in my abdomen. Tension grows in my face and my limbs. My breathing becomes shallow, and I have to remind myself that it's going to be okay. She can't do anything. I've spent the last twenty-four hours documenting every-thing that's happened in this firm since Pierce left. *Deep breaths, slowly, take air in and out.*

Once I calm down, I pack my personal belongings while I finish backing up my external hard drive.

When I arrive home, I feel lost. What am I supposed to do now? I pull out my computer and stare at the black screen. It's as if someone just pulled off my limbs and I don't know how I'm going to function anymore.

I'm not sure what time it is, but it's dark outside when my phone rings. Pierce's name appears on the screen.

"Brassard here," I answer, my mouth tastes like metal and my throat is dry.

"You okay there?" Pierce asks. "You hung up on me when my mom entered your office and I haven't heard from you for hours."

I don't have the energy to answer and he speaks, "My mother called me. They need help with a case that *you* fucked up. I'm assuming Eddy blamed you, and he's using you as his scapegoat. Which brings me to my next conclusion. They fired you."

"Well, counselor, two out of two," I say, and it's as if they are the magical words to open the dam. I begin crying, and I can't stop myself.

The crying seems like yet another way to disrupt my stomach and I'm puking again. This time I run to the kitchen sink. Once I clean myself and get ahold of my emotions, I grab my phone.

"Sorry," I sniff. "It's been a bad week."

"And it's just Tuesday," he informs me. "Did you document everything as I told you?"

"Yes, I barely slept because I worked on it all night. I had a bad feeling. However, she threatened to take away my license."

"She won't have time to do anything. She's too busy with Eddy's fuck up. We need to move fast," he says and adds, "Can you please go to the doctor soon?"

I hear voices in the background and then he asks, "What are your symptoms."

I give him a brief history of my nausea, fatigue, and mood swings. He repeats them to whoever is around him and the guy says, "Sounds like what Blaire has."

"Who is this Blaire, who are you talking to, and what does she have? Dad diagnosed me with stomach cancer," I say, yawning.

"I'm with my oldest brother. He's a doctor," he answers. "Blaire has hyperemesis gravidarum."

"English, please?" I ask, hoping the guy can send me the prescription to the pharmacy and I can skip the doctor.

"Excessive vomiting during pregnancy," Pierce responds.

"No, I can't be pregnant, "I protest. "Your brother is wrong."

"Defensive," Pierce highlights. "So, there's a possibility."

"Fuck!" I grunt. "I'll call you later."

I TAKE A SHOWER, change my clothes, and head to the pharmacy. Once I'm back, I stare at the boxes I bought. One of these seven tests has to be right. All of them say that they can give results as early as the first missed period. Checking my calendar, I realize that my last period was two weeks ago. It was light, but I had a period.

This is a waste of time.

Why am I even listening to Pierce and his brother?

Because he's the second person who suggested the possibility, and unlike your mother, he is a real doctor.

Instead of taking the test, I head to the kitchen and look for some food. It's to no surprise that I only find leftovers growing green stuff on top of them.

"This is a wakeup call," I tell myself. "You're not pregnant, but you're unemployed. This is your opportunity to reinvent yourself."

When I pick up the phone, I find a notification from Nate.

Nate: *Call me when you're back from work.*

Nyx: *It's eleven your time, are you still up?*

Nate: *Heading back home from the office. It was a long ass day and it made me think of my favorite workaholic.*

Reading his text, I start crying because I'm unemployed. My phone rings and it's him.

"Hey," I sniff.

"What happened?"

Between sobs, I tell him how my week has been going, and I can't stop crying as I tell him that my boss threatened to take away my license.

"She won't be able to touch you. Trust me. Her firm will be

closed before she tries to file any documentation against you," he assures me. "I need you to take a breath."

"I'm trying, but I can't stop crying," I say angrily. "It's like someone opened the fucking dam and the water flows freely. There's no valve to stop this insanity. Let me call you when I feel less...or more...I'm not even sure what I'm feeling anymore."

"Call if you need me, okay?"

After he hangs up, I find some courage to grab the boxes, head to the bathroom, and use the first test. According to the box, two lines means pregnant. The longest sixty seconds of my existence pass, and after I look at the small window I feel my blood draining, so I try the next test. Then another one. And when I'm done with the seven, all of them agree. My entire world just flipped.

SIXTEEN

Nyx

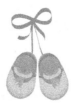

AND JUST LIKE THAT, my world went sideways. I don't think it's upside down. Perhaps it is downside up, and there's no way to put it back in the right place.

Ever.

I've heard that having a kid is life changing and when one learns about them, it is the happiest day of one's life. My future has gone from frightening to scary as hell. I cried for an entire night—and I've yet to find my happiness. On Wednesday morning I can barely open my eyes. My phone is dead, and when I have enough energy to charge it, there are several texts from Nate.

Nate: *Are you okay?*

Nate: *Answer your phone.*

Nate: *Why is my call going to voicemail?*

Nate: *Nyx, I need to know that you're okay or I'll call the National Guard.*

Nate: *Please, call me.*

Nyx: *My phone died. Please, don't send anyone to check on me.*

Nate: *How are you?*

Nyx: *I'll be fine.*

Nate: *I don't like the sound of that.*

I stare at the phone that begins ringing. I decline the call.

Nyx: *I promise to call you once I can talk.*

Nate: *Why can't we talk now?*

Nyx: *I'm not in a good place.*

He doesn't respond and I sigh with relief. I'm usually the stubborn one who doesn't let go until I am sure the person on the other line is okay. My siblings drop it the moment I say I need time. This guy takes more than one text to give me space. In all honesty, I'm not sure if I want the space.

My life has gone from perfect to terrifying. This is one of those times where I'd appreciate if someone could lie to me and say, it's going to be okay. I mean, it might not be a lie, but there's no guarantee that they'll be right. Our future isn't set in stone so who really knows how my life will be in a year.

I place a pin on my feelings because it's a lot easier to focus on objective goals. But before I start working, I place chilled black tea bags over my eyes to get rid of the swelling. This is something I learned from Mom. I might as well start following all her home remedies if I want to survive these next nine months. Once I feel ready to sit down to find a new path, I get lost in the possibilities.

Twenty-four hours later and two days after my life crumbled, I feel more confident about my future. I shower, go for a jog around the neighborhood, and even stop at the coffee place to buy a vanilla steamer and a pastry.

Around lunch time, I go to the grocery store with a list of what I plan to eat for the next couple of days. Skipping meals for the sake of my career wasn't smart. Now, I can take better care of myself—and my future baby.

That's the one part of my life that hasn't sunk in yet. I'm going to be a mother. This is one endeavor I hadn't planned yet. Just last weekend I was wondering if thirty-five was too early to have a kid. It's not a choice if I wait or not. I decided to have this baby. Since I like to read and learn while reading, on my way back home, I stop at the bookstore.

When I arrive at my place, I spot Nate's truck parked in my driveway. There's just enough space for me to slide my car into the garage. So much for *let me call you when I am up for it*. The strange thing is that my shoulder muscles relax when I drive close to him and he smiles at me.

When I turn off the engine, he opens the door and says, "I was about to call search and rescue. Where have you been?"

I pop the trunk open and answer, "Grocery store?"

He takes me into his arms and rubs my back. "Fuck, I couldn't sleep for two days. You said you'd call me, and I haven't heard from you."

Resting my head on his chest I close my eyes and let myself indulge in this moment. For a second, I want to forget everything that's happened since the last time I saw him. Since the kiss we shared. That perfect kiss when our lips met for the first time, our hearts beating at the same rhythm, and our souls lost in the abyss of the other, if not forever, at least for a moment.

Talk about unforgettable first kisses, exciting destinations, and unfortunate detours. No, it's a roadblock, and we each have to go our separate ways. We'll always have...what do we have?

Nothing. What could've been after Sunday is completely gone. For a long time, we don't say anything. We stay still, holding each other, or maybe he's the one holding me.

I'm not sure how much time passes but at some point he kisses my forehead and says, "Let's get those bags inside the house, and then you can tell me what's happening."

When I move, I realize that Brock is right beside Nate, quiet, sitting like the good boy that he is. I squat to pet him.

"How are you, boy?"

"Ruff!" he says and licks my cheek.

"I'm glad you guys are here, but you shouldn't have come," I say, trying to hold the tears because even this gesture makes me want to cry.

"The last time we spoke you were...in a bad place. You ignored my calls and texts. I couldn't leave you like this. Since I was on my way to Seattle, I decided to stop by," Nate explains.

I look up and smile, "Thank you for coming, but I'm fine."

Nate arches an eyebrow and crosses his arms. "You don't look fine, sweetheart."

"Well, I'll be fine soon. I'm just trying to figure out my future. Are Persy and Ford back too?" I ask, hopeful, because I need to speak to my sister.

"No," he responds. "They'll be back on Sunday. In the meantime, why don't we go inside? I'm not Persy, but I too can be a good listener."

Nate carries the grocery bags and sets them on the kitchen island. I close the trunk, grab the bookstore load, and set it next to my planner and all the printouts I have from earlier today. In silence and without prompting we begin to fix the groceries. He pulls out the trash can that's under the sink and starts tossing the takeout containers from inside the fridge. As I'm organizing the cans in the pantry, I hear Nate say, "Your reading material is...interesting."

I turn around and look at him, then at the book he's holding, *What to Expect When You're Expecting.*

"Mom was right," I mumble.

He nods a couple of times and asks, "You want to talk about it?"

Before I say anything, my phone rings. It is Kerry Sanders, the realtor I contacted earlier.

Lifting an index finger, I say, "Give me a second, I have to take this call."

For the next five minutes, I explain to Kerry my plans. She runs a quick search and gives me a house price according to the address where I live. She warns me that it's just an estimate that could be lower or higher depending on the condition of my place. We set up a time to meet this evening.

Nate shakes his head but doesn't say anything until I hang up, "You're selling the house. What's going on, Nyx?"

"I could use the equity," I explain. "There are a lot of expenses coming up and my insurance sucks."

According to the customer service rep I spoke with yesterday, I can't make any changes until the end of the year. Also, the cost of my health insurance is going up, since I'm no longer employed with Bryant, LLC. I tried to get a few quotes online from other health insurance companies, but everyone wants to speak to me to sell me their policies. Even though I plan on changing my insurance and getting coverage, I have to have a backup plan.

"So, we're keeping the baby?" he asks, more like mumbles.

I nod once in response.

Maybe Ed was a mistake, sex with him was as boring as getting a pap smear, and he's not the person I'd like to raise a kid with, but the baby is part of me. I want her or him.

"I'm over with the week, and it's just Wednesday," I whisper. "It's...overwhelming to even think about what's happening. There are so many things I have to do, including the lawsuit due to the wrongful termination of my employment."

"But selling the house..." he looks around the place. "Where are you going to live?"

"Until I find a place that is not too expensive but right for us, I'm moving in with my parents," I inform him. "Persy has Ford, and I can't be the third wheel. Eros and I would kill each other in less than a week."

He shakes his head and says, "Listen, I feel like you're making hasty decisions. Why don't you stop for a moment, take a mental break, and then come back to determine if what you planned is really what you want to do?"

I laugh at his suggestion. "I don't have time to think about anything. According to an online due date calculator I'll be responsible for another human being by Monday, April twelfth of next year. A Monday...can you believe it? It's like a sign that from now on my life is going to be an eternal Monday."

"Children tend to bring chaos, but I'm sure there's a silver lining somewhere in this predicament," he offers. "Which is why I suggest you pack your bags and come with me to Seattle. I have the perfect place where you can just relax."

"I don't have time to relax," I remind him.

"Do you trust me?" he asks.

"I just met you, and I'm positive that you shouldn't be here," I advise him. "Leave the dog and fly to Seattle."

He huffs and laughs humorlessly. "No, I am fond of Brock. But I promise to leave him with you while you stay with us in Seattle."

Instead of arguing with him, I go to the fridge where I have the ginger seltzer Dad made. I keep drinking a few sips during the day, and it's keeping my stomach somehow calm. However, there aren't many left, and I think I need at least ten boxes to help me with the morning sickness. If the medical websites are correct, I should be done with this nausea-vomit-fatigue period by September twenty-eighth, or as the professionals call it, the beginning of the second trimester.

According to my goal calendar, I should have a place and a job or steady cases by October first. After taking a few sips, I text Dad about needing a few more cases of his delicious seltzer.

He says he'll have at least two or three ready over the weekend. Right when I am about to put away my phone a notification pops up. It's a text from Pierce.

Pierce: *I emailed you the papers for you to sign. Send them back once you're done. The documents for Ed are in a separate email. I recommend you ask him to visit you at your home and settle this as soon as possible. Good luck!*

I turn on my laptop and print all the documents Pierce sent. Then, I text Ed asking if he could come to my house today.

Edward: *I'm busy. We agreed it was a one time.*

Nyx: *It's for a different issue. It's in your best interest to meet me today.*

Edward: *Are you threatening me?*

Nyx: *No, I'm telling you we have an important matter to discuss, and the sooner we fix it the better.*

Edward: *If you're going to tell me that you gave me syphilis, I'll sue you.*

Nyx: *Edward, be realistic. Just meet me at five. I'll send you the address.*

Walking back into the living room, I find Nate by the door with Brock right next to him.

"Ready to run away?" I ask and smile.

"No, we're going on a walk. Would you like to join us?"

I nod, grab my water bottle, and follow them.

SEVENTEEN

Nyx

"SO, how do you feel about all these changes?" he asks.

"Wow, let's start with the deep questions," I mumble and sigh. "I don't know how to feel yet. I've been so focused on my career that I haven't really thought much about children. Sure, I hoped that by the time I'm thirty-five I'd be in a serious relationship. Probably married or engaged and planning on having a family before I turn forty.

"In my mind, if I was ever pregnant, I'd be in love with the father of my child and thrilled about this new life we created—together. Edward Bryant and I slept together out of boredom or...something. This feels surreal. I understand what's happening, and I'm already getting ready for the event, but it hasn't sunk in yet. This baby deserves better than an unemployed, clueless, emotionless mother."

"That's different. Most of the women I've met have been planning their wedding since they were children," he explains. "Once I dated a woman who had a wedding book since she was twelve."

I don't remind him that I had a different life. My childhood consisted of traveling, climbing trees, learning about other cultures, other languages, and wanting to learn more and more.

We fall into an uncomfortable silence until he asks, "So the father... Are you planning on telling him?"

"Today," I mumble. "He's coming at five. I have the parental relinquishment documents ready for him to sign."

"So, you're not giving him a chance to be a dad?" he asks, sounding upset.

"Listen, I'm giving him the news, explaining to him how I see this working out for the baby, and giving him an out," I clarify. "It's up to him, but to tell you the truth, I hope he signs the papers. If he stays in my child's life there'll be expectations that I doubt he'll meet. It's going to be eighteen years of hell for everyone."

"You don't think he'll pay child support?" he asks.

"No...I haven't even thought about that," I mention. "That'd be a secondary issue. My primary concern is my child's emotional wellbeing. What if he's around for the first two years and then he disappears leaving a hole in their life? I'd rather handle his absence from the beginning than leave a kid wondering why their father never came back."

"Sounds smart. I'm sorry for judging you," he apologizes.

I arch an eyebrow. "I had no idea you were judging me." Then it hit me...his mother, or maybe his ex. Either way, this should be uncomfortable at least and painful the most. "I really think you shouldn't be around me. This situation is too close for comfort, isn't it?"

"It's not." He rubs the back of his neck looking toward the sky, then he glances at me and says, "I'm perfectly fine. I'm not the one unemployed, pregnant, and confused. Except, I am worried about you."

"I'm a big girl," I assure him.

"You are, but I bet you're one of those people who avoid asking for help," he argues. "I'm pretty sure that you're the kind of person who runs to save everyone, but when you need a life jacket because you're swimming in deep water, you don't reach out to anyone. You just keep swimming."

He's not wrong. I'm used to being the most levelheaded of the family. The one who saves everyone else. Persy is the only one I'd trust to give me a hand. Not today. She's too busy with her book and her new boyfriend to help me, which is fine. Because I am fine.

I am...

"If I interpret your silence correctly, well, I'm right, aren't I?"

"Maybe? I don't do it often. It's easier to look after myself," I ramble.

"That's a 'Yes, I'm not in a great place and I'll try to figure this out on my own,'" he pokes my nose and smiles. "I have some news for you. You're not alone, and I'm just as persistent as you are. It'll be impossible to get rid of me."

Those blue eyes look at me tenderly. I'm not sure if I like them seeing me without the fire of desire they had last Sunday.

This is for the best, Nyx. You have a lot of issues and he is...a friend. Having a kid is a lot of responsibility. Are you sure you can keep one alive?

"I don't know what I'm going to do with a baby," I say out loud, and not sure if it's to him or to myself. "Look at Callie. I did a crappy job with her."

"She's not your kid," he reminds me. "Kid sister, yes, but definitely not your child. She's in Boston by the way."

I come to a halt and hold my breath before I ask, "Is she okay?"

"Perfectly fine, and in case you're wondering, she's working at a bar and going to school part time," he informs me.

"Like grad school?"

He frowns. "No, like college. I take it she's finally going to get a degree."

"She finished college two years ago," I correct him. Maybe his people didn't do a thorough research, or they have the wrong Calliope Brassard.

"She dropped out after the first semester at Colorado University," he adds to his misinformation.

"You are wrong. I know she studied four years of journalism," I press. "Persy, Eros, and I paid for it, so she wouldn't have any student loans."

He smirks and crosses his arms, "Did you go to her graduation?"

"No, we went to our Parentcation instead," I explain what that is, a vacation from my parents, before we all go camping with my parents for a week where no electronics are allowed.

"Okay, then I don't know why she's back in college," he says in a condescending tone.

"You don't think she graduated?"

He's silent and we begin to walk.

"What do you know?" I ask, catching up with him.

"She quit her freshman year of college," he repeats. "Give me your email, and I'll send you the entire file I received from my P.I."

I want to continue fighting him, but my gut says he's right. Callie is capable of deceiving us, and we're too busy with our own lives to doubt her.

"No, we... See I can't be a mother. We supported her for four years while she misled us."

"She's not your child, and you can't compare her with your future children," he says. "I just met you, but from what I've learned so far, I think that baby is lucky, and you'll do great."

"Doubtful," I huff. "I'm unemployed, about to be homeless, and I'll have to raise this kid on my own."

"I could use you in my legal department. You can move into the penthouse that I own here, and you have a supportive family that loves you."

"I need flexible hours." Plus, my sister lives in his penthouse, and

I don't say that aloud because what if he kicks her out. I'd have to defend her in court and our friendship would be over.

"Well, then we have you in a consulting capacity, and I'll make sure your insurance covers the maternity. You don't even have to sell your house," he insists, and I feel as if we're trying to prove who is the most stubborn of the two of us.

We could discuss my future for hours, but I decide to be the bigger person or the one who ends this discussion with a good note. "I can use the friend but not the micromanaging,"

He stops walking, turns to look at me, and smiles. "Sorry," he apologizes and grabs my hand, we resume our walk. "It's not micromanaging but trying to help you. Like you, I'm a problem solver. The way I look at it, it's a simple fix. You're right though, everyone reacts and needs different things. I'm here for you in any capacity. The invitation to go to Seattle is open."

EIGHTEEN

Nyx

———

I EXPECTED Nate to leave for Seattle after our walk. Instead, he takes off the light jacket he was wearing and sits on the couch.

"Okay, walk me through your options," he says.

"What do you mean?"

"You said you've been working on a plan. I just want to listen to what you have in mind and be..." he scratches his chin. "A devil's advocate."

"I don't know if I should laugh or take you seriously with that arrogant smile," I say, but I grab my stuff and sit right next to him.

While I show him my calendar, the timelines, and the ideas I have to try to make a living, he focuses on my every word, but grabs a pencil to make some notes. More like puts initials in certain places.

"I should have a good nest egg by April twelfth. If I can, I'll take a month or two of maternity leave. By then I'll be able to continue what I've been doing," I finish.

"What are you doing with the baby once you're back to work?"

"I'll hire a part-time person to help me for a few hours and pray that the baby sleeps," I say, hopeful. "What are the holes?"

"It's all based on probabilities, and if one thing goes wrong, we have to have a fallback," he suggests. "If this Pierce guy has cases, if Persy has work... Those are way too many risks because what if they don't have anything solid for months. I think you should start a small firm. Brassard & Associates. You hire lawyers that can take the load when you're on maternity leave."

"Remember the part where I can't afford to take that big step," I remind him and add, "And I refuse to either get a loan or accept loans from friends."

"How about an investor?"

"It's a law firm. Things work differently," I clarify. "Thank you for trying to help though. I'm sure Persy will have something. I mean, she's been pushing me to be her agent."

He frowns and nods. "That's perfect. Sheila could work for Persy, raise her kids, and even plot on how to steal millions of dollars from her. You can do at least the first two things and have the side jobs for a rainy day."

When he points at September twenty-eighth on the calendar, I stare at his arm, trying to read one of his tattoos.

Life is either a great adventure or nothing. -H.K.

"Who is H.K.?" I ask, tracing the words.

"Hellen Keller," he replies.

"That's a..."

"Perfect mantra to follow," he answers. "I believe there's a gray area for everything except for life. You either live it or you don't. You see every experience as a learning moment, or you can repeat the same pattern and live with regrets."

The way he says it makes me think about all the years I've been neglecting myself. What I did yesterday opened my eyes to what I've been missing. Everything I know exists and have experienced from a young age I decided to push away for what I thought was stability. Just this week I learned that nothing is granted and in a blink of an eye, everything can disappear.

"Life is a choice," I say out loud, which is something I told myself yesterday. I either choose to see this period of my life as a new beginning or cry for what I never accomplished during my old chapter.

He takes a pen, and carefully writes on my wrist those four words, *Life is a choice*.

"You should get a tattoo of it," he says, while writing the same on his left wrist.

I stare at our wrists and wonder what choices we should make and if all the choices I've made so far are the right ones.

"Listen, this is scary, but you're going to be all right. We're here for you," he assures me.

He's right, my parents are going to love the baby. Eros and Persy will be the best aunt and uncle. I'm not sure what Callie will do, but I trust that someday she'll come back to us.

Nate points out a few more flaws and mocks that I drew fruits on the calendar for every week. According to one of the websites I consulted, they compare the baby's size with fruits and some vegetables. I thought it was a great way to remember how big she or he is getting. He can't blame me for having blueberries for this week. Next week it's a raspberry, and well, I'm not looking forward to having a pumpkin or a watermelon come out of my vagina. Thankfully, I'll have enough time to get used to the idea.

IT'S ALMOST five when Nate heads to the kitchen where he begins to look around the pantry and the fridge.

"You have food for Brock," he states with a surprised voice.

"In case he visits again," I announce, searching for the food bowl I bought for my favorite pup.

"Thank you," he says looking at everything I got for Brock. The mat, the toys and some treats. "We are touched—but you're not keeping him."

I laugh at his warning and ask, "Are you hungry?"

"Yes," he answers as he grabs a pot and starts filling it with water. "I'm thinking pasta, garlic bread, and a salad."

"You know how to cook?" I stare at him attentively as he washes the tomatoes. "There's a jar of marinara sauce in the pantry."

He gives me a grimacing look. "What's next? Frozen garlic bread?"

I laugh but he doesn't join. "You are serious about this, aren't you?"

"Uh-huh," he answers, going back to the tomatoes.

I observe him as he chops tomato, onion, and minces garlic with precision. He knows what he's doing and sadly, he looks hot while he's at it.

"You are...unexpected," I say, and maybe this is the second or third time I mention this since I've met him. "How... I'm not even sure what to ask you. Who taught you it is wrong to eat marinara from a jar? Are you Italian?"

"After my parents' divorce, my paternal grandparents came to live with us," he responds. "Grandma was Mexican. She used to say that 'Idleness is the mother of all vices.' So, during our free time, they kept us busy. When we weren't with Grandpa helping him fix things around the house, we were cleaning or cooking with her."

"They sound like interesting people," I say.

"They were awesome," he admits and glances at me as he sautés the tomatoes and onions.

He sighs and with a low voice he says, "Your parents remind me of them, but not exactly."

"Were?" I ask, curiously.

"They died when we were twelve," he states. "Grandma had

cancer and Grandpa died a couple of months after she did. A heart attack."

I wonder if maybe his grandfather lost the will to continue because the love of his life was gone? Before I can ask more about his family, the doorbell rings. When I check the app, I see Edward waiting.

"I'll get it," Nate announces, handing me the wooden spoon he's holding and turning down the flame.

I take a sip of my ginger seltzer as I watch the door.

"Can I help you?" he asks, swinging the door open. Brock walks toward them and growls at Edward.

I swear, Nate pats him the same way he does when he's done something good. They are a pair.

"I'm looking for Nyx Brassard," Edward's voice is somehow louder than usual but squeakier too.

Is he afraid of the dog? Brock attacks people with love.

"And you are?" Nate questions with a growl that sounds pretty similar to the tone Brock just used a few seconds ago.

I hold the laughter.

"Edward Bryant. She's expecting me."

Nate moves and I walk toward the living room area. Having an open house has its advantages and disadvantages. Anyone can see everything from almost every angle. It's aesthetic, but I have to keep the kitchen clean all the time. When I leave dishes around the house, the place looks messy, or maybe it's me. I'm too anal.

This is going to serve me well with a baby. With my luck it's going to be as messy as Eros and Persy.

"Edward," I greet him. "Thank you for agreeing to see me."

Edward looks at the seltzer bottle I hold and says, "No, thank you, I don't have much time. What do you need?"

Nate stands right next to me, takes the spoon and the seltzer, freeing my hands. "Go ahead. I'm here if you need me."

I nod and wait until he moves, but he doesn't. Shoving my hands in the back of my jeans pockets I look at Edward and say it, "I'm pregnant," pausing and taking a deep breath I add, "And by the way it's yours."

He gasps, takes a step back and shakes his head. "No, that's impossible. We used a condom."

His gaze is focused on the floor and then when he lifts his chin, he accuses me, "They were yours. You poked them so you could—"

"I'm going to stop you right there," I say, grabbing the documents Pierce prepared for me and handing them to him. "As I was saying, I am pregnant. I plan on keeping this baby. However, I don't expect anything from you. You can decide how involved you want to be. If you plan on being in the life of my baby, you have to commit one hundred percent. It's not a *today I'm in and tomorrow I'm out*. Children need consistency."

He stares at me and then at the papers. Nate turns around and marches to the kitchen. I wait while Ed reads each page and sighs.

"You can't spring this on me and demand an immediate answer. How do I know if this baby is mine and not his?" He points toward the kitchen.

I laugh. "He's a friend. I've never had sex with him so him being the father would be a miracle."

He huffs, walks around in circles and then stands up in front of me. "So, I can see the baby, but you don't need child support?

"Actually, if you want to have rights, you'll have to have obligations too," I warn him. "I don't expect you to support the kid entirely, but if you want to have visitations, share custody or have any relationship with her, I expect you to provide for the baby too."

He scrunches his face in disgust and says, "It's a she?"

I place a hand on my flat belly and snap, "It's too early to know if it's a boy or a girl, but if you'll be making a decision based on gender, you can just sign those papers and be done with this. My kid won't be raised by some misogynistic man."

He glares at me, puffs his chest and before he can say anything, Nate speaks, "I'd be careful with my next words if I were you."

Edward exhales harshly, and says, "I need a paternity test and time before I make any decision."

"If there's a non-invasive test before the baby is born, I'll get that done. It could be easier if you just sign the papers," I advise because it's apparent that we're going to have more problems than I anticipated.

He stares at the papers, then at Nate, and finally at me. "Easier for you," he states. "What if this is my only chance to be a father? Maybe I'll fight you for custody."

"Maybe it is time for you to leave because you're pissing me off, man." Nate walks to him and looks down. Edward is about four inches shorter and thin in comparison. I'm pretty sure little Eddy is trembling. "This isn't a game. It's the life of a person. The future of a child who wasn't planned but will be here whether you like it or not. It's not about you or Nyx, it's about a baby who will depend on her parents. A girl or a boy who needs love, attention, and you have to be sure that you're up for the task—which lasts a lifetime."

"This doesn't concern you," Edward argues.

"Nyx isn't alone, so don't think you can try to walk all over her," Nate states. "She's pregnant, not disabled. The next time you piss her off, I won't intervene. I'll let *her* bust your balls."

"And who the fuck do you think you are?" Edward challenges him. "I can take *you* down if you continue *pissing me off*."

"Nathaniel Chadwick," Nate answers followed by his arrogant smirk. "You can google me, if you're not sure who you're fucking with."

I hate to say that that was hot, because this was my moment and he stole it.

Or did he?

"This is bigger than any of us and not some legal case that should be settled in court, a bet, or a game. I expect you to be mature about the situation and mindful of my child," I say. "We can settle it easily, but if you'd like to do it the hard way just remember who has had to save your ass when you fuck up a case—also, Pierce is on my side."

If there's anyone he is afraid of, it's his cousin.

He turns around and dashes out of the house without saying another word.

Once Edward leaves, Nate turns around and apologizes. "I'm sorry for intervening, but he was starting to say things I can't tolerate, and you don't need to get upset. It's bad for the baby."

"You're cute."

"Damn woman, you like to hurt my pride. Let me finish cooking. When is the realtor arriving?"

Checking the time on my phone, I realize she'll be here in less than an hour. "Soon," I answer. "Let me help you so we can eat before she arrives." I kiss his cheek and repeat, "Thank you."

It wasn't necessary for him to bump heads with Edward, but I appreciate the sentiment. I appreciate even more that he's worried about the baby's wellbeing.

NINETEEN

Nyx

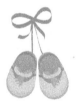

KERRY TEXTS that she's going to be thirty minutes late. That gives us plenty of time to eat and for Nate to start clearing the table and cleaning the kitchen. Brock and I go out for a quick walk and when we're back, she's by the door looking at the exterior of the house.

"Are you Nyx?" she asks.

"Yes, Nyx Brassard," I confirm, extending my hand. "It's a pleasure to meet you, Kerry."

"Do you own more than one pet?" she asks, staring at Brock.

"No, he's just a friend visiting. The place is pet free, smoke free, and brand new. The previous owner bought it and demolished the old construction."

She nods and types something on her tablet. We go inside where Nate is still cleaning the kitchen. Kerry doesn't pay much attention to him and focuses more on the house. She asks me questions about the rooms, the square footage, and other features. After an hour discussing prices, alternatives, and plans, I sign an agreement to sell the house and use her as my real estate agent.

Nate isn't thrilled about it, and after Kerry leaves, he repeats the same thing, "We can work things out without the need to sell this place."

He's a sweet guy, but he's a billionaire and it's obvious that if anything were to happen to one of his companies, he has a few others to fall back on. His brother could bail him out. I am the one who bails out my siblings.

"As I said, it's not only about the money but also the school district. According to my research, I should move south of the city," I inform him. "Plus, the asking price is twenty percent above what I thought they'd give me. You heard her, it might sell in a matter of days. This place is a hot commodity."

There aren't many houses for sale around the area and people are paying prime prices to live in this neighborhood. She's going to put the *For Sale* sign out tomorrow with a banner on top that says *Coming Soon* to stir interest.

I have a couple of days to pack and put my things in storage. She's hiring a person to stage the house and bring in her own furniture— Nate is the one who requested it.

"I'll support you no matter what," he states and then says, "We should start packing what you'll be taking with you. Demetri arrives tomorrow to take care of the rest."

"Your butler?"

"House manager and assistant," he corrects me.

I narrow my gaze, studying him. "You're dragging him from New York just to do this?"

"He's flying from Seattle," he clarifies. "D manages all my properties, and he's due to come to Denver soon."

"You have more than two homes?"

He shrugs. "I like to travel. Which reminds me, you should probably pack a separate bag to take with us to Seattle."

"I'm not traveling," I argue. "I haven't told my parents and I have to—"

"You already made a lot of decisions within the last twenty-four hours and are changing your life radically," he finishes my sentence.

"Come with me," he insists. "There's plenty of room, a pool, a dog who apparently is in love with you. I'll be working so you'll have the house all to yourself. I think that's better than living with your parents. Persy told me that they have zero regard for their guests and can be noisy at night."

I squeeze my eyes and shiver remembering the times Persy caught them having sex while she was staying with them for a few days.

"Okay, I'm going for a few days," I agree, looking at him and wondering if this is a good idea. My attraction to him is increasing, and at the moment my plate is full, and there's no room for him to be around.

Am I doing the smart thing?

He's a good friend. It's not like he's offering you an arsenal of orgasms while you're in Seattle. So far, he's been supportive about your situation, and he's focusing on the baby.

"But before we leave, I need to talk to my parents, and I'm not driving tonight to see them."

He grins and I stare at his lips, longing over that kiss we shared on Sunday. What if we do it just one more time before I have to become celibate for the next eighteen to twenty years?

"Tomorrow then?" he asks, taking me away from the trance.

"Can I think about it?" I ask because this might be a bad idea.

THE NEXT DAY, Nate arrives around six in the morning.

"Isn't it a little too early?" I complain.

"I'm still on Eastern time," he states. "I've been working for the past couple of hours."

"Too early," I complain. I sit on the couch and call Brock who jumps up next to me and rests his head on my lap.

"Get ready, I want to leave early," he prompts me before heading to the kitchen.

This is what I call a real friendship with benefits. The guy is a good cook. I wouldn't mind keeping him for a long time. Once he's done preparing oatmeal with berries, he calls me to join him.

Today isn't any different from any other morning this week though, I eat a little breakfast and within minutes I'm throwing up. There's something different about the routine. This time, Nate runs after me, holds my hair and rubs my back. It feels nice, even relaxing, to have someone by my side while I feel like I'm throwing my entire life into the porcelain bowl.

When I'm done, I brush my teeth. He looks at me with such tenderness I want to hug him, but I don't.

"You know what's sad?"

"That my oatmeal was fucking awesome and you wasted it?" he jokes.

I laugh. "Yes."

It is sad, but what I want to say is that I wish I wasn't doing this alone. Not that I want Edward involved in my life but...this should feel different, shouldn't it?

The baby book I read yesterday kept talking about what my partner should be helping me with, and I'm longing for this partner that I've never even had in my life. I was too busy building a nest egg that I never planned on a future.

Nate's phone buzzes. He growls and asks if he could use my computer.

"Of course," I respond. "I'll take a shower and while you're working, I'll drive up to my parents."

"Why don't I take you?" he asks, his focus is on the computer.

"Because you're working, and I think it'll be best if it's just them and me," I say but then rectify when I picture my parents smothering me with hugs and attacking me with all kinds of questions. "You know what, you're right. You should come with me."

He stops typing and lifts his gaze. His blue piercing eyes stare at me. "Why?"

"You might be able to help me dodge a few questions," I answer. "Let's say I'm using you as a shield."

He smirks. "Bring on the Brassards. I can take them."

My God, if this wasn't so strange and unreal I'd say that he's beyond perfect. Every guy I've dated ran scared when they met my parents. This guy saw them having sex, and he hasn't complained after the incident. He's even willing to come with me even when they might probably get a million times more weird after I give them the news.

I look up to the ceiling and send up a thought, *couldn't you have sent him a few years ago?*

WHEN WE ARRIVE AT MY PARENTS' house, Mom holds my arms carefully and studies my face. "We should take you to the doctor. At this point, you should be taking prenatal vitamins."

I laugh and roll my eyes. I haven't even told them about the baby, and she's already giving me advice. Thank goodness she doesn't have any baby clothes, or she'll be giving them to me along with the suggestion of a few names and...I should run now before it's too late.

Dad asks, "Are you okay?"

"I've been better," I answer.

Nate squeezes my hand and whispers, "It's okay. I'll deflect as much as I can."

With that reassurance, I enter the house.

"Nathaniel, what a surprise," Mom greets him. "I thought you were in New York."

"I'm on my way to Seattle, but I decided to stop by to check on Nyx," he answers.

"You're a good kid. She's been avoiding me since Monday. I'm surprised she came to visit us," Mom complains.

"I'm right here, Mom," I sneer. I hate when she talks about me in the third person as if I'm not nearby.

"Yes, you are," Mom concedes glancing at me again and sighing dramatically. "Should I sit down?"

"Let's save the dramatics, Mom," I suggest. "When are you going back to work?"

"Next week," she says. "And I'm glad you're here because we're working on a book proposal and I need you to help me."

"You mean pretend I'm your agent," I correct her, almost wondering if I should say yes but only if I get a small cut from their profits.

"Yes, you did it for Persy. I'm sure you can do it for us," she says. "Now tell me what's happening. You've been absent for three days, which means you've been plotting something and it's time for the big reveal."

Dad laughs and Nate joins.

"I'm glad my life gives you comedic relief," I say unamused.

"It's not funny that my kid doesn't need me as much, but we've learned to take it lightly," she confesses. "I'd like to be a part of the important decisions you make in life. But for some reason, you never take us into consideration."

"You raised pretty independent children, Mom."

"I'll subscribe to that answer even when we both know it's a bunch of bologna."

She's probably wrong, it might be a combination of both. They taught us how to be responsible, to take charge of our own lives, and to trust our instincts—not that our instinct is always right. There's the part where they can be overwhelming, and their ideas don't always fit into the real world.

"So, what is it?" she asks.

"I got fired on Tuesday," I begin the conversation and tell them what happened on Monday.

They've known that things haven't been going well at work since

May when Pierce hinted he'd be quitting the firm and leaving the state. The day he left, things just went from bad to worse, and here I am, unemployed.

"What can we do?" she asks.

"Well...since I'm selling my house, I might need to stay with you guys for a while," I answer, wondering if this is a good time to throw in the baby or if waiting until next year might be for the best.

Dad frowns, but remains quiet, observing me.

"But you love that house," Mom states.

"It's lovely, but I can't afford it, and the schools in that district are... I prefer to look for something in a different district."

She arches an eyebrow. "I was right."

"Yes, Mom, you were right. I'm pregnant," I concede, waiting for her to say something else, but as it's expected from her, she hugs me.

"My baby is going to be a mom," she repeats excitedly.

Suddenly, she's crying and then, I'm crying. This time I'm not sure why or if it's contagious, like yawning.

"Are you happy?" she asks, clearing my tears with the back of her hand.

"I'm getting used to the idea. It hasn't sunk in yet," I explain instead of saying I feel like a bad mother for not having any emotion whatsoever about the baby.

She smiles and says, "It won't be until you have everything in place. You lead with logic. What about the father?"

I brief her about Edward.

"What can I do for you?" Mom asks.

"Your love, that's all I need, Mom."

She hugs me, "Everything will be fine. I'm here for you and the room is ready for whenever you want to move in with us, and you can stay for as long as you need."

"I'm going to be a grandfather," Dad says, taking me into his arms. "Finally, one of my children is willing to give me a grandchild. But I don't see anyone congratulating me."

"Congrats, Grandpa," I say, hugging him back.

"I feel sorry for the others to come, because the first one is always the favorite," he whispers, but it's obvious that Mom can hear him because she protests, "We don't play favorites, Octavio."

Nate looks at me and smiles but stays quiet, just observing the scene developing in front of him. I'm just hoping that this is as far as they get, but I'm wrong because Mom starts, well, being Mom.

"We have to schedule a doctor's appointment as soon as possible. On second thought, you should move in with us today. We'll have to push the project for our book for next year," she doesn't even stop to take a breath. "Get the list of names, Octavio. We have so much to do. I think this one could be Hera."

They start throwing names, possible middle names, and even the idea of Dad building the baby's crib. I search for Nate's gaze but he's staring at my parents either highly entertained or terrified. When he finally looks at me, I try to desperately say, *take me away from these people.*

"It's time for us to leave, Nyx," Nate finally speaks with a firm voice that freezes my parents.

"You're not staying for lunch?" Mom asks.

"The plane is waiting for us, and we still have to go to her house to pick up Brock," he lies. He had someone come to my place to pick him up before we drove to my parents, and they'll be meeting him at the airport. "She's had a hard week, and I thought it'd be good for her to take a break before she embarks on motherhood."

"When will you be back?" Mom asks but doesn't give me time to answer. "We'll see you on Sunday. Won't we?"

"I'll call you," I answer.

"Do you need us to pack your things?" Dad asks.

"I have people in charge of the task, Mr. Brassard," Nate explains.

"Call me Octavio," he corrects Nate. "I appreciate your help, but I'd rather take care of my kid."

"Which is respectable, but Demetri has been working on the details all morning. I'll give him your number in case he needs help."

Dad glares at him and then says, "Your seltzer won't be ready until tomorrow."

"If you don't mind, I'll have Demetri stop by to pick it up," Nate offers.

"Be careful with what you're doing," Dad warns him.

"Of course, sir." He turns to look at me. "Ready to go?"

"Yes," I say, hugging my parents.

"When will you be back?" Mom questions.

"Soon. It's just a couple of days," I answer, but maybe I should stay with Nate until the baby is born, and then they can focus just on that poor little creature.

I look again at my parents, and I can't understand why they are so excited and full of love for this baby. While I'm still trying to warm up to the idea that I'm going to become a mom.

TWENTY

Nate

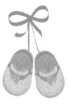

IT'S safe to say that I have no fucking idea what I'm doing. None whatsoever.

"You do realize that now I have to go with you," Nyx says as I'm driving toward the airport. "Or find alternative accommodations for the time being. If Persy was here..."

Didn't we agree she'd be coming with me? I had my people drop by her house earlier to pick up Brock and her belongings so they can set them up on the plane.

"We had agreed that you'd be coming with me," I remind her.

"No, I said I would think about it," she enunciates her words. "There was no yes implied. I'm not going with you."

"If not my house, then where will you stay?" I ask, more like challenge her. "D is coming in tomorrow, and I wasn't lying when I said he's been working on this project all morning. Your house will be empty by tomorrow night, and a cleaning crew arrives on Saturday morning. Are you going back to your parents?"

She makes a strange noise which sounds between a wounded puppy and an angry lion. "I feel like you pushed me to go to Seattle with you."

"No," I claim. That'd be really stupid.

And still, here you are, you fucking idiot.

When it comes to Nyx, I jump headfirst without thinking; and I just met her. There are several questions I've been asking myself since I arrived in Colorado yesterday afternoon. I haven't found an answer to any of them, yet.

Why the fuck am I here? happens to be the most important of them all. Followed by my favorite, *Are you out of your fucking mind?*

She's a complication with complications of her own. I don't like children, and she's about to have one. I'm still attracted to her, maybe even more than I was the first time I met her. That kiss we shared keeps playing in my mind—on repeat. Yesterday I didn't kiss her when I had her in my arms because she seemed to be vulnerable, and after she delivered her news, well...I should be jumping on a plane to the other side of the world and staying there at least until the kid turns eighteen.

"How bad will it be if I stay with my parents starting tomorrow?" she asks and then leans against the seat making whimpering noises. "I love them, but I don't think I can bear to be with them while I'm still trying to get used to the idea of having a baby. But...I should just live with them. Right?"

What does she want from me? Staying with her parents is a sensible option. In fact, that could be the solution to her current situation. I should stay quiet. I should just drop her at home and run far, far away.

I don't do any of those, and contrary to what logic dictates, I answer, "Do you think that's the solution to your problem?" I question and then respond automatically, "I doubt it. You might be upset, but think about what I just did for you."

"Excuse me?" she asks appalled. "You did what for me?"

"I saved you from naming the poor baby Artemis, Hephaetus, or Hera if it's a girl."

"Hephaestus," she corrects me. "He's the god of fire. Son of Hera and Zeus. That's a—"

"Don't lie to yourself. With all due respect to the Greek mythology, it sounds like Heffalump," I point out and she laughs. "You know I am right."

"Still, I'm not sure if I should be going with you."

"So, you plan on lying to your parents and living under a bridge so they can't find you?" I ask, picturing her living in their shed at night to avoid them and then going into the house during the day while they are at work.

Honestly, I don't like the picture. She'll be better at my house where she can use any of the guest rooms. I can set up a desk in the loft area, and if she's bored, she can use the pool. Brock can use the company—he'd love to have her around.

"Think about what's best for the baby. You love your parents and they are looking after you, but...do you think you can deal with morning sickness, mood swings, and them at the same time?"

"You are a pushy man," she grunts.

"No, I'm right," I argue.

"Maybe," she grunts.

"Let's go then?"

"Fine, but you're going to have to deal with a puke-y, unattractive roommate."

"Yes, but he's a great dog, and you'll be watching over him, won't you?"

She laughs and the magical sound makes me forget all the doubts and the questions I had before. This is going to be okay.

BEFORE WE LEAVE FOR SEATTLE, we stop at a Greek restaurant nearby Centennial airport to have lunch. Unfortunately, Nyx pukes right as we enter, and we flee the joint as soon as the owner offers to clean for us.

We stop by a smoothie place where she washes up and I buy her a few drinks and a parfait. There has to be something that she can eat at least until we arrive home. During our flight to Seattle, Nyx falls asleep and it gives me plenty of time to work. She's pretty self-sufficient, but I'd rather hang around her during her first day at home. I don't even know how long she plans on staying.

At any rate, she can live with me for as long as she wants to. It won't be easy, but I'll convince her to stay with us for at least a month. The house is big enough for a family of six. We can share and not even worry about cramping each other while working. I can take care of her while she's pregnant.

Wait a second, is this some kind of savior complex?

Shaking my head, I answer automatically, no, she doesn't need rescuing.

Nyx already has a plan, and it's a lot better than sticking the baby to her rich boyfriend and hoping she never gets caught. Fucking Bronwyn. I think she left me bitter.

On second thought, my reaction to Nyx's pregnancy was a lot better than my reaction to my ex. I run a hand through my hair and let out a harsh breath. It feels like it was just yesterday when I arrived from a trip, I drove to Bronwyn's house and as she opened the door she said, "We're expecting a baby."

It felt surreal, and I was quiet for several minutes while I digested the news. Of course, my timing was terrible because after a long silence tears rolled down her cheeks.

"I knew it. You don't want us," she declared between sobs.

My immediate reaction was to hug her and tell her we'd get married and be a happy family. In retrospect, I think she said it to make sure I didn't ask questions. Not that I'd doubted her. After all, according to what we had established from the beginning, we were in a committed, monogamous relationship.

She was my world and having Wyatt became our dream. A dream she pushed so hard I couldn't imagine my life without him. The same dream she snatched abruptly away after tangling me in her web of deceit.

I should let him go. Stop holding onto a kid that'll never be mine, harboring the same amount of hate and love for a woman that might not have loved me at all, and wondering why I wasn't enough for my mother to at least call me on my birthday. It's starting to affect me more than I ever imagined.

I should be a lot more like Nyx and analyze everything that happens in my life before I take a step. Keep my heart and my life out of reach of everyone. Then, I'd be fucking Ford.

Is this why I'm trying to be a part of the Brassards? Because I'm afraid that Ford, the only person who I can trust, might be leaving me behind, just like everyone else?

Or I understand Nyx really well because she's a lot like my brother?

Turning to look at Nyx who is sleeping, I wonder if bringing her to my sanctuary is a lack of judgement or a way to hold onto a sliver of hope.

What is it that I'm hoping for?

TWENTY-ONE

Nyx

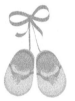

"NYX, WE'RE ABOUT TO LAND," I hear Nate's voice. When I open my eyes, his blue piercing gaze stares at me fondly. "Come on, we need to make sure your seatbelt is secured, and your seat is in the right position."

I stretch and swing my legs down to the plane's floor, readjusting my seat belt. I never take it off, not after that one flight when I was eight and there was a lot of turbulence. I disobeyed my parents when they said, "Nyx, sit down and adjust that belt." Needless to say, I almost hit my head when the plane jolted.

Once I'm ready for landing, I realize that Brock is back inside his kennel, which is secured to the floor of the plane. According to Nate, traveling is his second nature. I wouldn't know, since I fell asleep as soon as we took off from Colorado. I should follow Mom's advice about taking prenatal vitamins. Well, I find yet another reason why I should've stayed at home.

I'd be lying to myself if I said I came against my will. Nate voiced what I was feeling. Overwhelmed by all the changes that are yet to come. Upset by everything that I lost. Dazed by my parents' advice, which I know they are well intentioned, but I don't have the mind space to think about names, food, or anything else that affects my kid. I need a small break. A few days without having to think about my future should be enough to energize me.

Still, I'll take this down time to research doctors, prenatal classes, and maybe even places to exercise while I'm pregnant. My doctor retired back in February. I should text Persy and see if she has a new one. Why bother. I said I'd be the one finding us someone new. I'm sure she's waiting for me to do it.

Once we land, Nate announces that the car is already waiting for us. The driver welcomes us and then takes care of the luggage we brought. Nate keeps his computer with him and once the car drives away, he says, "I hope you don't mind. I have to answer some emails."

"Don't worry about me. I swear, I'm pretty independent," I assure him.

So much so that I can go a couple of days without communicating my whereabouts. I'm the one who reaches out to my siblings most of the time. I guess that's our dynamic. It occurs to me that I should text Eros and Persy about... I frown at my phone, realizing that for the first time we haven't spoken to each other for this long—since Saturday.

They haven't noticed, which isn't strange. Persy is in the honeymoon period of her relationship, falling more and more in love with Ford.

While Eros...what is his excuse?

When I look at Nate, I remember that he's working hard to make sure that his business not only takes off, but soars. All of us are too busy to think about the others, and as the glue, I make sure that at least I reach out to them.

Nyx: My life sucks. I'm taking a break. Let's talk once I'm back in town.

Persy: Where are you going?

Nyx: Out of town.

Eros: Evasive. You either robbed a bank or kidnapped Nate's dog.

Persy: Nate is in Seattle. It has to be something else.

Eros: He was here yesterday and visited our parents today —with Nyx.

Nyx: How did you know?

Eros: I was pulling into the house when you two were leaving. Dad said you have some news for us.

Persy: You're pregnant, aren't you?

Eros: What? Who knocked you up? If it was Nathaniel, I'll kill him.

Persy: She just met him. Unless he has some kind of supernatural sperm, I doubt he's the father.

Eros: Where are you going, Andromeda?

Persy: To Seattle with Nate.

Nyx: How do you know?

Persy: He's texting Ford and said he saved you from our parents.

Nyx: They are hovering.

Persy: I wouldn't expect less from Edna. Octavio...Dad...well, it's you. You're his unrecognized favorite. Do you need me to meet you in Seattle?

Nyx: Thank you, but I need some me time.

Persy: Why there and not at home?

Nyx: Oh, I got fired on Tuesday. I'm selling my place. Demetri is packing the stuff I left behind and storing it.

Persy: Work for me and don't sell your house. You love the place.

Nyx: The school district is terrible. There aren't many parks around for the kid to play. Though I might accept the job if you don't mind letting me have a couple of months of maternity leave.

Persy: Yay, I get to exploit my sister and finally pay her. When can you start?

Nyx: You're ridiculous. Let me...

Persy: I know. You have to trace a plan before you can restart. Are you okay about the baby?

Nyx: Yes, but I feel...I don't feel anything yet. You know how you see those mothers that are gushing about their unborn child as soon as they learn they are pregnant?

Persy: What does that have to do with you?

Nyx: I'm not like them. So far, I don't feel like a mother. What if I can't love this baby?

Persy: I'm sure it works differently for everyone.

Eros: Dude, you'll be fine. You're the most maternal of my three sisters. You just need time to get used to the idea of having a baby. Congrats by the way.

Nyx: Love you both.

Persy: Call us if you need us.

Eros: Same.

THE CAR COMES to a roundabout with a fountain at the center, sweeps around it, and continues up toward a fantastic sprawling house. It is a Mediterranean style home with a stucco exterior, covered with tile rooftop, and oriented around a central courtyard. It's twice as big as my house and surrounded by trees that seem to hide the place.

"It *is* right by Lake Washington," I state as I spot the waterfront.

"You thought I was exaggerating?"

"No, just...this is beautiful," I say in awe.

Though the place is beautiful, the interiors make it feel...cold. "Needs some TLC."

"What does that mean?"

"It's elegant. Don't get me wrong, but it doesn't feel as if someone lives here," I conclude.

"The interior designer—"

I glance at him judgingly. "Seriously, you hired someone to tell you how to fill your space?"

"Yes. I was too busy working to worry about those superfluous details. It looks good, it's functional, and I like it."

"But do you love it?" I ask.

He stares at me and shakes his head. "Next thing I know this place is going to be filled with bright, blinding colors like my penthouse."

He scrunches his nose and I laugh. When he leased his Colorado penthouse to Persy, she redecorated the entire place, giving it a boho new-age style with bright pinks, oranges, and earthy tones. My sister and I are a lot alike, but she's louder, bolder, and likes to express herself with dazzling colors.

"You're confusing me with my sister. I like some color but with moderation," I clarify. "Not that I'd just change your decor arbitrarily. I'm just suggesting that you add a few details that make it yours. Fresh flowers would be lovely, but that's of course, up to you. Wouldn't you rather live in a place that feels like home?"

He rolls his eyes and shakes his head. Brock runs toward the double door that opens to the backyard and barks.

"Let me get him outside and right after, I'll give you the grand tour."

So far, I've been in two of his places. His homes are gorgeous, but I wonder if he even enjoys them.

Between this one and the penthouse, I think I prefer this house. It's tucked in a corner and far from people. As we walk through every room, I observe that there's nothing that says, "This is my home." It could easily be a house decorated for one of those architectural magazines that lay on the coffee tables of medical offices, dentists, or waiting rooms in general. There's something missing. Like pictures of him, his brother, and maybe even his father.

"You can choose any of the guest rooms," he offers, then points to the one at the end. "That one is mine."

"What if I want that one?" I joke.

"We'll have to share the bed," he answers and then grins. "Just so you know, I sleep naked."

"Start wearing pajamas. What if I accidentally enter your room and..."

I trail my gaze and press my lips together regretting what I just said. My life has changed, and I can't just flirt with him. Playing with fire before was acceptable, but now... There's too much going on with me to even entertain some playful banter.

He narrows his gaze, "You like to challenge people and play with words, don't you?"

I scrunch my nose and nod. "Sorry, it's a habit of mine. Try having an older brother, a chatty younger sister, and an annoying baby sister. It's about survival. Eat or get eaten. Be the smartest or... you get the idea."

"It's all good," he answers. He walks me to his office, and then to the other side of the house where there's an indoor pool, a gym, and the media room. Finally, he takes me to the living room, the dining room, and the kitchen where Demetri is staring at the open refrigerator."

"D, we're home," Nate announces.

"Hey, Demetri," I greet him.

"Ms. Nyx, it's a pleasure to see you," he says, turning around and looking at me. "I stocked the fridge and the pantry. Nate, I should be back next Wednesday after I take care of your properties in Colorado. Is there anything I need to know about your house, Ms. Nyx?"

"No more than I emailed you," I announce and give him the keys.

"It'll be fine," Nate assures me, taking my shaky hand. "D, if you need anything, you know how to reach me. Make sure to take Nyx's belongings to the guest room that's closest to my room."

"So, you're taking the risk of having me close," I joke.

He looks at me and blinks a couple of times, leans close to me and whispers with a low, husky voice. "The question is, can you have me close?"

I shiver and press my legs together trying to ignore the ache in my core. As I said before, he's not a guy I should be playing with, and now that I'm about to be a mother, it'd be a terrible idea to acknowledge the fire between us. There's a little person I should be putting first.

It's not just you anymore.

TWENTY-TWO

Nate

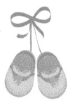

NYX'S first night at the house is different from anything I've ever experienced in my life. I've lived on my own for years. Unless my brother drops by, it's just me and Brock. Nyx and I have dinner, which for the second night in a row she finds endearing that Grandma taught me how to cook to keep me busy. When we finish, we clean up the kitchen and take Brock for a walk around the neighborhood.

That dog is on cloud nine. He acts as if Nyx walks on water and she's the only person who deserves his love, attention, and loyalty. I'm not sure what it is about her, but having her around is refreshing. These couple of days she's been less guarded. I like this version of her, or maybe I like the version of myself when I'm around Nyx. It's all too complicated and simple. The ambiguity of the situation doesn't go unnoticed. Though it's best if I ignore it—for now.

I can say that I enjoy her being around as much as I enjoy when Ford visits, but I'd be lying. Nyx is different. She's fun, I love our chats, and she's gorgeous. My brother grunts. We have the best time when we're skydiving, or as he likes to call it, channeling my inner Evel Knievel. I'd like to say he's ugly, but that'd be calling myself ugly. One thing he never does is spend half of the night with morning sickness.

The first time I hear thumping, running, and grunting is around one. As I get out of bed and put on a pair of boxers, I regret not giving her my bedroom where I have a private bathroom. Since she's using the bathroom across from her room, I can hear everything—and it ain't pretty. When I hear some heaving, I rush to her. I hold her pony-tail, rub her back, and say, "It's okay. I'm here."

Once she's done heaving, I grab a hand towel, wet it, and put it on her neck the way I saw her mother do it last Saturday.

"Sorry, I'm..." she laughs. "I swear this is worse than when I go out drinking with Persy."

"You always get so drunk you end up puking?" Someone should teach this woman to drink or avoid drinking.

She laughs, "That's what everyone thinks, and I make them believe that it's true. My brother and sister swear I'm super hammered when I start puking, but I am not. After a few shots, I begin to feel sick and if I continue, well... I spend thirty minutes puking everything I drank. Sometimes I think that my stomach is too weak and...maybe I'm alcohol intolerant."

"But you're not that drunk when it happens?"

She shakes her head and takes a deep breath, then she finally brushes her teeth. "Nope, and the next day my hangover is not as bad as Persy's."

"Maybe we have to take you to a nutritionist. I can't have you like this for the next seven to eight months. The blueberry needs food to grow."

She blinks slowly as she looks over at me and smiles. "Blueberry?"

"According to your drawings, right now it's a blueberry," I remind her as I lean against the wall and study her. She looks adorable, with her hair coming undone and falling down her neck. Her face is flushed, her eyes sparkling. "Have I mentioned you're cute?"

"You're weird. I just flushed down my entire dinner and all the yummy popcorn I ate during our movie night, and you think I'm cute," she says, trailing her gaze toward the door and back at me. "Thank you for being here for me. I...this is better than the last few days."

"You should've called me before," I say, reaching forward with one hand and sliding it along her waist. I pull her to me and hug her. "If I had known, I wouldn't have left you on Sunday."

"I can be on my own," Nyx mumbles.

She doesn't sound ungrateful. I'm guessing she's fighting her instincts. I just met the Brassards in person, but I've been watching them from afar since they appeared in Ford's life. They are all independent. However, they support each other, and the one who is always pulling the weight of the world for them is Nyx.

"You can, but for the sake of the blueberry, you're going to lean yourself a little on me," I suggest. "Nothing that'll make you feel uncomfortable."

"That's not me," she confides with a sleepy voice.

Her head rests on my chest, her eyes are closed, and her heart beats slowly against mine. There is something about this moment that feels right. I want to pick her up and take her to my bed. Just hold her all night long to make sure I'm there when she gets sick.

She yawns and says, "Thank you again for watching over us. I'll try to sleep and not wake you up if..."

"Please, wake me up," I appeal and kiss her forehead before releasing her. "Sweet dreams."

She turns to look at me, giving me a shy smile. "You too."

MY DAILY ROUTINE consists of spending an hour in the gym, rinse, swim ten laps in the pool, and then shower. Fridays are casual days at the office. I normally arrive early with boxes of bagels and trays of fruit for the employees. This time I ask my assistant to pick them up at the coffee shop for me. I also warn her that I'll be late. I want to make sure Nyx eats breakfast. She woke up at least two more times that I heard. I should have her sleep in my bedroom to keep an eye on her.

"How are you feeling?" I ask as I hand her a cup of yogurt and one of the last ginger seltzers.

"I texted Demetri to see if he can find something similar to these drinks while we wait for your dad to finish the next batch," I announce.

"Thank you," she sighs. "I'm grateful to you for taking care of me, but I also hate you a little."

"Not a morning person?"

She gives me a glance over and says, "Look at you. It's as if you're ready for your photoshoot looking all hot, fresh, and sexy. I...I look like roadkill."

I laugh and shake my head. "You look beautiful," I correct her. "Tired, but beautiful. We should find you a doctor. Marcia, my assistant, is already searching for a nutritionist."

"That's on my list of things to do. Maybe I can get an appointment as early as next week," she says. "And don't worry about booking me a flight. I'll do it later today. I just need to decide when it'd be best to leave."

"Why are you leaving?" I frown. "You should stay here longer."

"You're so sweet, but I'm sure having someone waking you up in the middle of the night because I can't keep any food in my stomach must be aggravating to you."

"Not at all," I assure her. "I had no idea what morning sickness was all about until I met you. Not sure if my life will ever be the same."

"So romantic," she jokes and frowns. "What about...? Sorry, I shouldn't be asking personal questions."

"We're friends," I observe, knowing where her train of thought was heading to. I had a pregnant girlfriend. She's wondering if I'm handling this well because of my previous experience. "We should be able to trust each other, don't you think? Now, to answer your silent question, Bronwyn didn't have morning sickness or if she did, she never told me. I...when she gave me the news, she was about thirteen weeks pregnant."

"Hmm," Nyx says, and I wonder if she's thinking what I am thinking.

Who waits so long to tell the father, and why didn't I question any of this from the beginning? I'm an inquisitive man, but during that time I wasn't thinking at all. As of today, I don't have any answers about my behavior while I dated Bronwyn. I took everything she told me without questioning if any of it was even true. The biggest issue about those years is, *who the fuck was I?*

"But you're a pro living with a pregnant woman, and that's why you're so calm about this," she states.

"Kind of," I respond. "Bronwyn and I didn't move in together until Wyatt was born. She lived in Midtown. Her place was closer to work. I lived in Brooklyn, and the commute was too much for her to handle. We decided that once the baby was born, she'd quit and live with me, but until then we'd live apart. I was also traveling a lot. So no, I think I've dealt with more stuff during the past week with you than with her."

I sound like a shitty boyfriend and a terrible father. I was excited about my son, committed to them, and I visited her as much as it was possible unless she drove down to her mother's place in Philly. Then I wouldn't see her during the weekend.

Nyx watches me, and I'm not sure if she's judging me or...

"What are you thinking?" I ask instead of assuming.

She shrugs. "Nothing really, I'm just..."

"Judging?"

"No, analyzing. Because when you talk about your relationship it sounds one way but then, you swear she's the love of your life. Was she really?" she asks. "It feels like you were keeping each other at a distance. In my experience—watching others dating—when things get so serious, they... Never mind, maybe I've been hanging out with Persy for too long."

"Almost all your life," I joke, and wink at her.

"My point is that I appreciate what you're doing for me and the little berry."

I smirk.

"What did I say?" she asks, wiping her mouth and tucking her hair. "Do I have something—"

"You call the baby *berry*."

"Well, it's a lot better than not having a name," she answers. "After hearing you call her blueberry it just...I don't know. It sounds catchy. Next week it is raspberry so I might as well stick to something for two weeks."

"So, do you think you're having a girl or hoping that the baby is a girl?" I ask.

She frowns and scrunches her nose. "Neither one, but you're right I keep calling the baby a she. This tiny one needs a name, so I stop stereotyping it."

I suggest other names and she's laughing at every stupid thing I mention. Fetus Cletus is her least favorite.

"You can call it B.o.B.," I suggest.

"Battery operated boyfriend?" she asks, and I laugh.

"No, baby on board," I clarify, but still laugh because I should've thought about the first one before I opened my mouth.

When we're done eating breakfast, I say, "I'm heading to the office, but text me if you need anything."

"Like double chocolate ice cream?" she asks, giving me a mischievous smile.

"Are you craving ice cream?"

"No, but I'd like to know what the limits are," she explains.

"Anything goes. You're my guest and I'm committed to providing you with anything you need while you stay with me."

"For what's worth it, Bronwyn missed a great man."

"Did she?" I ask. "Maybe I was a terrible boyfriend."

"If you had been that terrible, she wouldn't have tried to pass Wyatt as yours," she suggests, and I wonder if she's right.

Before Bronwyn, I've never had a long-term relationship, and after her, I slept my way around the world. Now, I don't even know what I want when it comes to my romantic life. Is it even worth it to put myself out there?

My life is good. I don't have the time or space to contemplate the possibility of another heartbreak. There's nothing I can offer, and I'm pretty sure love is about reciprocating. I'm content. No, I'm happy, living my best life.

"Maybe I was a shitty guy, but I had money and that was enough for her."

"Were you the perfect boyfriend? I can't answer you that question, but maybe she could've talked to you about what she was feeling, what she was missing, or how she wanted the relationship to be. Some people don't like monogamous relationships, and if that's the case, they should be looking for someone who shares her ideologies and not... I'm sorry. I'm talking too much, aren't I?"

I shake my head, "Everything you say and ask is valid."

Those are the questions I should've asked back then. Why is it that during that period I just took whatever Bronwyn gave me without inquiring anything further?

"Again, call me if you need me," I repeat, kissing the top of her head.

"Frozen yogurt when you're on your way back home," she calls after me, and I smile wondering if she's trying me or dead serious about the craving.

TWENTY-THREE

Nate

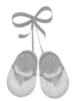

ON MY WAY to the office, I receive a call from Ford.

"T'sup?" I answer through the Bluetooth.

"Are you twenty?" he mocks me.

"Ford," I grunt. "I'm not in the mood to deal with crap."

"Did a mean kid bully you in the sandbox?" His taunting tone is not sitting well.

My assistant just called to let me know that I received a package from the New York office. A package from Bronwyn, to be exact. She doesn't know where I live, but she can still reach me through my corporate offices.

What does she want now?

The last time she sent something was over the holidays. It was an ornament Wyatt made especially for me. Also, a request for a loan. She's still freelancing because paying childcare so she can go to work isn't worth it, and *I made her quit.*

He's five. Shouldn't he be in school already? How would I know? He's not my kid, and I'm not privy to what he does. I didn't fall for her blackmailing, nor will I fall for it this time. She's lucky I didn't take away the trust fund I set up for him when he was born, which he can't touch until he's twenty-five.

"Love you, man, but you're not the funny one of this duo," I remind him. "What can I do for you?"

"Can I ask what the fuck are you doing?"

"Yes, as soon as you give me some context," I answer.

"Nyx," he answers. "I told you to stay away from her and now she's living with you."

I laugh, because really, he makes this sound like a love affair when it's only just lending a hand to someone in need. I'm doing it for Nyx but also for him. After all, if things go well with Persy, he'd want me to get along with his in-laws, right?

"Man, I love you, but you're getting it all wrong. There's nothing between us. This is a favor to a friend. If you think puking leads to sex, then you're in for a treat when you knock up your girlfriend."

He growls. "This still sounds like a bad idea."

My brother isn't too social. I have to speak his language.

"It's pretty simple and nothing bad. I offered her my house because she needs time to think about her future. She reminds me a lot of you."

"Me?" He sounds doubtful.

"Yep. Before she can deal with shit, she needs time to think. I'm providing her a safe space away from her family," I explain. "The same way I do for you. Not sure how much you know about your in-laws, but they are a handful."

A handful is putting it mildly, but I'd be lying if I said I don't appreciate them. I could see myself hanging out with them often.

They are a riot. Octavio and I could spend hours crafting beer, hiking, or maybe even building stuff. He's fun.

"They are different," he says, and I'm wondering if this will be a deal breaker for him.

Mr. and Mrs. Brassard have no boundaries. I caught them having sex, and from what I learned from Nyx and Eros, it's not the first time and they don't give a shit about it.

"Not sure if you'll be able to handle them, but they are cool," I reassure him. "Just nosy..."

"Persy has warned me a few times. They aren't the problem. I just need you to swear that there's nothing going on between you and Nyx, Nathaniel." he insists.

"Nothing," I assure him, but maybe the word comes out harshly.

Am I lying when I say I sound so definitive? We shared a kiss almost a week ago.

Just a kiss. Nothing more than that...but was it really just the meeting of two sets of lips, the fusing of two mouths, or am I trying to play down what really happened that night?

Oh, fuck. She made me doubt everything, even the meaning of the few beats we shared during the kiss.

I still question what really happened between us that night. Did I kiss her because I wanted to feel something or because there was a real pull between us that made it happen?

Have I entertained the possibilities of what could happen if I insist on pursuing this? Is there really something going on between us?

With her current situation... I force myself to stop thinking about her.

"Who pissed you off?" he asks.

My fucking head that's confused as fuck, your call, my ex...

"Bronwyn keeps trying to reach me," I growl, deciding this is the safest subject to discuss with him.

If I avoid his questions, he's going to drag his girlfriend to Seattle and take Nyx away from me. I'm not ready to see her go.

Again with the convoluted thoughts and ambiguous feelings,

Nathaniel. Stop it.

"Not that I know much shit about feelings, but you're still hung up on her," he concludes. "Maybe you should talk to her."

What the fuck does that mean? Is he telling me that this woman he just started dating is his forever? This is exactly why our parents divorced, why divorces are on the rise. We don't think and just pull the trigger. I almost became a statistic. Also, Nyx just told me I'm making Bronwyn out to be more than she really was. Both thoughts crash against each other, and I feel as if my head is about to explode.

Since he can't understand me, I can explain to him what's happening. I try to put him in my shoes. "If Persy did what Bronwyn did, would you forgive her?"

"I can't see myself without her, but I also don't think she'd fuck me the way Bronwyn did to you," he replies. "I'm not saying go back to her and patch up your relationship. I'm saying get closure and find a good therapist. It might help you look forward to something more. You might not fall in love the way you did with Bronwyn, but that doesn't mean there's no one else worth loving."

I stare at the dashboard, making sure I'm speaking to Langford Chadwick and not some friend or a computer program he created. Some days he makes me think that computers have more emotions than him. The name on the screen says, Ford. My jaw almost drops because really, who is this guy?

What he says compliments a lot of what Nyx was telling me earlier while we were having breakfast.

"What happened to you, man?"

"Persy," he answers, and I swear I could almost see emoji hearts coming out of the speaker.

This is so freaking hilarious, and I'd be mocking him if I wasn't in the middle of my own existential crisis.

"Dude, you've been listening to your girlfriend's shit for too long. I swear I feel like I just went to the shrink. At least you didn't charge me a penny for that," I try to joke, but really, I feel like he just gave me a lot to think about. "So, why did you call me?"

I'm so distracted I can't even remember how we began this

conversation. Should I reach out to Bronwyn and tell her to stop trying to contact me? Then, I could figure out her real motives and get closure.

What if she never married Wyatt's Dad? Would I forgive her? Doubtful. Is there someone out there for me that will take the little I can offer?

And the only person I can think of is Nyx. Would she even entertain the possibility of having anything to do with me?

All these thoughts might be Ford's doing.

This is definitely the result of my twin's newfound life. He has never fallen in love in his entire life. Now that he's with Persy, he's making me feel like I'm going to be left behind. He's messing with my head. Am I holding onto Nyx because that'll keep me closer to him?

It's just for a breath that I entertain that thought because really, Ford and I barely saw each other while we were in New York. Being with one sister doesn't guarantee that the other will be around, and I'm perfectly fine with it.

What is it then?

Just live and forget about everything else.

I don't need a therapist, and I definitely don't need to reach out to Bronwyn. I have to plan a vacation where I spend half of the time jumping from planes, rafting, and finding extreme activities while during the other half I fuck women that will help me erase the uneasiness inside my chest.

"Listen, my woman is worried about her sister, so please keep an eye on her," he says, and his voice comes out harsher than I care to listen to. "I'm not sure why Nyx trusts you but...just be mindful, okay? Don't fuck this for me."

There it is. He's concerned that I'm going to break his new toy.

"I don't think I've ever heard you talk this much in my life," I conclude. "Yes, I'll take care of her. Talk to you later."

I hang up because we can be on the phone for hours discussing the many ways I can fuck this up, how he's not thinking straight, or... We get along well, but we also know how to fight. After all, we are brothers.

TWENTY-FOUR

Nate

_____

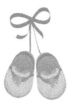

MY DAY GOES AS USUAL. When I arrive home around six, I find Nyx and Brock on the couch. She's asleep with another open book laying on her chest. Instead of waking her up, I march to one of the guest rooms and grab a blanket to cover her.

Brock is right behind me.

"Hey, boy. Did you have a good day with Nyx?"

He barks once and nuzzles my leg as I pet the top of his head. I don't know what this dog is going to do when she leaves, but I hope he survives her absence. He's too enamored with her. Last night, after all the back and forth trips from her bedroom to the bathroom, he ended up sleeping with her. I wanted to tell her that he's not allowed to sleep on beds, but I didn't have the heart to take that away from either one of them.

Demetri isn't going to be happy about Brock's behavior, but this time he can only blame Nyx.

"We can convince her to stay longer," I suggest, and he gives me a skeptical look. "I agree, that might be impossible, but we can try."

Once I'm back in the living room, I snag the book carefully and set it up on the coffee table. I lay the blanket on top of her. When I pull it down to cover her feet, I realize she has a ring on her pinky toe, an anklet with an infinity symbol charm, and a tattoo on her ankle. It reads,

Joie De Vivre

It makes me wonder if there's more underneath that she's hiding. I don't speak French, but I know that phrase. It means something like *joy of living*.

There's no doubt in my mind that there is a lot more of Nyx Brassard beneath what she lets everyone see. How am I supposed to find out if I'm right when we're in an awkward place? Her life has shifted permanently; I'm the fucking tin man.

I wish we had met a few years ago, or—

Stopping myself from thinking anything further, I kiss her forehead. Focusing on the ifs is just a loss of precious time and energy.

"Come on, boy," I whisper to Brock. "Let's take you outside."

I open the door for him and watch him run around the backyard chasing birds. The sound of rustling inside the house makes me turn around, and I spot Nyx watching me from the couch.

"Hey, sleeping beauty," I greet her.

Her lips stretch showing me that sweet, breathtaking smile that I'm growing fond of as we spend more time together.

"How are you feeling?" I ask her.

"Tired," she answers with a yawn. "What time is it?"

"Only a few minutes past six," I answer.

She gasps, "I meant to cook dinner for us. My plan was to read a chapter. I swear it was two o'clock just a few minutes ago."

"You didn't sleep much last night," I remind her. "Don't be harsh on yourself, okay. What else did you do today?"

She briefs me about the wrongful termination lawsuit they'll be serving her former employer late next week. And she found a place where they can do a non-invasive paternity test.

"We can't do it until I'm at least eight weeks pregnant," she states.

"Which according to your calendar is on the thirty first, if I recall correctly."

"You have an amazing memory. I scheduled my appointment, and Edward's," she adds. "He was avoiding me until his cousin threatened to involve the courts if he didn't agree to provide us with his sample."

Sounds like bluffing to me, so I ask, "Can he really force him to do it?"

"Doubtful," she answers and grins. "We'd have to wait until the baby is born and by then, it'd be Edward pushing for it to show me that he has no part in the baby's life and he doesn't have to pay child support—which I don't need him to do. In most cases, you wait until the baby is born to establish paternity. This is different. There aren't any precedents that we could find in the state of Colorado.

"Waiting until this can become a mess isn't an option for me though. I just want him to either sign the papers or think about his part in the baby's life. Though, since Edward is pretty ignorant about family law and fearful of his cousin, he agreed," she informs me.

"Remind me who this Pierce is," I ask.

"My mentor and the guy who is helping me with the wrongful termination case," she answers. "He asked me if I could drive down to Oregon this weekend. Would you mind if I borrow one of your cars?"

I want to tell her that he should be the one dropping by Seattle, but instead, I offer to drive her. "We can leave early in the morning."

"Thank you so much. I don't want to inconvenience you. However, Pierce and I have to discuss the lawsuit and also his employment proposal." She pauses and takes a long sip of air. "He might be able to provide me with a good insurance that'll cover the maternity expenses."

I rub the back of my neck, turning to check on Brock who is still sniffing around the grass and say, "I'm not sure how to feel about your rejection. You're accepting work from everyone but me."

She lifts an eyebrow and waves her hand. "Sometimes I'm not sure if you're joking or being serious."

"This is me being totally honest. I want you on my team because you're damn good. I've seen you work," I pause and look toward the backyard and then back again at her. "Remember that time when my lawyer was working on Persephone's lease contract and you ended up knocking a chunk of the rent to make up for the fact that my stupid brother was trying to add illegal clauses to it?"

She fights the grin. "I can't even with that contract. There was no logic to it. I'm pretty sure your lawyer was just trying to keep Ford happy."

"Yeah well, in theory, that cost me. If I hire you, those mistakes won't be happening again," I say, hopeful. We have great benefits, and I really want to help her.

"It's nothing personal, I assure you. While the blueberry is a baby, I'd rather choose my caseload. Having a permanent job is demanding and won't give me the room I need to take care of my newborn. Pierce gets it and is willing to work with me. I know it doesn't make sense, and you might want to match whatever he offers, but the thing is I know Pierce, and I won't have that need to throw myself into my new job to show that I'm capable. If I take something new, I'll be fighting with my instincts all the time, and it'll be too stressful."

Judging by her worried expression, I decide to drop the subject— for now. This isn't about handing her something because I feel bad for her. It's about hiring the best for my companies. She's that good.

"Fine, I'll stop pushing you, but if you ever need a job, I'll hire you in a heartbeat."

She chews and licks her bottom lip and as much as I keep fighting with my common sense, the craving for her is beginning to push away the logic.

I know she's talking, but I can't make out the words over the blood that's pumping hard and fast. So, I shake my head, control myself, and say, "What was that?"

Her brow lifts, and damn. Can she stop playing with her lips and her teeth? I swear one of these days I'm going to slam my mouth against hers and she won't be able to blame anyone but herself for being so sexy.

"When did you stop listening?" she asks suspiciously.

Right about the moment I wanted to be the one fidgeting with your lips.

"You mentioned something about an appointment."

"Yes, I need to go to the doctor," she says, and I almost high five myself because it was a great guess. "It's in my top ten things to do soon. The at-home test said yes...well, the seven I used. Mom confirmed I am, but what if it's a false positive?"

"Is this denial or just wanting an official yes from a doctor?"

"The second," she confirms. "It's just a technicality. I really want them to say, here, you're expecting a baby, and you'll be popping this beautiful pumpkin out of your vagina around April twelfth, and it's in perfect health. Because if you recall, I drank wine while I was in New York. What if something happened to her?"

"Do you want me to get my assistant to schedule you an appointment?" I ask. "She's researching the nutritionist by the way. I should have more information Monday. Maybe I should ask her to just make you an appointment with both."

She asks, confused, "Here in Seattle?"

"We have doctors here, too," I tease her.

"Well, yeah, but I have to..." She trails her voice and her gaze toward the coffee table where her phone and the book she was reading earlier sit. "On second thought, I'm not sure when I'm going back to Denver. I might as well do this here, next week. I should get that positive sooner rather than later."

I want to throw a fist to the air and celebrate the news.

Trying to sound neutral and not in the least excited, I ask, "What made you decide to stay with us longer?"

She grins. "Mom. She called asking me too many questions all at once, and Brock and I decided it'd be best if we remain with you for a little longer."

"Sweetheart, let's make sure you remember this. Brock is mine. If you want to hang out with the kid, you have to stay. You're not taking him with you," I warn her with a light voice. "You can just move in with me. I could use another roommate. As you can see, I have plenty of room for you too."

Her throaty laugh makes me shiver with desire. That sound is just like everything about her, arousing. "Your place is gorgeous, but too far from home. I can't imagine living in another state."

I want to tell her that you get used to it. When Ford realized that he couldn't live in New York, he moved to Miami first. A year later he jumped to Chicago. Then there was London for a year...or was it first to London and then Chicago? I can remember every place he lived because we own a house there, but not the length or the order. The only thing I clearly remember is that we had to learn to live apart.

She's going through too many changes, and it's not the time to tell her that maybe she should try living somewhere else. My place might be the wrong choice. What am I supposed to do with her?

I rub my temples as the images of her on top, under, or beside me while I'm making love to her appear in my head. What the fuck is wrong with me? This is what happens when I don't sleep enough. We need to leave the house before I do or say something stupid.

"Do you feel like going out to dinner?" I ask.

"Where would you be taking me?"

"I can get us a reservation almost everywhere," I assure her. "We've yet to celebrate the little blueberry, or should we call her Helios?"

"Stop calling my baby weird names."

"Sorry. Your parents started it."

"I accept your dinner invitation. Let's just hope my stomach behaves while we're out."

TWENTY-FIVE

Nyx

———

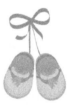

EATING out at a fancy restaurant is overrated. I talk myself into believing that the hype of going to a five-star restaurant is so last century.

Really. There's nothing better than dining on the veranda with a view of Lake Washington, enjoying Nate's company, and devouring the most delicious French onion soup I've ever tried in my life—that he prepared—and realizing that it will take me months to find a new normal.

Until I can get this nausea under control, I think eating out is off the menu. Earlier, when we entered one of the finest steakhouses in

Seattle, I got nauseous. I'm not sure if it was the scent of the food, the place, or the people wearing all kinds of perfume.

Who would've guessed that my life would shift so much in such a short time? Just a couple of weeks ago, I was worried about drowning and feeling lonely. Tonight...well, here I am, having dinner with a guy I swore would be a distant memory, and in a different state where I'm planning on staying for at least a couple of more weeks—when I can start searching for a new house.

Do I miss my family?

Mom's making sure that I don't miss her at all. She keeps texting me and calling me. I love her dearly, but she's hovering more than usual.

"I have to ask," I say.

"Not really, but hit me with your next question," he responds. "They're highly entertaining at times. I like inquisitive women."

I narrow my gaze, trying to understand his statement, but I choose to disregard it and ask, "How often do you throw a romantic candlelight dinner for your dates?"

He rolls his eyes and almost laughs. "Never. You and Ford are the only guests I've ever had in this house. What makes you think I've done this before?"

"It's perfect," I explain. "The twinkle lights webbed over the roof, the view, the meal...even the company."

His gaze moves around between the lake, the setting, and then me before saying, "This is the first time I have had such lovely company. The lights were here when I bought this house. Well, I had them replaced with new ones, but the setting was already a part of the place."

He skips the food, but we've already discussed that he's a great cook, so I have to ask, "How long have you lived here?"

"Four, almost five years," he answers.

I'm tempted to ask him more, like what made him move to the suburbs instead of buying a place in the city. "Why..." I trail my gaze toward the city lights.

"We used to own a place downtown," he answers. "Ford wasn't

166 • CLAUDIA BURGOA

visiting often because it was too close to the offices. I decided to move to a quieter neighborhood that would contrast my life in New York."

"Which one do you like best?"

"I like living in Manhattan, with moderation," he answers. "It's one of the few cities where you can get food delivered at any time of the day—or night. It has everything. It's diverse, and you can get lost too. From all the world cities, I think that's my favorite."

Looking across the lake, I can see why he'd choose this house. It has a fantastic view, the commute is short enough to travel to Seattle every day, and the silence is relaxing. But, is it this place or us that gives me peace?

There's an intimacy we share when we don't say words that calms me. Maybe that's the biggest reason why I am here.

Being at home, trying to organize my thoughts, my future, and my present felt so lonely. Nate makes everything bearable even when all I'm doing is pondering about what's coming up next and running scenarios to decide what's the best way to go.

With him, I feel as if I'm not alone trying to survive. Before yesterday, I felt like it might be easier to sink than breathe and stay afloat.

He's not pulling me out of the water. He's handing me a float that I can hold onto until I know where I'm heading. That's what I decide to focus on for the foreseeable future: Nate, the friend.

I refuse to acknowledge the way his touch makes my skin tingle. It's not easy to ignore his smoky-gravel voice as heat spreads along my body. He's too alluring to ignore. His charm can be spellbinding if one isn't careful, but I am. I keep telling myself that if I can get past this attraction, we could be the best of friends.

"Penny for your thoughts," I offer, wondering why he's been less chatty than usual.

"Why do people offer their two cents when they are about to speak but just a penny when they want someone else's thoughts?"

I chuckle and grab some of the freshly baked bread we bought on our way back from the city.

"Probably because when you offer your two cents, it's advice, a critique, or life-changing. While in my case, I have no idea what you're thinking and it might not be worth my time?"

"Way to kick my pride," he jokes and winks at me. "Stop wounding my ego, woman."

"Just keeping you grounded. I don't want to inflate your ego so much that you won't fit in the house," I tease him.

"My ego grows with touch, not with words." He smirks widely. "Let me know when you'd like me to demonstrate."

"Well, now I have to ask," I say, diverting the conversation to a safer subject because I'm not discussing his length, girth, or stamina. Not when I'm having trouble not picturing him naked. "If my memory serves me correctly, I recall you propositioning me the night we met."

"And the offer is still open, sweetheart," he answers, crossing his arms as he watches me.

"Don't you have, like, friends with benefits or...someone to go out with? I mean, it's Friday, and you're stuck with the pregnant lady who cramped your style in the middle of one of the best restaurants in the city."

He's about to speak when I add, "After all, you're the famous Nathaniel Chadwick. Playboy, adrenaline junky, and businessman."

"That's not exactly how they describe me," he corrects me and laughs when I roll my eyes. "Our outing was—I'd be lying if I say that you looked cute at the restaurant, but it wasn't pretty. However, I enjoy your company more than I enjoy the company of many people. To answer your question, I was a serial dater before Bronwyn, and after her, I was sleeping my way through the world. I stopped because it gets fucking old and lonely."

I scrunch my nose and agree with him, "It does get lonely. Not that I sleep around, but the couple of times a year that I managed to find a guy, it never lasted more than a night or a weekend. If you still love your ex, why don't you...?"

I stop myself because I doubt suggesting going back to her is the way to go, but what is it that he needs to do to move on with his life?

He combs his hair with one hand and lets out some air before he speaks, "Why do I keep getting bombarded by things like questions, packages, or discussions that end up bringing up my past?" he asks, aggravated. "It's not only your questions but also the memory of my old home in New York. I loved my house in Brooklyn. It was far enough from the city, but close enough too."

It sounds like he had to move because she lived close by, and that's shitty. "Did you sell it?"

"I didn't have the heart to kick Bronwyn out of it," he answers. "It's still mine, and she's probably living with that asshole and their kid—or kids if they had more. I pay taxes, the insurance, and... Today, Ford reminded me that I have yet to find some kind of closure from that relationship—and recover my house."

I try not to scowl at him when I ask, "Like getting the house back?"

He glances at me and asks, "What would you do?"

"If I was in your place?" I take a piece of bread and munch on it while I think about the answer. "I think you refer to the betrayal, and I honestly don't know if I'd forgive him—whoever this guy is. Now, her deception went further than just cheating, she passed a kid as yours and then said, 'Oh well, he's not yours so never mind, I'll just snatch him away from you, and we'll go our separate ways.' It upsets me just to think about what she did to you. Since I'm not close to her, I can coldly say, let me hit her with a notice of eviction to recover your place."

He closes his eyes briefly and shakes his head. "It's not just the place. She's been asking me for financial help. I doubt she can afford to pay for rent."

This kind of talk helps me shake any feelings that I might be developing for him. Earlier I wondered if he really loved her and if they were really *that couple.* I lied to myself when I believed that maybe he was infatuated with her. But now...

Well, I can see that he is still in love with his ex and will never love anyone the way he loves her.

"Is Wyatt still registered as your child?"

"No, we took care of that almost immediately. I was deleted not only from his life but also his birth certificate."

"But she's still reaching out because she knows you love that kid as if he's your own," I mumble. "This might not be what you want to hear, but it's time to let them go and move on. If you want, I can handle the eviction and give them plenty of time to find a new place. It's not about you being heartless, but you need to heal, and the best way might be by cutting all ties to them."

"Something about this reminds me of my mother, you know," he says.

"What is it?"

He stares at the table, grabs his wine glass, and takes a sip. After a few beats, he says, "I'm doing this all wrong. As you mentioned, this looks like such a romantic dinner. I should be trying to woo you and get you in bed. Instead, I'm babbling shit that you must find irrelevant."

I reach out and grab his hand. "Not at all. First of all, we know how we'll be spending the night. With me having morning sickness and you assuring me that I look pretty even when I look like a demon possesses me."

"A blueberry sized demon," he jokes, caressing my hand's back with his thumb.

"We're becoming friends, and I'd like to help you in any capacity. It's the least I can do, really, for all you've done for me. Even if it's by being the bitch who draws the papers to remind Bronwyn that she made many bad choices and she should let you move on. Now, tell me about your mother," I plead, squeezing his hand to give him a little courage. "How is it that one thing relates to the other?"

"Mom left us and created a new family," he states.

"Did she just leave or did your parents get a divorce?"

He nods before replying, "After a couple of years of fighting like sworn enemies they divorced, and she left us."

I want to ask if there was a custody fight or if he's just assuming that she didn't fight for them. Maybe his father had a better lawyer that left her without the right to have her children during the weekends. It happens. I've seen it many times. These parents never think about their children or the consequences.

"She has a new family. My brothers are twenty-eight and twenty-seven. I have a younger sister who is twenty-five," he offers. "It's obvious that, for her, it wasn't because she didn't want children. She just didn't want us."

I'm about to open my mouth when he waves his hand. "If Mom had wanted us, she'd have requested visitations. At least a holiday every other year. Since the moment she left, I never heard from her. Sometimes, I want to knock on her door and ask 'What the fuck was so wrong with us that you had to get a new family?'"

"Which translates into what the fuck was wrong with you that Bronwyn got another man and had a child with him and not you?" I question as my heart squeezes because women have fucked with this guy a lot.

These two are the most significant players in his life, but what if there had been other women using him and never loving him.

No wonder he's so jaded.

"Yes, that's exactly it. There's something wrong with me for thinking that, but I just can't seem to let it go."

"Well, you're a catch. If you ever need references, send them my way."

"Says the woman who keeps rejecting me," he teases me.

"If we had met under different circumstances..." I shrug. "I'm pregnant and you have a lot of emotional gunk that you have to sort out before letting anyone in your life."

"My brother would be killing me if I make a move because he's afraid that I'll fuck up his relationship with Persy."

"I'm not in the practice of listening to others, so we'd be doing a lot more than holding my hair while I talk to the porcelain goddess in the bathrooms. And well, on the couch...the action would be different from just tucking me in when you find me asleep because it seems like I'm developing some kind of pregnancy-narcolepsy," I say, but would I break the sister code for him?

No, I'm too loyal to my sister to mess with her relationship. Probably.

"Really, just the couch and the bathroom?" His voice has an energy that makes me want to say yes, and let's just do it now. "We'd have gone through all the surfaces in this house and be heading to some tropical island where it'd be just you and me. Just say the word."

My sensible side says, "No. We're both in a bad place. I'm starting a new life, and you—"

"Do you think I need a therapist?" The change of pace feels like a whiplash.

One moment he's telling me that we could have sex on any surface of the world, and the next we're discussing...therapy?

"Talking to a professional about your unresolved feelings is always a good idea," I answer, because having a sister who does that for a living has taught me many things, and I can respond to this better than discussing his tour le sex. "That said, you need to want to go. If not, it's a waste of time for you and the therapist."

"Do you have a therapist?"

"I do, and I speak to her every month. I have a lot of issues when it comes to my job. Mostly when I have to deal with family cases where I win because I'm good, however I shouldn't have taken the case because I worked for the wrong parent." I sigh, remembering all those cases I won because I'm a damn good lawyer. However, the child was placed with the wrong parent in my opinion. They make me sad. It's hard to live with the guilt and harder to move onto the next case.

If I had the money, I'd have a firm that works to help parents who can't afford a good lawyer but need to get their children away from their exes.

"You know what," I suddenly say. "Losing my job hurt my pride and changed my entire life, but it might be a blessing in disguise."

"For what it's worth, I'm glad that it brought you to me."

"But I shouldn't be here," I argue.

"Maybe this is where we belong. In this exact moment in time when we are somehow lost and in need of direction. We might be able to help each other find the way," he claims while his gaze traps mine, and all I want is to be that guide and maybe stay with him once he finds a new path.

"You know what they say about blind people leading each other..." I close my mouth because I can't recall that saying. "Anyway, I'm sure it's a pretty bad idea."

"No," he argues. "I'm an emotional mess. You're just trying to figure out how to live better with your new situation. Two different concepts. You can lead me into the emotional light, and I'll just make sure that you and the blueberry demon settle down. It's a win-win situation. What can go wrong?"

I stare at him, wondering if anything could go wrong. We're not offering anything out of the ordinary. I can be a pretty good emotional support. He seems to do well financially and really, he is helping me sell my place and giving me a safe space to get away so I can relax.

Does it matter that he's male model gorgeous with an amazing bone structure, captivating blue eyes, and a wicked smile that makes it hard not to smile back?

"Then, I'm happy to be here—*as your friend.*"

His grin widens, and God if it doesn't make me weak in my knees.

I'm not sure if the last three words are for his benefit or mine. One of us has to remember that this roommate arrangement can't go any further than maybe a couple of weeks. That we're both vulnerable and we could easily confuse a heart twinge with falling in love.

When my gaze finds his, I freeze because the expression in his eyes is back to that wildfire burning from the inside out. My heart speeds up fast. Thankfully, I'm saved by my phone. I see it's Pierce texting me. I shouldn't answer, but this is the best excuse to walk away from this romantic discussion before he says something more or I expect more than an accidental caress.

TWENTY-SIX

Nyx

PIERCE: Can we change plans?

Nyx: How?

Pierce: I need you here for more than just a Saturday afternoon. We have a lot to cover. Can you come on Monday? I'll secure your transportation. I promise.

Nyx: What kind of transportation?

Pierce: A private jet to Portland and a helicopter ride to Baker's Creek. You can stay with us until next Friday.

Nyx: That's an entire week of work. What do we have to cover?

Pierce: Trust me, this is going to be good.

Nyx: *I agree, but it better not be a face to face meeting with your mother.*

Pierce: *None of that, no worries. We'll work on that lawsuit too.*

When I give Nate the news, he doesn't love the idea. But there's nothing he can do to stop me—and he can't join me. He needs to be in New York by Monday. We spend the weekend together. He drops me at the airport and makes me promise him that I'll come back to Seattle instead of going back to Colorado.

I'm not surprised that the first words Pierce says when I enter his office are, "Let's open a law firm. We can be partners."

"Well, hello to you too," I greet him.

He smiles and says, "You look like crap, sweetheart. I heard that pregnancy gets better with time."

"Charming as usual. No wonder your wife is divorcing you," I dish back. "Tell me all about this firm you want to open."

There's a lot more to the fact that he wants us to start a firm. He wants me to oversee his father's company and Merkel Hotels, his brother's hotel conglomerate, since none of them can leave Baker's Creek until the end of next year.

First, he needs me to be in New York for the next couple of months so I can familiarize myself with Aldridge Enterprises, assist with the transition they are undergoing, and keep an eye on Merkel while they move their corporate offices from New York to Portland. After that, I can work from wherever I want as long as I can travel whenever he needs me.

"It feels like you're hiring me as your spy," I say as I stare at the page with all my duties for the upcoming months.

He runs both hands through his hair and says, "You're doing two jobs in one. We need a person who we trust overseeing this. I trust you, blindly."

"Your brothers don't know me, and if I recall, you don't know much about them either," I remind him.

"Things change, and you need to keep up," he states. "And yes, you're our eyes and also my legal partner. So...what do you say?"

Before I sign on the dotted line and we become Aldridge, Brassard & Associates, LLP, we discuss the baby I'm expecting, and how that will affect traveling during the last trimester of my pregnancy. He hopes that by then we will have a strong team that can represent us anywhere.

I spend an entire week learning more about Aldridge Enterprises, handling some personal cases for his brothers, and working on my lawsuit against Bryant, LLC. By Friday, I not only have a job, but Sarah chooses to settle and pay the emotional damages she caused me by the highly unprofessional, unfair, and unexpected dismissal.

The only thing I have pending is the paternity test that hopefully will persuade Edward to sign away his parental rights.

My morning sickness doesn't improve. On Wednesday, Pierce's sister-in-law, who is a doctor, drags me to her practice to draw blood so she can confirm the pregnancy. On Thursday, she tells me the bloodwork not only confirms that I am expecting a baby, but I'm healthy. She prescribes me prenatal vitamins and recommends the same thing as Mom, that I eat tiny meals often. Nate calls in the morning and at night. He texts me during the day. It's just to check on the blueberry demon and me.

This would be swoony, if it wasn't sad. His attention reminds me that I don't have anyone to be there for me and the baby. The books I read keep talking about my partner and...someone has to rewrite those books because they are not only outdated but definitely depressing. Sometimes I want to yell at the book, *"There's no partner to hold my hand while I'm going through this freaking journey. How about you erase those stupid lines?"*

By Saturday, I'm ready to leave Baker's Creek first thing in the morning. I have to be in New York by Monday. I decided to arrive a couple of days early to fight the jetlag, play with Brock since Nate is still there, and go shopping for new clothes.

All my work clothes are currently in storage. I could go and fetch them, but what is the point in going through all that trouble when they won't fit in a couple of months. According to a blog I've been reading, it makes more sense that I buy baggy clothes and a few maternity basics like jeans and black pants. Last night, when I spoke with Nate about it, he agreed to take me shopping later today or tomorrow.

As I close the door of my hotel room, I receive a text from Nate.

Nate: *Are you awake?*

Nyx: *Yes, I'm leaving the hotel soon. I want to arrive at the airport with plenty of time to buy a ticket, check-in, and eat something before I board the plane. I'm dreading the five-hour flight. Why are you up so early?*

When I look at the time, I realize it's just a few minutes before eight o'clock his time. That man needs less coffee. I bet he already went for a run, hit the gym, and showered. If I video chat him right now, he's going to look handsome, well rested, and probably ready to go and jump from a plane.

Nate: *Well, you said you wanted to leave early for New York. I had to be at the airport at midnight to make it on time.*

I stare at the phone and frown. Has he been waiting for me at the airport since midnight?

Nyx: *Where are you?*

Nate: *I'm downstairs, waiting for you.*

Nyx: *In Baker's Creek?*

Nate: *Yes. Do you need me to come upstairs?*

My heart is racing fast at the prospect of seeing him, and my lips stretch into a wide smile. I push the lobby floor button three more times hoping it'll make the cart go faster.

Nyx: *I should be downstairs soon.*

Nyx: *Why are you here?*

He doesn't answer. When I step out of the elevator, Nate is right outside. He receives me with a big smile and open arms.

"Hey," I greet him, walking into his embrace.

"How is the blueberry spawn and her mama?" he asks, kissing the top of my head.

"We're doing well," I answer, placing a hand on my soft belly. It's still strange to think that there's a tiny person growing inside me. "I wasn't expecting to see you."

"Well, I didn't like the idea of you flying commercial," he says, nuzzling my hair. "Plus, Brock and I missed you."

"You did, huh?" I ask, snuggling closer to him so I can listen to his heartbeat and breathe in the scent of his cedar and sandalwood cologne.

Why did I miss him?

I shouldn't have, but God, this week was too long and too exhausting. Nate makes everything more bearable—and Brock too. There's something about having them around that makes everything easier, even breathing.

"Ready to go?" he asks, taking a deep breath.

"Yeah," I answer, opening my eyes and moving away from his warm embrace. "Where's my boy?"

"He stayed with Demetri in New York. But I promised the pup I'd bring you with me," he says, grabbing my luggage and taking my hand.

All week long, I've been thinking not only about Nate but also the *not just friends* feelings I've been experiencing for the past few days.

The more time passes, the harder it is to convince myself that there's no space for him in my life. And he just showed me that he doesn't have a problem boarding a plane and flying to the other side of the country to pick me up because...why did he do it?

"Why are you here again?"

He looks around and throws his sexy grin at me. "You have selective hearing. I told you, I missed you, I didn't want you to take a commercial flight, and I couldn't wait to see you."

"Nate..." is all I can say because all of those reasons are sweet.

They also make me think that maybe we could try to act upon my feelings, but what about his?

Bronwyn will always be the love of his life. I'm expecting a kid, and he has issues when it comes to children. I won't neglect my baby to spare his feelings, and I know he can never care about my kid enough to accept her into his life.

"Before you protest, we need to discuss your living arrangements," he says as we walk toward a black sports car that sits almost in front of the entrance. "It's nice of Pierce to offer you his brother's brownstone, but that's a long commute to Manhattan."

"That's one option. The other two are his father's home, which is across from Central Park," I inform him. "Or one of the suites of Merkel's hotel."

"Living in a hotel sounds stressful. The father's penthouse might be a good choice, but you can just stay with me where you have a twenty-four-seven cook at your service, Demetri to assist in case I'm not in town, and as a bonus, you get Brock," he says with a voice that sounds more like a game show host than himself.

"I forgot how ridiculous you are," I claim as I get in the car.

"Stop denying it. You missed me," he argues as he turns on the engine.

So much so that I'm starting to worry about the feelings I refuse to acknowledge.

"How's New York?" I ask, changing the subject because even though I missed him, we shouldn't be discussing the possibility of an emotional entanglement that is going to leave us hurting.

"Hot, rancid, and humid," he answers.

"Rancid?"

"There's a putrid smell characteristic of the city that increases during the summer," he explains.

"If you had a choice, would you just stay in Seattle?"

"Probably," he responds. "There are times when I want to move everything to Washington."

"Why not Colorado, your brother lives there?"

"It's something I can contemplate soon. He moves so often that I can't just make the decision to uproot thousands of employees when he might just say, well now, I'm going to North Dakota," he answers.

I laugh. "I doubt that Persy would follow him there."

"What if they break up?"

I consider it for a couple of seconds and say, "I've never seen my sister so in love with someone."

"Good, because my brother has never been in love before your sister, so if they break up...I'm not sure he'll survive."

"That's impossible," I argue. "How can a thirty-five-year-old man... Really? Persy is his first?"

"Yep. Believe me when I say he got the brains and I got the heart," he confesses.

"So now that they might settle down you could entertain the possibility of moving everything to Colorado?"

"At least the New York staff. My commute would be shorter, or... Ford can take care of that part of the company while I stay put in Seattle."

"You wouldn't move?"

"I'd commute. There are too many affiliates in Seattle and packing would be too costly and not worth it in the long run," he answers. "Where are you opening this law firm?"

"Oregon, but we're going to be able to practice in several places since we both passed the Bar exam in New York."

"But you studied in North Carolina," he amends.

"Yes, but if you take the test in New York, it has reciprocity with several states," I explain lightly. "Back then I had no idea where I wanted to work."

"What made you decide to move to Colorado?"

"You can only be away from the parents for so long?"

"The ones that drive you crazy?" he asks mockingly.

"Those," I confirm. "I love my parents, which is going to make it hard to be away from them for the next few months."

"What if you have to live permanently in New York for this job?"

My heart stops because that's not something I would ever consider. There's a huge difference between needing a few days alone and not seeing my parents for weeks at a time.

"I don't have to. Pierce and I discussed it already. We're opening a firm. While we decide where we're setting it up, I'm working on this special project. He needs me there for the next three months, but after that I can be anywhere," I explain, while I remind myself that this isn't permanent.

"Can you work from Seattle once a month for a week during the next three months?" he inquires, and I stare at him confused.

"That's a strange question. Why would I want to do that?"

"I don't want to leave you alone, and I have to go to Seattle at least once a month for a week," he explains. "Can you negotiate that?"

"You're cute, but I'm a grown woman, and I can be on my own."

"Damn it, woman!" he protests. "Stop calling me cute."

"Adorable, then," I rectify. "Let's backtrack and explain to me, why can't I stay in New York without you?"

"Because..." he huffs. "I don't want the blueberry demon and you living on your own, okay?"

When I think about the past five days, I realize that not having him around wasn't pleasant. I could use a friend, and he's by far the best candidate for the job.

"Thank you." It's all I say because asking more questions might lead me to something I don't want to discuss now—or maybe never.

TWENTY-SEVEN

Nyx

———————

I LOVE to stare at the clouds, whether I'm on the ground or while flying.

Clouds make me wonder about life and the future. Ever since I can remember, I've been on a plane. Mom kept us pretty entertained during our flights. She'd have us coloring, looking for shapes in the clouds, or playing games she and Dad made up.

It's no surprise that when we're above thirty thousand feet, I push open the shade of the window and stare at the blue sky and the puffy clouds we are flying over. There's nothing else in the surrounding area but the blue and white shades.

This reminds me of how small we are and how little our problems really are in comparison.

After two weeks, I can safely say that I'm getting used to my new normal. Queasy stomach, fatigue, and having some extra time to just relax. That's never been me. Ever since I can remember, I have to be on the go doing something, keeping myself busy. I think Eros, Persy, and I were restless while growing up.

If Persy and I were bored with our dolls, we'd join Eros in his eternal search for bugs. He collected bugs while growing up. Well, he collected the pictures since we couldn't carry them around, and they weren't pets.

Now that I'm older, I realize that we were pretty difficult children. Most kids are fine with just listening to their Mom say no.

We required a logical explanation—or at least logical to us. I'm sure not many boys have to hear an entire explanation of how gathering insects and keeping them is wrong. Dad explained several times to Eros that beetles were integral to ancient Egyptians. We should treat them with respect. Or how bees are essential for life to exist—without them, there wouldn't be pollination and without pollination, the entire world would stop existing as we know it.

The list goes on and on. He was allowed to trap mosquitoes because Mom hated them. But he never cared about them. Just thinking about my brother and my sisters makes me wonder how this little one is going to behave. If I'm going to need a degree in science to make sure I can keep up with her, and if she'll be fine without a dad. I'm sure plenty of children do well enough with a single parent, but I can't imagine my life without Mom and Dad.

Maybe this is why Mom kept *me* busy because I'm always thinking about the future, worrying about not getting it right, and fearing that things won't go the way I envisioned them. I've been driving myself crazy since we boarded the plane, and Nate has been working with Ford. They are working on some secret project.

"What are you worried about?" Nate asks.

I turn around and find him studying me with such interest I feel like a piece of art on exhibition. I've noticed that he's always watching me, observing me, trying to figure out how I work or...I don't know why it is that he's so fascinated by me.

"Why do you think I'm concerned?"

He takes a seat next to me and traces a line on my forehead. "That cute frown line deepens when you're worried about something."

I pat my forehead wondering what else I do that I never pay attention to and ask, "I do?"

He smiles and presses his lips while nodding. "Yeah, just like the little line that forms between your eyebrows when you're curious about something. You have a lot of tells. Soon you won't be able to feed me any bullshit."

I blush and say, "I'm not sure if you're ridiculous, cute, or just plain weird."

He winks, "I'll keep you guessing too. Now tell me what is worrying you so I can help you solve it."

"Well, while growing up we were a handful. Mom had Dad to help her with us...or vice versa. I'm not sure if I need to go back to college and get a degree in education or..."

He laughs, and that rich sound makes the apprehension on my belly dissipate, and why do I have that need to get closer to him and kiss his jaw and then his mouth. I have this strange desperation clawing its way to my head and trying to convince me to take what I need. Him. I fight it because I don't want to ruin my time with him. He's an amazing friend.

"I'm glad I amuse you, sir," I growl, faking anger.

"Sorry, but imagine if every parent in the world had to go back and get a degree just to raise their children—no one would have kids," he concludes. "My guess is that you're terrified about the future and if you'll be able to do it well on your own. Now, this is the part where I remind you that you have a great family that is there to support you. You also have me."

"You," I repeat wanting to ask more but also afraid about his answers. "Sure, volunteer while there's no wailing child. I bet by the time this little one is screaming bloody murder you're going to be thousands of miles away from us, which I understand. I'm not trying to guilt you."

He laughs and shakes his head when I yawn. "Why don't you take a nap. We still have three more hours to go."

I want to say no, but my eyes are closing so I agree to doze off but refuse to go to the bedroom. There's something about having Nate around that feels just, right.

"So, the narcolepsy is still going on, huh?" Nate wakes me up before we land in New York.

"Umm, you told me to nap and I woke up too early to remember anymore," I joke and sit upright.

"I forgot to ask, did you sleep last night?"

I shake my head and remind him, "My morning sickness is worse at night."

"We got you an appointment with the nutritionist for Monday, an OBGYN, and a sonogram since you said the doctor at Baker's Creek recommended you schedule one just to confirm your due date," he announces.

I reach out for his hand. "You didn't have to, but thank you very much for doing that for us. I really don't know how I'm going to repay you for everything that you've done so far."

He puts a hand on top of mine, holding it tenderly but firmly. "You don't owe me anything. This is what friends do for each other. I'm sure if I was pregnant, unemployed, and confused, you'd be giving me a hand."

"No, I'd be selling your story and representing you," I correct him. "First pregnant man. That's gold. I'd make a fortune off of you."

We both laugh.

"I walked myself into that one, didn't I?"

"Yep," I answer, my body still shaking. I can't stop laughing because his laughter is contagious.

"I'm glad I amuse you."

"I like you, Nathaniel Chadwick," I confirm.

Above all these crazy things I feel for him, I love his company and cherish his friendship. I genuinely like this guy. This is just the beginning of the storm, but it's so easy to walk through it because he's beside me.

"Glad to hear, because I like you too, Nyxie," he says and then adds with his voice dropping to a whisper. "I like you. A. Lot."

My eyes stare at his lips that are approaching me. My pulse accelerates and just as I feel his warm breath, the flight attendant's voice comes from the speaker.

"Please make sure your seats are adjusted, your—" I tune her out and busy myself pretending to get ready for landing and trying to steady my pulse. We shouldn't engage in more than holding hands or we might ruin what we have.

TWENTY-EIGHT

Nyx

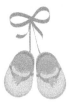

AFTER WE DISEMBARK THE PLANE, we march to the parking lot. I'm surprised that he drives an Audi A7, nothing too fancy. His brother has a car collection that I envy. Maybe Nate isn't too much into cars like Ford. What does he collect?

Instead of inquiring about that, I ask, "Did you get any sleep at all?"

"During the flight from New York to Oregon," he answers.

"I'm thankful that you picked me up, but you could've waited at home."

He opens the door of the car and helps me inside. "Yes, but then I would've missed you for six more hours." He kisses my cheek and closes the door.

I'm not sure if I'm confused or playing dumb. Is he flirting with me or doesn't he know the boundaries between friends?

I fidget with my phone during the drive to his apartment. He leaves the car in front of the building and tells the doorman to park it in his garage. Nate interlaces our fingers and we head to the penthouse.

The elevator doors open right on his floor and waiting for us is Demetri who bows slightly and gives me an unwelcome glare, "Ms. Nyx."

"Good afternoon, Demetri," I greet him and ask, "What did I do?"

"Brock isn't allowed to be on the furniture," he says firmly.

I laugh and Nate *tsks* at me.

"Well, he's my buddy. We read together and take naps. I can't just let him do it on the floor, can I?" Then I glance at Nate and narrow my gaze. "You ratted me out."

His blue eyes look at me mischievously. "Not intentionally. D complained about Brock's behavior and I said, 'I have no idea why he's acting up. Take it up with Nyx. He spent most of his time with her.'"

I sigh and say, "If needed, I'll take him with me. Now, where is my boy?"

"The terrace," Demetri answers in such a snippy tone I almost laugh. "He's on the couch taking a nap."

I stretch and say, "I should join him."

"The shopper from Bloomingdales is waiting for you in your room, Ms. Nyx," he indicates, tilting his head toward the staircase. "You have an hour with her. The shopper from Neiman Marcus should be here at six."

I look at Nate. "Why?"

"You mentioned you wanted to shop. I simplified things in case you were tired." He throws one of his simple answers that annoy me because they make sense. There's not much room to argue, but I can't just let it go.

"I can go to the store...and I was planning on going somewhere less expensive."

"She is here. Let's see what we can get or at least get a few ideas of what you want to buy," Nate argues, taking me by the hand.

His personal shopper shows me catalogs, guides me through the easy to use system where I can input all my preferences so she can find me the right styles, and she also brought some clothing items along.

Most of the clothing I try on is loose enough that if I gain weight it should still fit me. She makes a list of everything I like and leaves. The second shopper is not much different. Both leave every item that fits me, and I love them. They order the rest. Everything should be here by mid-week.

"I feel like Cinderella or Julia Roberts. You have to tell me how much you spend, Nathaniel Chadwick," I chide him because he's the one who tricked me into telling him if I liked the stuff or not and kept on piling it.

"Sure," he says dismissively. "I mean, it's nothing, Nyx."

"Clearly those stores are nonprofit, and they just gifted me thousands of dollars' worth of clothes because it's giveaway day," I say mockingly.

"Why don't you let me take care of you?"

"Because I can take care of myself," I answer.

"Well, too bad. I want to do it and I will do it," he challenges me.

"You can't just say, 'I'm going to be your sugar daddy' and think I'll be okay with it," I protest, and he laughs.

"Well, according to this blog I've been reading, I should be able to make my own choices. This is my choice. I am taking charge. Plus, I give zero fucks about being conventional."

"You're quoting my sister, aren't you?" Those are three of her ten life mantras. "Well then, think before you act, mister."

"Her philosophy is pretty similar to mine. I can get on board with what she says—sometimes," he argues. "Thinking before acting is overrated."

Nate's words make me miss my sister, and instead of fighting about the clothing, I'm afraid that he might bring up number four, *always feel*. I say, "You just reminded me that I have to call Persy."

"Do it while I make us some dinner. Soup or sandwich?" he asks.

I glance at my phone and then at him, asking, "You're not making anything fancy?"

"Nah, I'm trying to see if a light dinner and maybe a late snack will help you," he replies. "I've been reading that the less processed the foods—"

"Wait, you've been reading about morning sickness?" I ask, and my heart makes a double flip.

He smiles, kisses the top of my head and leaves. Instead of staying in the room, I head to the terrace. Brock is laying on the couch until I call him. He comes running toward me with a huge grin and fast strides.

"I missed you, boy," I say, petting him and giving him a hug, and I swear he hugs me back. This dog is so much like Nate. When they are around, they make you feel like the world isn't a scary place.

"Let's call Aunt Persy, boy," I suggest, giving him one last pat before I dial her number.

"Finally," she answers. "How are you doing?"

"Better," I reply with a steady voice that doesn't give away my worries, the fear of the uncertainty, and the doubts that are plaguing my heart.

"Really? You're going for *better*. I've been worried sick, and Nathaniel isn't helping," she says snapping.

I fight the frustration building inside me because I told her to give me space and she was contacting Nate? I breathe and give her a chance to explain herself.

"Why would you need help from Nate?"

"I keep telling Ford to ask him how you're doing, and Nate doesn't give him a good answer," she protests. "It's not any different from your, *better*."

"So much for giving me space," I remark trying to hide the annoyance.

"I'm trying, but it's hard not to worry about you," she explains. "There're too many things going on with you, and what if tomorrow I find out that you're working for some Joe Schmo on the other side of the country. You're pretty independent, but I want to be there for you and the baby. Plus, you're living with a stranger."

"Your boyfriend's brother," I remind her.

"Still, you don't know who he really is," she presses.

"My brother is trustworthy, Persephone," I hear Ford objecting. "Take your drama down a notch, babe."

"We spent a week with Nate," I recall. "Then he came to visit for a weekend—I'm impressed that he didn't run away after the parents' incident."

"That has some merit," she agrees.

"Listen, Persy, I'm a pretty good judge of character," I continue. "I wouldn't just accept an invite from some weird guy while I'm hitchhiking by the highway."

She huffs and then asks, "When are you coming back?"

I tell her everything that happened with Pierce and what I decided. That I'll become her official agent but charge her less than what Sheila was making. We settle for fifteen percent of her earnings instead of twenty.

"Hearing that you have a plan makes me feel better because now you can relax a little. I'll talk Ford into visiting his brother next week. Make sure you send me your calendar so I know when you'll be in Seattle or New York. If you need anything—"

"I'll reach out," I promise.

"This feels weird. You're always here for me, and now that I feel like you need me, you just disappeared," she says with a worried voice.

"It was the timing, Persy. If this had happened a week before or a week later maybe you would've been there for me instead of Nate."

"Are you two...?" she didn't finish speaking but her boyfriend did. "Fucking. It's called fucking, Persy. I told you they are not."

"Having hot, dirty sex at night while I'm puking? Oh yes, we are," I assure her. "We can't get enough of each other."

"Sorry, I'm just... This is new to me, Nyx."

"Having a pregnant sister, feeling like you need to help me but not being here, or...fill in the blank here, because I can only have one person mothering me," I say and add, "I need my sister and my best friend to be her usual self."

"Well, then you should let me blog your pregnancy," she laughs. "What? That's what I would always ask, Langford. Don't judge me, grump."

"I'm trying to get Edward to give up his parental rights," I explain. "I'm not sure how he'd use this against me, but...I can't."

"What if I keep your name under wraps and just call it a friend?"

Usually, I let her post my bad dates. I'm not sure how to feel about letting her post about my baby. Would she post about hers if she ever gets pregnant?

"Fine, but can you please be honest about Nate? Do you like him?" she insists, and God if she's not annoyingly persistent.

"He's attractive, funny, and easy to talk to. He also has a lot of baggage and I have a baby to worry about. I'm pretty sure I remind him of his situation."

"You know about the ex?"

"Yep."

"Be careful, okay?"

"Hey, I'm the big sister, not you."

"Well, someone has to take care of you. I just wish you are starting your firm."

I remind her about my plans and that being in New York is just temporary.

"Where are you going to live?" she continues with the inquisition.

Looking around the terrace, I wonder if I should take Nate's offer and stay with him. This place isn't home, but Nate and Brock make things better.

"Living in Brooklyn doesn't seem practical. I might stay here," I respond adding the logical explanation Nate gave me earlier.

It's simple, and hopefully she won't try to dig deeper until she finds those feelings I'm trying to bury.

"Hmm," she mumbles.

"What?"

"Nothing," she answers too fast. I'm sure there's a lot on her mind but I'm thankful that she's letting it go, at least for now. "I just wish I was close by. Please, don't forget I'm here for you."

"Thank you. Talk to you soon?"

"Yes, I really want to see you. That baby needs to hear my voice often if I want to become her favorite person."

"Don't tell that to our parents or they're going to ask for a sabbatical and follow me everywhere I go," I say alarmed.

"Well, I should give you a heads up. They mentioned the possibility of retiring after the school year is over to dedicate their life to their grandchild. Helios, or was it Hanover?"

I laugh, and just like that I'm running to the bathroom to puke. Thankfully there's a powder room next to the terrace.

Brock is suddenly barking and Nate's yelling, "Coming!"

Seconds later, he's holding my hair, rubbing my back, and assuring me that it's going to be okay.

"I have to bring hand towels from upstairs. In the meantime, I'll use toilet paper." I feel the wet compress on the back of my neck, and he places a kiss on my shoulder. "It's okay, babe. I'm here."

Once I'm done, I rinse my mouth, and he holds me. "What were you doing?"

"Talking to Persy and laughing."

"I have to add this to my notes."

Before I can ask him what he means by *notes*, his phone rings, "Yeah? She's fine. It's called morning sickness. Google it and learn. Yes, I'm with her. No, there's no need to jump on a plane, but you and your girlfriend are welcome to visit—*without* hovering."

He nods, kisses the top of my head while embracing me tighter and says, "I am looking after her. If you can ask Octavio to make more ginger seltzer though. I don't think we have enough, and that stuff is a godsend. Yes, you can fly them to visit just...I'll send you the calendar once we know where we're going to be every week."

He stays quiet for a long time and finally says, "Yes, Persy, I'll make sure to keep everything you just said in mind. Now, if you don't mind, I need to feed your sister."

Once he hangs up, he pushes me slightly and looks at me. "Are you sure you are okay?"

I nod.

"Okay, I got food and your seltzer is ready."

"Nate, what's happening between us?"

He gives me a sad smile and shakes his head. "Nothing. I'm just taking care of you, okay?"

"Thank you," I say, and I wonder what Persy and Ford said to him.

TWENTY-NINE

Nyx

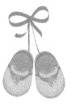

THE NEXT MONDAY, I visit Aldridge Enterprises. It's just a quick meeting to walk through the facilities and meet the interim CEO. After we're done, we agree to meet on Tuesday to start our project. I also make an appointment with the human resources director. Apparently, Pierce and his brother cleaned house and we need to hire new personnel.

As I'm leaving the building, Demetri is waiting for me. Marcia, Nate's assistant, crammed my day with appointments. The OBGYN is first, followed by the nutritionist, and ending with the imaging place where I'm getting to meet my baby.

The doctor's appointment takes almost two hours. Between lab tests, a pap smear, and getting all my medical information, I am out around two. Demetri, who had given me chicken soup when he picked me up, hands me an apple.

He drives me to the nutritionist who asks me about my likes, dislikes, allergies, and eating habits. After an hour of asking me questions regarding my parents' trips and all the exotic foods I ate while growing up, she promises to have a menu ready for me by tomorrow. She asks me to call her if there is something that doesn't work for me and to also visit again after the baby is born to change my diet.

When I arrive at the imaging center, Nate is waiting outside the modern steel and glass building.

"Hey," I greet him.

"How are you feeling?" he asks, handing me a sandwich.

"You have to stop feeding me."

"Have you eaten anything since Demetri gave you that apple?"

"How did you know?"

"I asked him to give you a snack because you forget to eat."

I glare at him, "And what about the soup?"

"That was lunch," he says, giving me a sly grin. "Did you eat anything else?"

"It's hard to remember."

"Which is why I'm trying to be here to remind you. You know what they say, you make a habit after twenty-one days."

"You are spoiling me. The habit I'm building is having you looking after me—all the time," I joke as I eat my sandwich, and he leads us to the twentieth floor where the imaging center is. "Are you going to keep doing this after it becomes a habit?"

"What did the doctor say?" he asks as we ride the elevator, avoiding the question.

"She can do the non-invasive paternity test and send it to the lab too. The nutritionist will send me a menu that I should follow religiously."

He nods a couple of times, "Forward it to me since I am working on that bad habit of pampering you."

"Which you should stop," I insist.

"You secretly love it," he argues and asks, "What's happening at work? Do you like the place?"

"It was like the first day of school. There was nothing important and a lot of information that I have to assimilate," I answer, wondering if we're avoiding each other's comments and we should just sit down and talk about what is happening between us.

Last night, he set up a baby monitor in my bedroom so he could hear me if I got sick—which I did. He was right by my side the moment he heard me rustle and run to the bathroom. After the fourth time, he just stayed with me in bed until I fell asleep. At least, I think that's what happened. I have no idea when he left the room.

"How about you? Did you take over the world, or not yet?"

"No, but I have a couple of new ideas in the works. I have to figure out production and marketing while both products are in development."

The elevator doors open to the lobby of the imaging place. The receptionist greets us.

"Hi, Nyx Brassard," I announce. "I have an appointment at—"

"Yes, we have the room ready for you," she answers.

"Do you need my insurance, credit card...ID?" I ask, a little put off by her prompt service. Maybe I'm used to crappy customer service and this is how it's supposed to be.

"No," she hands me a paper. "I need you to confirm that the information on there is correct."

I look through the paper that has everything and frown. "Yes, it's me, but how?"

Giving her back the paper, I also take out my credit card.

"It's already paid for and your doctor sent all your information," she explains. "You're all checked in. Just follow Alicia. She'll give you more instructions."

I cross my arms, press my lips together, and narrow my gaze at Nate.

"They are waiting for us," he says, giving me a slight squeeze and guiding me toward the back offices.

"You can't just pay for everything I need," I whisper shout.

Alicia hands me a paper sheet. "Strip from the waist down and cover yourself with this. The technician should be with you soon. She points to the big machine in front of me. "That's the main screen. On the left is the second one, a bigger one to appreciate the ultrasound best."

"I'll give you a couple of minutes," Nate announces.

I want to stop him and give him a piece of my mind because he can't seriously think that this is all right. He paid for the nutritionist too. Since the insurance doesn't cover the services, she requires a card before making an appointment, and Marcia just paid for it. Of course, he leaves too fast and I can't say anything.

I'll find a way to repay him for everything that he's spending. I get it. He has money, but I can pay my way through this rough patch.

A couple of minutes later there's a knock on the door. The technician and Nate enter. He approaches and whispers, "I didn't ask if it's okay to stay with you."

We didn't discuss this before, but I truly assumed he'd be by my side, just the way he has been since this journey started.

"Can you stay?" I ask. My heart is pounding, and I'm not sure why I am so nervous about this. "It's...overwhelming." *And you always make everything bearable.*

"I'm here for you," he whispers, brushing my hair to the side. His blue piercing eyes stare at me tenderly. "I like it when you wear your hair down."

"Good afternoon," the technician greets us. "I'm Stella, and I'm here to introduce you to your little one. Are you ready?"

I nod, watching her take a seat, grabbing a wand that looks like a thin dildo and placing a condom on it. "It's going to feel slightly uncomfortable, but this is the best way to get an image of the baby since he or she is too small for a regular sonogram.

"Here we are, our little passenger," the tech says. "Say hi to Mom and Dad."

"What's that noise?" I ask, confused.

Nate smiles, "Is that the heartbeat?"

The technician nods. "Yes. It's beating pretty fast, almost 170 beats per minute. That little one is already moving. She's almost an inch long."

"It's a girl?" I ask.

"No, we can't know that until the baby is about fourteen to sixteen weeks," she says, taking some screen shots. "That should be around five to seven weeks from now. According to the sonogram, your due date is on April tenth."

"See, the baby is not coming on a Monday. She's arriving on Saturday," Nate whispers.

The brightness and excitement in his eyes are just as thrilling as the sound of my baby's heartbeat through the speakers.

The silhouette of the baby is more like a peanut, a tadpole, or a bean held by a thread. It's strange how I feel attached to her...or him. Tears stream down my face, and it's not sadness but the many emotions that suddenly explode inside me.

Nate kisses my forehead and says, "You okay?"

"I'm going to be a Mom," I whisper between sniffs. "Look at her. She's so little."

He smiles and nods while cleaning my tears. "It's pretty awesome, isn't it?"

"I can't even describe what I'm feeling. It's...this is the best thing ever," I say.

"Wait until you hold her. That'll be the best moment of your life."

He kisses my forehead and says, "Thank you for letting me meet the little blueberry demon."

A gasp sob escapes me because this moment would've been so much more perfect if I had shared it with the man I loved. But it's okay because at least I have Nate, don't I?

THIRTY

Nate

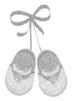

AS WE LEAVE the imaging offices, I'm emotionally exhausted or...I can't explain what just happened in that room. One moment I'm there to give emotional support to Nyx, and the next, my heart is pulsing just as fast as the baby's heart. My stomach roils at the memory of the first time I heard Wyatt's heartbeat.

That's the moment when I realized he was a person and not some unexpected news. Now, something I wasn't ready for during today's sonogram was Nyx. Well, her reaction and everything that transpired in that room. I witnessed the exact moment when the baby stopped being her new project, and she fell in love with her child. I felt sucker punched. Nothing had ever prepared me to witness such a powerful moment.

What concerns me most is that I think there was some bizarre exchange of hearts, souls, and shit going on inside that room, and I'm not sure what it is that I have inside me. There's a lightness and yet a heaviness inside my chest. Addressing anything would be stupid because Nyx was extremely vulnerable after what just happened.

Trying to add a lightness to what I witnessed, I grab one of the grainy pictures the technician gave us out of the plastic folder and study it.

"This isn't a blueberry," I protest as we make our way outside the building, and I'm trying to figure out exactly what we can call the baby based on this image. "A peanut, maybe?"

"We're not calling her Peanut."

"Thumper?" I ask. "That heart was beating pretty fast."

"What's wrong with Berry."

"Like Barry Manilow?" I say. She frowns, and I enunciate, "Berry and Barry sound almost the same. Do you want people to sing "Copacabana" when you tell them about Berry?"

She rolls her eyes. "I'm sure you're the only ridiculous person who can compare berries to Barrys, but now you just ruined it for me. Fine, we'll find something new."

"Thumper," I repeat in case she didn't hear me the first time.

"Nope. It reminds me of Thumbelina, and I didn't like that story while growing up. It's a pretty dark tale if you analyze it. I'm pretty sure there's human trafficking involved in it. Maybe Bean?"

I stare at her for a beat. She got that from a children's book? *Who are you kidding. You do the same with movies?*

"Thumper as in the rabbit in Bambi," I clarify. "The best friend."

"Oh right. The one where the mother was killed in the middle of the woods and the child was left an orphan," she answers. "Such an uplifting tale. We should call my child something after a joyful movie."

"It was just a movie," I insist.

"They killed the mom. That's not a happy feel good movie—"

"Okay, let's try something else. This looks like a smudge," I mention, working harder on deflecting the emotions that are just pushing against each other.

Because in my story, they killed off the fucking father and gave the boy a new one. It's like I never existed. Fuck, I'm still angry, and listening to her baby just brought everything up to the surface.

I'm not only angry at Bronwyn, or myself. I'm fucking upset at Edward because he doesn't care about his baby or this moment. My blood is boiling the most because this isn't my moment to share with Nyx. This isn't my baby. And I might never get to have this again. Also, because I want to kiss her hard. Hug her and twirl her around and celebrate that we just met her beautiful baby.

"We're not calling her Smudge," she contends.

"I never said that. I just brought it to your attention that it looks like a smudge," I correct her. "We can try something like Sweet Bun."

"That's...cute."

"Just like her mother."

"The flattery won't get you out of the doghouse," she argues. "I'm not happy about your 'help.'"

"So, are we coming back after the sixteen weeks to find out if it's a boy or a girl?" I deflect, again. She lost her job. I'm still unsure that the new project she's working on might be right for her, and her house hasn't received any offers yet. She has to save as much as she can in case things don't work out for her. "Listen, I think we could get one of those 3D ones. Maybe those are for when they are older? We have to ask about it."

"I...I don't know," she answers. "Should we learn if it's a boy or a girl? It can be a surprise."

"That's a great question because there's the nursery, the clothes, and most importantly, the name," I offer.

She sighs, I can feel the tension creeping in as the muscles in her jaw begin to twitch. I take her hand, wave at Demetri when I spot him driving right in front of the building, and walk with her to the car. After opening the door for her, she slides into the back seat and I follow right behind.

"Listen to me. We can't stress out about those simple details. I can have someone get the nursery ready within a day, and just like we did this weekend, I can get the clothes with a snap of my fingers. We can have a list of names for boys and girls."

"You..." She looks at me strangely and shakes her head.

"What are you thinking?"

"I'm not sure if we should be friends while I'm going through this. What if I get the wrong idea? What if—"

"Are you getting the idea that I want to be there for you and Sweet Bun?"

"Well, yeah," she answers and opens her mouth.

"Good, then we're on the same page. The way I see it, I'm your best option." I show her my index finger. "Persy is busy with her book, her rebranding, and my brother. Take it from me, that guy is a full-time job."

"I wasn't going to mention her."

I show her now two fingers, "Eros is busy with the business, and he's going to Costa Rica."

"We're not joining him?"

"We could if you want to, but I'm thinking that with your pregnancy it might be safer to travel during your second trimester—and I'm not leaving you alone."

She sighs and nods. "That's sensible."

"Your parents..." I shrug.

"They want to visit me."

"I'll get them plane tickets for the weekend if you want," I offer.

"Only if you let me pay you back," she counteracts.

"That's a no. You have to save your money for the blueberry demon," I remind her.

She stares at her hands and then asks, "Do you think I should start searching for a place in Colorado?"

"What do you want?"

She laughs. "I want a house like the one you have in Seattle. It's close to a lake, has a pool, and it's so big that the master bedroom faces east and west so you can watch sunrises and sunsets. Since that's impossible, I'll take a property I can afford in a good school district."

"That's easy. I'll get Demetri to search for that."

"You're like my fairy godfather."

"More like Jaq," I correct her.

"The mouse?"

"Yes, but that mouse made the impossible happen to get everything for Cinderella because he adored her," I explain. "If he had been a guy, he'd actually be the one she would fall in love with and not the prince who had nothing going on for himself."

"That's too deep for a children's movie, but true. You analyze movies...a lot," she complains.

"When you grow up with a grandfather that couldn't watch a movie without discussing the actors, the plot, the music, the lighting, the editing, the meaning of each scene, and what the screenwriter failed to notice and would have made the movie a lot better...let's just say I can ruin almost every movie for you."

"You miss your grandparents," she states, grabbing my hand and squeezing it.

Usually those gestures are welcomed, but right now I can't handle it, so I smile and take my hand away. It's not that I don't want her to touch me. It's because I have this craving for her that's becoming harder to control. If I'm not careful I'll cross the line and as I promised Ford, I won't do anything stupid until I fix my shit.

Not that kissing Nyx is stupid, but doing it when I'm in a bad place will just hurt one of us, or both.

"Some days," I agree.

"Are you going back to the office?"

"No, I left for the day. I want to work from home and keep an eye on you. Brock must be missing his Nyx, and we can show him the picture of the blimp."

"Blimp?" she squeaks.

"I am more convinced that we can call her Helios."

"It's Helium," she corrects me.

I smirk. "See you're even warming up to it."

"Stop taunting me."

"Now, where is the fun in that?"

During the drive home, we keep discussing nicknames for the baby. It's hard not to get sucked into the idea of being a part of them. This isn't me, or what I should be planning. I know how this exact story ends. Maybe Nyx hasn't met the love of her life, but she will. When it happens, she'll just wave at me and say, this was fun but it's time for me to have a family.

Earlier, Ford and I had a long discussion. He's concerned that I'm with her just because I might want to play house while pretending that I have Wyatt back. I told him that what's happening with Nyx is nothing like what I felt for Bronwyn. The only thing he said was, go to fucking therapy.

This time I didn't tell him that I would if he did. We are both pretty fucked up, but he was able to get past his issues and find Persy. I...I need someone to help me because what I'm feeling could be a mirror of what I lost, or it could be the real deal. And until I understand which one it is, I'm just betting on the wrong horse and losing what can be the best thing in my life.

THIRTY-ONE

Nyx

———

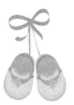

THE FIRST WEEK at Aldridge Enterprises is easy, and by Friday I am able to work part time from Nate's apartment. He had Demetri set up a small office in one of the guestrooms. When I told him he was like a fairy godfather, I wasn't kidding. There are times when I am thinking about getting a cup of tea and before I can even walk into the kitchen, he's already setting up the kettle for me.

He's beyond sweet. Under different circumstances, I could easily fall in love with him.

Every day, I arrive home before lunch. That gives me a couple of hours to rest before I jump into my daily conference call with Pierce.

This is part of our routine, at least until we have a structure, more employees, and less fires to extinguish.

We are officially establishing the law firm in Portland. He doubts he'll be moving back to Colorado. Nate is hoping that by Thanksgiving, I will just work from Seattle—which is only an hour flight from the offices.

Nate is having a contractor build me a space next to his home office. I'm not sure what he's doing, or more like why he is doing it. As I explained to him several times, once I'm done with the project in New York, I'm heading back to Colorado.

I don't think he's listening. He swears I'm his permanent roommate.

Maybe he feels alone in that big house and he's trying to fill it with strays. Soon, I have to sit down with him and explain to him that I can't be a placeholder to stay around while he's waiting for the next best thing.

The second week isn't that much different. We wake up early, and I drink whatever smoothie is on the menu. We head out for a thirty-minute run. He goes to the gym while I shower, and when I'm ready to leave for the office there's a small breakfast waiting for me.

Now Saturday morning is the day we sleep in—and by that I mean wake up at eight.

Today isn't much different from every single morning. I wake up next to Nate. I blame this sleeping non-arrangement on the blueberry demon. If I didn't have morning sickness, I wouldn't be where I am right now.

We should stop this insanity. It's almost like an unspoken understanding between us. The entire routine is just a pretend game where we say goodnight and head to bed—in separate rooms. But at some point during the night, morning sickness hits me. Brock barks like a possessed dog. Nate swoops inside my bathroom to hold my hair, make sure I'm all right, and holds me after I clean myself.

I don't understand why he has to hug me for a long period of time after I'm done brushing my teeth and rinsing my mouth, but I don't complain because being in his arms is almost magical. After the second time I get sick during the night, Nate stays with me in my bed. Because, what's the point of going to his bed when he'll have to come back running a couple more times?

Now, the huge problem I encounter happens the next morning when I wake up next to Nate. His arms are around me, lips against my bare shoulder, and his morning wood pushing against my ass.

Every day, I have to remind myself that this doesn't mean anything. Sure, this is what any guy would do if he sleeps with a woman. Isn't it? I wouldn't know because the last time I had a steady relationship was back in grad school and we slept naked most of the time.

I glance over at Nate whose long lashes are shut, and his breathing is steady. His torso is bare, and God if I don't want to trace his tattoos, but I stop myself from doing so many things. Soon, this morning sickness will be over, and I won't have to wake up reminding myself that he's just a friend. I won't have to control the need to run my lips along his rough stubble. I won't have to have a long chat with my heart while I shower about being safe.

We don't mean anything to each other. And most importantly, I have to pretend that I don't like the feel of him sleeping next to me. So, like I do every morning, I wiggle myself out of his embrace, head to the bathroom, and take a shower.

Dressed in one of the cute sundresses I got from the last shopping spree, I step outside the walk-in closet and find him sitting on the bed looking at the nightstand where I have the framed picture of my Sweet Bun.

"According to the sonogram, today is week twelve. If I'm lucky I should stop puking right about now," I say excitedly.

"If that baby is as stubborn as her mama, it won't happen until she feels like it," he jokes.

His raspy voice, that *just woke up* rustled hair and sleepy eyes leave me speechless, so I resort to the childish stick out my tongue gesture.

"You should just move into my bedroom. My bed is more comfortable," he suggests, and I laugh.

"Morning," he greets, throwing that sexy smile my way and making my knees wobble.

He's so handsome I want to cry. I should tell him that my room, my rules, and he should be wearing a shirt because with that body, that face, and that voice, it is super difficult not to jump him.

He pushes himself out of the bed and gives me a hug. "I'm glad you're ready. Ford just texted me. Your family should be here in about twenty minutes."

I frown and stare at him. "What family?"

Taking this opportunity, I step away from his now familiar too-comfortable-hard-to-resist embrace.

If I'm not careful, one of these days I'm going to kiss him *accidentally*. One kiss will lead to another and...I can't be responsible for not jumping on top of him and getting my way. Which is a big no in the rule book of temporary roommates.

He arches an eyebrow. "Seriously, you forgot about them already. This is why you're never leaving my side. What if you forget I exist a day after you leave me?"

"No, but..." I blink a couple of times trying to remember if I discussed a visit or anything with my parents. Mom and Dad kept saying they'd come as soon as they had free time.

Mom would've told me if she was planning to visit, wouldn't she?

"Is it just Ford and Persy?" I ask.

A part of me hopes that it is just them. Then there's a bigger part of me who wants to see her parents. We have daily calls via Face-Time, but it's not the same as having them in the same room.

"Let me get ready. I'll have Demetri walk Brock so I can make you breakfast. Today is mango and avocado smoothie day."

"You're making this stay better than any five-star hotel. I might just move in with you forever," I joke.

He smiles at me, his eyes stare in a way that makes my heart skip several beats, and he says, "We're happy to have you with us for as long as you want to—always is a good choice by the way."

"You say that now, but wait until the wailing child is born," I warn him. "You'll be kicking us out of the house before we're out of the hospital."

He smiles and leans closer to me, kissing my cheek. His lips brush the corner of my mouth so lightly I shiver. Without a word, he walks out of the room and leaves me confused as fuck.

JUST AS HE PROMISED, twenty minutes later, my family is parading through the door.

"She's alive," Eros says, walking to me and giving me a hug. "Let's go home. There's no need to live in some stranger's palace. Unless... he invites me to live with him too."

"You're such a big concerned brother," I joke.

"Why are you here again? Because I've been hearing a lot of versions from everyone, even Ford."

"What is his version?" I ask curiously.

"Grunt, grunt, grunt...she's safe," he answers and Persy slaps his arm.

"Ouch, I'm kidding. He only grunted once," he corrects. Persy sneers and I laugh at them. "Persephone's version is better. She recorded a podcast but it hasn't aired yet."

"Did he drink coffee?" I ask, because he's acting weird.

"So, what's your version, Andromeda?" he asks, rolling his eyes. "Why are you here?"

"I actually have a real job," I clarify and tell him all about Aldridge Enterprises, Merkel, and the firm I'm opening with Pierce. "Nate's kind enough to let me stay at his penthouse free of charge."

He turns around and glares at Nate. "Dude, I'm watching you."

"Just keeping an eye on her," Nate says innocently.

Mom, who is standing next to Nate and Dad, waltzes over to me and hands me a present. "Something for my grandchild."

"She's been knitting all month," Dad warns me.

I open the hemp bag and take out a beautiful white, teal, and pink blanket. "This is gorgeous, Mom. Thank you."

"How have you been, Nyxie?" she asks, hugging me. I hug her back, and that's exactly when I start crying.

I'm not sure if it's the term of endearment, the fact that I cry about everything, or just because I miss her and I'm not going back home just yet.

Dad joins the hug. Then it's Persy and Eros. That's when Mom says, "I wish Callie was here."

"Fuck, don't speak to Nyx. Apparently she's crying over anything," Eros complains.

When the embrace is over, Nate walks to me and takes me in his arms. "You okay?"

I nod, grabbing the handkerchief he carries around for me.

"So, what has everyone been up to?" I ask, hoping that the water works are over.

"I'm building the baby a crib," Dad announces.

"Thank you, Dad," I sniff.

"Are you okay?" Mom asks.

I nod. "Sorry. Lately, everything makes me cry."

"It's like someone broke her," Persy jokes. I glare at her and she smiles. "What? You're the hard ass of us, and now...well, look at you. So, how's the sale of the house going?"

"The realtor mentioned there are a couple of people interested," I tell her. "We don't know what's happening. Demetri is going to check it next week to ensure the staging looks good and there aren't any issues that might be swaying away any potential buyer."

"Well, I'm moving in with Ford. You can have the penthouse," she offers.

"Of course, let's just shove her into the apartment you don't own and ignore me, the owner," Nate complains, pointing at himself.

Persy glares at him and says, "It doesn't bother you that she lives in New York with you, but it upsets you that she can use the place you never lived in? My God, you Chadwick men are infuriating."

"One of us is a handful," Nate agrees. "Fortunately for your sister, the annoying one isn't me. So, when are you two moving in together?"

"We're looking for a place," Ford grunts and keeps glaring at Nate.

"Demetri is helping us look for a place for Nyx. Why don't you talk to him?" Nate offers and then looks around the room.

He sighs, kisses the side of my head, and releases me.

"Follow me, Langford. We need to discuss a few things."

Persy and I look at each other and shrug while they leave for the terrace and shut the door.

"Let's go and take a walk around the park," Mom suggests. "I love sightseeing around this city. In the meantime, you can tell me more about your work."

I look towards Nate one more time before I agree on leaving the house with them. Nate sounded too serious and concerned. Ford looked pissed, but what do I know? I barely know the guy.

THIRTY-TWO

Nate

"WHAT PART of don't fuck this for me didn't you understand?" Ford questions as soon as I close the door. "I fucking told you to stay away from her. But you didn't give a shit. This is exactly why we can't have nice things."

I cross my arms and glare at him as he paces around the terrace. This is why I told him to come out with me. I'm not sure if his girlfriend knows him this well, but fuck if I don't know exactly what his red face and murderous gaze means.

He's pissed at me because I was holding Nyx.

"You done with the temper tantrum yet?"

"I fucking warned you," he repeats flustered.

"Warned me about what, Langford?"

He points toward the house, fuming. "Are you unaware of the little show you had going on in there?"

"Do I need to ask you to forgive me for holding my friend because she was crying?" I laugh and shake my head. "You are priceless, man. Obviously, you have no fucking idea what's happening between us."

"You hugged her and kissed her," he continues.

I facepalm and say, "I keep forgetting that emotionally, you're a toddler. Friends can hug and kiss too. There's nothing wrong with that."

"So, if I ask you to swear that there's nothing between the two of you..." he trails his words and looks toward the house. Then he frowns. "Where the fuck are they?"

"Focus, Langford," I redirect his attention.

He exhales harshly. His hands open and close into fists. "Okay, then tell me, what is going on between Nyx and you?"

"You sound like a fucking broken record," I complain, walking toward the end of the terrace.

I rest my arms on the stone wall railing and stare at the park.

Nyx loves the view. Not as much as she loves the one from Seattle, but she can spend hours outside just staring at the park.

"Nathaniel, don't ignore me," he orders.

I look over my shoulder and glare at him. He wants me to answer a loaded question. I have five words for him: Nothing, everything, I'm fucking confused. Which I don't say because he won't like them.

A few beats later, I turn around to face him and say, "At the moment, we're friends and roommates. She's going through a lot of changes. I can't offer her anything more than a place where she can stay, my friendship, and my badass cooking skills."

"But you're still attracted to her," he states, serving me with a nasty glare that would frighten others, but it just pisses *me* off. "Which means there's nothing innocent about those hugs."

"Funny that you mention that. They are indeed innocent," I clarify. "Am I attracted to her? Yes. She's gorgeous, smart, and most importantly, she understands me. Am I going to act on that? No, because I'm not in a good place. That reminds me, I am going to California next weekend to visit Mom."

He blinks a couple of times and repeats, "Mom?"

"Yes. I started therapy, and you know what I realized?"

He stares at me, mouth open and eyes wide. Well, I surprised myself too when I began searching for a counselor. Two and a half weeks, six sessions, and four books haven't transformed me, but at least I realized that it's time to confront my mother.

"Please, don't say that we have mommy issues?" he responds.

"No, but maybe we do. I have abandonment issues, and I need closure from her."

"She has a new family," he growls.

"We know," I agree. "She's still the woman who up and left us without even a goodbye. There has to be more to our parents' divorce."

"You are hoping that there is more because if not, it makes her the bitch who left her children," he roars.

"I need to know what that *more* is, Langford," I claim. "You might be okay not solving your past, but I am not."

"Everyone copes differently," he claims.

I narrow my gaze and ask, "Are you going to therapy too?"

He shakes his head. "No. I'd rather read and then discuss my shit with you or Persy. Which brings me to, I want to talk to Dad about his new family."

"What about it?" I ask instead of reminding him that they aren't new.

Dad remarried almost twenty years ago. There's nothing new about them. My stepmother is fine but awkward as fuck. She has no fucking clue on how to treat Ford and me. Clyde, her son, is a leach who sucks us dry any time he can. If I had a choice, I'd rather not deal with them. I love my dad, and that's why I put up with his family.

"We have to stop having these awkward reunions with his wife, Ruby, and Clyde. They don't like us, and we hate them. Why not leave them at home and hang out with just us, his sons?" he suggests.

"I like that," I agree with him and say, "We can go to L.A. next weekend. Play a round of golf with Dad, then have a cup of coffee with Mom afterward."

He exhales harshly, takes a look around the terrace and asks, "What if I don't want to see our mother?"

"You can wait for me at home while I'm with her, and then we can spend the weekend with Nyx and Persy," I suggest.

"Again with Nyx," he protests.

"She's my friend," I argue.

"Dude, Eros is my friend, and you don't see me hugging him and kissing him. Do you?" Good. He's joking.

Since his temper has simmered down, I take the opportunity to say, "I have a lot of shit to work through before I can make a move."

"So, he thinks," he mumbles. "Man, you're drooling for her. It took you a lot of self-control not to push her family away from her so you could be the one hugging her. But you're fucked up, and she deserves someone better."

"You're an asshole."

"So they say."

"Listen, I'm not sure if what's happening with Nyx is real. I won't know until I get closure," I emphasize.

"From Bronwyn too?"

I nod.

"Call if you need me," he offers. "Just, don't fuck with Nyx or I swear I'll push you down the Grand Canyon and claim it to be an accident."

"With a brother like you, I don't need enemies."

He shrugs and we go back inside the house. Since the place is empty, I text Nyx.

Nate: *Where are you?*

Nyx: *The park.*

Nate: *I'm going to do some work, but if you don't come back in a couple of hours I'll catch up with you.*

Nyx: *It's Saturday. You shouldn't be working. The anti-workaholic rules apply to both of us.*

I look up at Ford, who seems like he needs a few hours without the Brassards, and I fire up a text.

Nate: *Since when did we come up with those rules? Though, I'm doing this for Ford. Miss you.*

Nyx: *It's one of those unspoken rules. Don't work much, okay?*

THIRTY-THREE

Nate

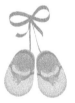

NYX IS RIGHT. I shouldn't be working on Saturday. Instead of going to the library, I give Ford a few options to let out some steam. Skydiving on Long Island, flying to Jersey to the racetrack, or playing video games. Surprisingly, the racetrack option wins. He's one to shy away from doing something extreme given a better option. We drive to LNCWare where the helicopter waits for us. In less than thirty minutes we're on the track pushing the gas pedal.

Two hours later, we're back home, and there's no trace of the Brassard family. I decide to prepare a snack for Nyx before we search for them.

"What are you doing?" Ford asks as I grab a ginger seltzer from the fridge.

"We have to find Nyx and feed her."

He tilts his head and furrows his eyebrows. "Why?"

"Because she needs something to eat," I explain.

He scratches the back of his neck and says, "I don't remember you doing this for Bronwyn."

"You weren't around," I scrub a hand along my jaw. Fuck, this entire conversation is a mix between a counseling session, the Spanish Inquisition, and a kid afraid to lose his favorite toy.

I'm not saying that Persy is a toy. By now, I understand he adores her, but could he trust their relationship a little more—and me too? He's right though. I don't think I ever worried about what Bronwyn ate, if she had a good night's sleep, or if there was anything I could do to make her comfortable during her pregnancy.

Am I doing this out of guilt for what I didn't do for my ex?

"I was around," he reminds me. "See...you two were close, but I don't think you were as devoted to her as you are to Nyx. The way you look at her is different. How you speak about her and the baby... Dude, I've seen you yawning during conference calls because, and I quote, 'Nyx and the *blueberry demon* had a bad night. I just need another cup of coffee.'"

"Your point?" I blow out a frustrated breath.

"Don't do anything stupid," he states.

"Like running away from her if there's a misunderstanding instead of communicating with her?" I ask, bring up what happened between him and Persy only a few weeks ago. It's a low blow, but I have to find ways to stop him. "We're mature enough to have an adult conversation."

"When are you going to have this so-called adult conversation about your feelings? I'm just going to throw this out there and remind you that she's expecting someone else's baby," he says, punching me with a fucking low blow of his own. "What if *he* swoops in and says, 'Let's try to become a family?'"

I text Nyx to check where she's at. She responds that they are close to Bow Bridge. I ask her to wait there for me.

"Don't ignore me," Ford growls.

"I need to know where she's at, okay," I respond. "If I know her, she hasn't eaten anything since the smoothie I gave her earlier."

"Don't deflect," Ford orders as I text the driver to meet me downstairs because I need him to drop us by Bow Bridge.

"I'm not," I respond, fucking annoyed with his attitude. "Obviously you don't know Nyx well enough. I met Edward, and I doubt there'll be any trial period. Your scenario sounds scary, but not for me. I know where I stand when it comes to her. I'm her friend."

"Denial," he barks.

"That's what we are at this moment," I press. "Being in love with her doesn't change what we mean to each other at this moment. If at some point I can offer her more, I don't know how she'll respond. I don't plan on professing my undying love for her, because as of right now, I'm not sure if what I feel is the real deal. Keep up, Langford. I am fixing my shit, and I can't rehash this conversation again. Any other questions before we meet them?"

He glares at me and shakes his head.

"Good. Let's pin this conversation for a later time. Maybe when I know what I feel, or never. I like the latter better."

Is Ford right about my behavior toward Nyx? Yes. Nyx has a different hold on my heart than Bronwyn did. I don't know if it has to do with the circumstances, the person I am today, or the fact that Nyx is different.

Either way, I am taking my time analyzing what's happening between us. I can't be reckless with her, even when at times I wish I can just kiss her and act upon my desires.

She's too important to be careless. I'm finding myself, hoping I emerge from the debris that was my old life, guided by her voice. She's becoming my guide. Perhaps the feelings I have for her are real—and as I learn to love her, I'm discovering to love myself along the way.

The driver drops us close enough to Bow Bridge. We walk toward the center of the park and find the Brassards taking pictures and pointing at the ducks.

"We've never been that happy with our family, have we?" Ford asks.

I shake my head. "Our family is us, Langy," I remind him using the annoying term of endearment Mom used for him. "We had something when Grandpa and Grandma were around."

"But never with our parents," he remarks.

"If you play your cards right, you can have that with them," I suggest.

"And you?"

I look at Nyx, who turns around and smiles when she spots me. My heart drums inside my chest with the same rhythm it always does while she's around me. No matter what time of the day it is, she's the sun shining upon me. The best part of my day.

"What about me?" I ask, because that's not a question I have to ponder upon since Nyx became a part of my life. I am an afterthought. She's the only one who matters.

"Will you ever have a family?"

The silence stretches for a couple of minutes. Just a few weeks ago I wouldn't have entertained the question, let alone the possibility of having someone to love—and a kid. But there she is, an intelligent, fun, gorgeous woman. I just need to figure out how to fix myself and how to convince her that I'm worth giving a chance.

"I'm working on it, Ford. Keep up, won't you?" I say exasperated and walk to Nyx handing her the lunch box I brought for her.

"Here. Let's keep the little fig fed," I say.

"You're ridiculous, and this week she's a plum," she says, placing a lingering kiss on my jaw. I love when her eyes look at me like I'm the only person around her. It'd be so easy to bend and capture her lips.

"Sometimes I lose track of the fruit of the week," I say, trying to lighten the intensity between us.

She stares at my lips, then looks at me and whispers, "Thank you."

"Just making sure the little fruit is growing strong."

Eros glares at me and shakes his head. Ford goes to Persy, who hugs him tight and kisses him like a woman who hasn't seen the love of her life for years. Nyx's parents hold hands while they continue sightseeing.

I grab Nyx's hand and walk her to an area where we can sit so she can eat.

"What happened between you and Ford?" she asks.

Taking a deep breath, I glance at where my brother stands and then at her.

"We decided to visit our parents next weekend," I skip everything we discussed before it. "Would you like to join us on this quest?"

She tips her head to the side, with a curious expression. "You're visiting your mom too?"

I pinch the bridge of my nose and nod. "It's time to get some answers. You mentioned that maybe she lost custody of us, and if that's the case, I want to know what happened."

She opens the container with carrots and then the one with the dip. She grins and licks her plump lips. Fuck, I need to stop watching her eat. Even that looks fucking hot. Lately, everything about her makes me want to strip her naked and...I remind myself that I can't screw this up, literally and metaphorically.

"And you're just visiting your dad?" she asks between bites and then adds. "I never thought avocado, green salsa, and yogurt would taste so good."

"You will eat anything that has avocado."

She gives me a strange look, licks her lips, and chews her lip. A part of me wonders if she's feeling sick. The perverted part wants to think that she wants to drizzle me with that sauce and lick me. And I like the idea a lot.

"True," she agrees and clears her throat. Those hazed eyes look toward the bridge. I want to ask what she's thinking, but when she turns her attention to me, she's wearing her poker face. "So, back to your dad. Are you planning on just visiting or is there an agenda?"

"We can't stand his wife and Clyde so...we want to let him know that as much as we love him, from now on our visits have to be just the three of us."

She nods approvingly. "That's pretty grown up of you two. However, I'm sure that's not why Ford was about to blow up and you were trying to control him with your *powerful* gaze."

"You noticed, huh?"

"Yep," she glances at me, then offers me a dipped carrot. "It's all in your eyes. They're pretty expressive. So, tell Nyx what happened."

I roll my eyes. "He thinks I'm fucking with his future."

She looks at me and rolls her eyes. "Because he swears we are *fucking*."

I nod. "We don't need to have the talk yet, do we?"

"The one where you tell me we're just friends and I assure you that I know it?" she asks, waving her hand dismissing me. "It's cool. We can have it now or never. We probably have to stop sleeping together."

I sigh and correct the former statement, "No, the one where I tell you that I want more, and you tell me that I'm too fucked up to even consider being with me. We don't sleep together. We share a bed because the little demon keeps you awake all night. It saves time and energy to remain with you."

She dips another carrot and glances at me tilting her head. "I'm pregnant."

"I've noticed," I confirm and open the seltzer for her.

"Good, I was starting to wonder if you were forgetting about the tiny elephant growing inside me," she says, taking a few sips of seltzer. "Which brings me to...we don't need a conversation at all."

"Nyx?" I lift her chin with my index finger connecting our gazes. "I need a little more than deflection here. There's something happening between us. Denying it isn't healthy."

"I don't think we're ready to discuss anything beyond the fruit size of my child, my food intake, and what book we'll be reading at night."

"Do you think we'll be ready for more than that?"

She gives me a sad smile. "I wish I had an answer."

"It's a pretty easy question, but you're right. The answer is complicated since we have so much going on that prevents us from settling into something...serious," I agree with her but add, "We'll find it though—together."

I seal my promise by caressing her jaw and kissing her nose.

THIRTY-FOUR

Nate

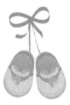

THE WEEKEND with the Brassards is an experience. Listening to their daughters warn them to keep their sex behind closed doors was frightening—and funny. Nyx threatens them, saying they'll never be invited back to the penthouse. On Sunday morning, Eros, Ford, Persy, Nyx, and I go to the tattoo parlor. Nyx agrees to get the *Life is a choice* tattoo with me.

When Persy sees it, she wants it too. As I pay for everyone, I realize that we all ended up with the same tattoo on the inside of our left wrist. The only difference is that Persy and Nyx have a heart on top of the *i* in life.

Edna loves to cook for her children. Unfortunately, her grandchild isn't crazy about her cooking because just the smell makes Nyx sick.

By the time everyone leaves Sunday night, Nyx is happier but really tired. She didn't take one single nap while her family was in town. She goes to sleep before eight, but like every night, her morning sickness wakes us up several times. The next week goes by fast. We don't change our routine. Well, she doesn't. I, on the other hand, spend more time working from home, and with her.

I get it. She can take care of herself, but I like watching over her.

Friday night, Nyx and I fly to California and stay in the house Ford and I own in Santa Monica. We spend the evening by the beach with Brock who loves to play catch.

We don't see Ford and Persy until the next morning since they arrive after midnight. By nine A.M. we're with Dad at the golf course.

"Are Persy and Nyx going to be okay by themselves?" Ford asks as we watch Dad swing his golf club to warm up his arm. "We should've canceled. It's not like you enjoy playing this dumb game."

"I'm going to ignore your question," I answer. "If either one of them heard you, they'd be glaring at you."

"Well, your girlfriend is puking all the time," he protests. I give him a dismissive glance. "We heard her hurling last night. I swear I wanted to drag her to the ER."

"She's not my girlfriend," I remind him. "Still, she can handle herself. I just like to watch over her."

"At least you accept that you are a bit too overbearing when it comes to Nyx." He stretches and yawns. "So, you two sleep together, huh?"

I glare at him and ignore his stupid remark. "I'm visiting Mom around four. Are you sure you don't want to join me?"

He shakes his head. "I'll wait for the Spark Notes."

We each take our turn, go to the next hole, and while Dad takes his sweet time, Ford asks, "When did you talk to Mom?"

"I had my assistant make the appointment," I explain.

"Nothing says, 'I missed you, Mom' better than a call from your assistant," he mocks me.

"At least, I'm doing something. How about you?"

He shakes his head. "I don't have it in me to see her. She let me go, and I let her go. Now, you are different. You..."

I hold onto feelings more than he does, he doesn't say. I'm not sure why that is or why I can't be more like him.

As we go from one hole to another, Ford and I talk to Dad about work first and then Ford looks at me expecting me to start the *other* conversation.

"Listen, Dad," I begin. "Ford and I...well, we don't get along with Ruby and her family."

"They are my family too," he corrects me, squatting to fix his golf ball and then looking at the horizon. "The next time we should bring Clyde. He could use his brothers."

"We're not brothers," Ford jumps into the conversation. "He's your stepson, but we aren't related."

"We could be a family," Dad insists. "You are just not giving them a chance."

"We've tried for years," I remind him. "How many times have we let Clyde and his wife get away with nonsense?"

"Is this because of what Sheila did?"

"It's not, but that's also as bad as what they have done to us for the past twenty years," I assure him.

"We are family," he repeats.

"No, they are *your* family, and we're done with them," I say firmly.

"If I ever see Clyde again, I might kill him," Ford adds.

"It was his wife, not him," Dad defends that asshole and Ford's jaw twitches. "So what if she took a little more commission that the contract said?"

"Sheila stole from her client, Dad. Stealing is a crime," I growl, not adding that this client is Ford's girlfriend.

Ford taps his temple a couple of times and his face turns red. Okay, so I have to defuse this or he's going to blow up and instead of never seeing Dad's family again, we won't be seeing him.

"Well, then drag her to jail," my father responds with some fucking logic that I can't understand.

Ford and I stare at him and I say, "Just like that?"

"As I explained to my wife, who I adore, I can't be paying for every fucking thing those two break," he clarifies to us. "She broke the law, and it's not my damn business."

"Still, Nate and I are thinking that it'll be best if we meet *with you* once every other month. Make it a guy's weekend," Ford explains.

"What about Clyde?"

"He's not your kid, Dad," I remind him and let out a long breath along with the frustration. "If you want to have a weekend with him, plan it separately."

When we arrive at the eighteenth hole, he finally understands that from now on it's just the three of us.

"So, if I invite you to lunch with Ruby today?"

"Persy and Nyx are waiting for us," I use them as scapegoats.

His eyebrows knit together, and he asks, "And who are they?"

"Our girlfriends," Ford answers. "Who you'll meet once we think you are worth the invitation."

We walk away without another word.

"That last part was harsh," I mention as we drive back to the house.

"It was honest," Ford corrects me. "Are you introducing him to Nyx?"

"First, she's not my girlfriend and will never be."

"I thought you two—"

"We're not teenagers. I'm sure we can come up with a better terminology when we agree on having a romantic relationship," I say, to annoy him.

"Whatever," he huffs.

When we get home, we find Nyx standing next to a blackboard.

"Are you taking mugshots?" I ask.

She turns around and smiles at me and I swear that face makes my heart rate speed twice as fast.

"Hey, baby," I greet her.

"My name is Nyx," she corrects me and points at her abdomen. "This is the baby."

I stare at what used to be her flat belly and smile.

"There's a bump," I announce, marching toward Nyx. "She's so tiny. The size of a..."

Nyx taps at the board and there it is, the number thirteen. *Baby Brassard I'm the size of a peach.*

I bend and touch her belly, then kiss it, "Hey, are you peachy? Happy thirteenth week."

It's obvious I have no idea what's going to happen between Nyx and me yet, but how I wish that I can call this baby mine. To be a lot better than my father was to me. To love this life with all my heart and to protect it to my dying breath.

"Persy and I went shopping for this board. It's perfect to track the bump size and changes she is going through."

"Hashtag-bump-watch," Persy sings.

"We're not posting this on social media," Nyx warns her.

"Fine. Let me take a couple more shots of you and you can choose your favorite one. We'll print it and start a scrapbook."

"We officially entered into the second trimester," she announces.

I pull her to my arms and hug her tight. "Congratulations. Do you want to go out to celebrate?"

"If by out, you mean the beach, yes. I'm about to change into my swimsuit and rub sunscreen all over my body. I have a date with your swimming pool."

"I'm leaving at three to meet my mom," I remind her.

She frowns. "You want me to come with you?"

"No, I'm just giving you a heads up."

"I'll come if you want me to."

"Thank you. That means a lot to me, but I think it's best if I go alone."

She squeezes my hand. "We'll be here."

THIRTY-FIVE

Nate

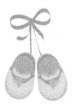

IT'S BEEN a long time since I've seen my mother in person. Twenty-nine years to be exact. When I arrive at the restaurant, the hostess walks me to a booth in the far corner, as Marcia requested. Five minutes later, the hostess walks to the table, a tall woman wearing a pair of big sunglasses walks right beside her.

She has dark hair cut into a bob barely brushing her shoulders. Her black dress is a tad on the formal side for a cup of coffee on a Saturday afternoon. I can't recall how she used to dress back when I was younger.

"Nathaniel," she confirms.

I nod once as I watch her take off her sunglasses. She doesn't look like a woman in her sixties. More like late forties.

She looks at me and smiles. "You look exactly the same way you do on the internet."

"Thank you for meeting me," I say, pointing toward the bench.

"I was surprised when I received your assistant's call. Are you okay?" she asks, concerned. She tries to reach my hand, but I frown and move it away.

"Why would you ask that?"

"Well, I think that you wouldn't call to ask for money," she states. "According to Jim, my husband, you and Ford are wealthy. Another possibility is that maybe you need a kidney and—"

"Let me stop you there," I say.

The waitress approaches the table and says, "Hi, I'm Tiffany, and I'll be your server. Are you ready to order?"

"Just water for me," I request, while my mother says, "I'll have a latte."

So, that's where Ford got his nasty habit of adding frothy milk to his coffee.

"Well, there has to be a reason you called me," she says when Tiffany is out of earshot. "Unless you're filing for bankruptcy and you need help. I'm sorry to tell you that unlike you, we live with a pretty tight budget."

"I don't remember much about you, but I do remember you spoke a lot," I say, trying to stop her because she hasn't let me say shit.

"Your dad was the quiet one. You and Langford were also quiet. How is he doing?"

"Ford?"

She nods. "He... When my kids were in elementary school, there was this boy who reminded me a lot of him."

I glare at her. "If you're about to spill some shit that is going to piss me off, don't do it," I warn her.

"So, you're still protective of him," she looks around. "Why is he not here?"

"Because he's the practical one," I respond. "He moved on with his life, unlike me. I'm still wondering what happened to you. Why did you leave us?"

"Of course, the inquisitive one," she states, looking at her hands for several beats. "That was my other guess."

She finally looks up and stares at me. "It's complicated."

"I'm smart enough to keep up. Why don't you try me?"

"How much did your father tell you?"

"My father's version isn't up for discussion," I say. She doesn't need to know that he doesn't talk about her. Once she left, her pictures disappeared, and we never mentioned her again.

She nods. "He's a difficult man," she leads with the best-known fact about my father. "As an only child, his parents raised him to believe that he was perfect. The rest of us had to worship him, and for years I did. I...I saw him as a deity until one day I woke up and realized he was a man with flaws and I had become one of his groupies. I lived to serve him and his children."

"We were *your* children too."

"I was Chuck Chadwick's wife. The Chadwick twins' mother. What happened to Ursula Lindt?" she argues. "He was a mama's boy. I didn't sign up to be his mother, yet I was there picking up after him, dealing with his absence, because playing golf was all that mattered to him."

"I remember you fighting a lot about that, even throwing things at him."

She fixes her hair, lifts her chin, and says, "You can't judge me. You have no idea how hard it was to be with him. I met Jim, and...he showed me that life can be different."

"I lived with Dad. If you believed that being with him was unbearable, why did you leave us with him?"

"There's no gray area for him. Either I stayed with him or I wouldn't be allowed to be around him again."

"Why didn't you take us with you?" I ask, frustrated.

"You're going to judge me," she states.

"Probably," I agree with her. "I don't know how to tell you this, but so far I'm not hearing anything that sounds remotely close to a grain of remorse."

"What were you expecting?" she asks.

"My...I have this friend who is a lawyer, and she said, 'What if she lost custody of you during the divorce,'" I explain. "It gave me some hope. It pissed me off that you wouldn't fight for us, but knowing Dad..."

I release a humorless laughter. "He's harsh and hard-headed. It's fucking hard to get him to understand that the world isn't his playground. But with patience, you can make him see things from a different perspective. You just didn't care about us, did you?"

"I was sinking in that house," she defends herself.

"Was he abusing you?"

"No, but...I wanted to start over with Jim," she explains and then adds. "I regret what happened. I could've handled it differently, but look at you. You grew up to be a successful businessman. If I had dragged you with me, you would be a nobody."

I raise an eyebrow, lay my palms on the table, and lean closer to her. "Do you really think I am where I am because of my father's money? That I would take my grandfather's legacy over having a happy family?"

I lift my palms as if giving up. What's the point of having this conversation?

She stares at my wrist and reads out loud, "Life is a choice."

I read it too, twice. This reminds me of not only Nyx, but last week when we went to get these tattoos. Ford and I have been making choices throughout our entire life guided by my grandparents.

"That's exactly it. You have to choose because you can't have everything," she insists. "You either have money or you have a happy family. You can't have it both ways. Either I had enough money to travel around the world or...I chose happiness. I'm sorry I had to shut you down to be able to reach it."

What she says reminds me of the Brassards. They don't have

much money, but they sacrifice everything for their children. They still do it, even when they're all grown and independent.

"Sometimes you can have success and happiness," I contend. "Sometimes life is about the moments you miss with the people who matter because you were too busy piling a fortune that won't feed your soul. You're right, I have no idea what you felt back then, but maybe Ford and I would've been happier with just a pile of clothes that fit in a backpack and someone who taught us the real value of love."

Which maybe we learned from our grandparents. We just never thought about it before. Maybe my father sending us to do community service felt like cruelty, but we learned a lot from every person we've met since then.

"I don't understand," she claims.

"My parents were too selfish to think beyond their needs," I answer. "I've lived wondering what is wrong with me. I should focus on my grandparents who gave us the foundation. I should focus on what I have and not what I think I need. I hope you're happy, and if you're not, I hope you find happiness."

MY NIGHTS ARE BETWEEN A NIGHTMARE, bliss, and a fantasy. I can't sleep because of Nyx. It's not the morning sickness as much as my mind keeps replaying everything that we do during the day. I remember her eyes twinkling and her smile brightening every room when she enters.

Tonight though, I keep remembering how hot she looked while she sun tanned by the pool when I arrived from my chat with my mother. I wanted to kick my brother and Persy out of the house. To pull her into me. Wrap my arms around her while I kissed her slowly. She's a beautiful goddess but unattainable for the moment.

Instead, I explained to Ford what happened. He wasn't surprised. Nyx was by my side comforting me, but the only thing I wanted was for her to kiss me. To let me love her and make everything go away. It didn't happen, and like every night, I'm aroused and completely dissatisfied.

All I can do is take a cold shower while I imagine her on my bed, by my side. Tracing her delicate curves with the tips of my fingers. As I palm my length, I think about caressing her full breasts. Sucking on her nipples until they are rock hard. I want to kneel between her legs, forcing her inner thighs to open wide apart for me.

I grip my cock, moving my hand up and down faster, wishing it was her delicate hand holding me. Or her luscious lips sucking me dry. I want to be inside her, loving her. Her naked body pressed to mine. Lips brushing our bare skin. Teeth biting and longing kisses between us.

As the crave for her intensifies, my hand quickens its movements. My body tenses. The thrust of my hips intensifies. The muscles in my legs strain as jets of cum spurt, washing down while I shower. The music playing on the speakers muffles my moans.

When I come out of the shower, I hear noise coming from her bedroom. Brock barks, alerting me that she's sick again. I hate to see her like this. If I could, I would take her place, but I can't so I do what I can to make it better.

"Hey," I say, as I arrive at her bathroom and she's already brushing her teeth. "Sorry, I feel like I'm late."

Her eyes look at me tenderly and she shakes her head before spitting. Once she rinses with mouthwash she finally speaks, "Sorry for waking you up."

"You can't be sorry for keeping me awake," I reword. "Why don't I just stay with you? It's silly for me to go back to my room when we know this is going to happen a few more times."

She bites her lip and nods.

I trace my thumb along her frown and ask, "What are you thinking?"

"Let's call it not safe for tonight," she mumbles, wiggling her nose. "I like you, and it's kind of hard to stay on this side of the line. Not sure if you've noticed this roommate arrangement is becoming a little blurry."

I set one hand on her hip, the other rests gently on her shoulder. I move forward pushing away every thought of why this is stupid. My eyes lock on her mouth as I move close, and as I'm almost brushing her lips, she inhales sharply.

We kiss, and this time is soft, tender. I crave her, but I control the desire to possess her. I just want her to feel safe and loved tonight.

This is our routine. Well, except for the kiss. I fantasize that she's mine. I take care of her, and at the end I tuck her under my arm and watch over her and her baby. Do I wish she was mine? Of course, but most of all, I just want her to be fine.

THIRTY-SIX

Nyx

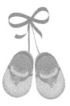

"TIME FLIES when you're having fun," Nate says while he takes the sixteenth week picture of the little terror.

"She's still small," I claim, placing my hands on top of my belly.

"You look like you ate a whole avocado and it's stuck in there," he jokes walking to me and kissing the baby. "Are you okay in there? Kick once for yes and twice for no."

I glare at him. He keeps talking to the baby and inciting her to kick for him. "Every book says that you don't feel much movement until the baby is—"

"Sixteen to twenty-five weeks," he answers, kissing my lips. "If we had a baby trivia night, I might win."

I want to tell him that he is cheating because he has some experience, but bringing up Bronwyn might not be a good idea.

He's working on what he calls his emotional issues. Three weeks ago, he began with his parents. The visit with his mother left him angry. He hoped that like many parents, the one with money had taken the children away but, in her heart, she cared for her sons. He's working on not hating her because the last thing he wants is to drag negative feelings about her. On the other hand, he helped me take Sheila down.

She's spending a few months in jail for stealing money from my sister.

We still haven't discussed our feelings. That's frustrating and yet fine because we're not in a good place. Still, since that day we've been stealing caresses and kisses. They are just lingering, not full blown erotic embraces, but I'm so horny that some nights I spend an hour with my sex toys getting myself off while I think about him.

"What do you want to do today?" he asks, handing me the little board with the number sixteen. "Ready?"

I nod and call Brock who runs toward me. "Sit boy."

He does and I hang the board, placing myself close to him so Nate can take a picture of Brock and the baby. A second later, he's shaking his head and trying to take the board off. I help him and he huffs at me.

"Sorry, but I promise these pictures are worth it."

Brock glares at me and marches toward Nate.

"I love him, but I swear he throws tantrums as big as Simon," I mention, and since I brought up the feline, I text Persy.

Nyx: *What are you up to today?*

Persy: *I couldn't convince Ford to take me to New York.*

Nyx: *Next weekend?*

Persy: *Are you and Nate still 'friends'?*

I stare at the phone for a long time, wondering how I should respond to her. Normally, I'd tell her the truth. There's a fire between us that threatens to consume our hearts if we're not careful. We shouldn't act on it, but I'm dying to be reckless and...

"You okay?" Nate asks, and I shrug, trying to erase all those naughty thoughts that keep me distracted most of the day—and all night.

Before I can answer his question with one of my own, Demetri walks outside the terrace.

"Happy Saturday, D," I greet him.

"Ms. Nyx, as always, it's a pleasure to see you," he greets me. "Since you are both here, I'll take the opportunity to remind you that Brock has a bed in the downstairs area."

Nate and I laugh because Brock has no regard for furniture or any other surface in this house. He's a well trained dog, just spoiled by us.

"It's perfectly obvious that neither one of you care for him enough to show him how he should behave," he snips. "Just don't expect me to help you if you bring another dog home."

"How can we help you, D?" Nate asks.

"The appointments with the realtor are set for next week," he answers. "Also, Ms. Bronwyn Davis is downstairs, looking for you, Nate."

Nate takes a deep breath and shakes his head.

"You okay if she comes upstairs?" he asks me.

I frown, "Me?"

He nods.

"If you want, I can stay out here," I suggest.

"I want you with me as long as this doesn't make you feel uncomfortable," he explains.

"Then, I'm fine."

Demetri nods and goes back into the house. Then I ask, "Why is she here?"

"My lawyer served her with an eviction notice. My physical address is on there. I expected her to come by and try to persuade me to let her live there for another ten years," he answers.

For a moment, I want to remind him I wanted to be the one serving her with that, but then I remember that it was too long ago.

Now I'm emotionally invested with him and it'd be not only unethical, but messy.

"We should go inside because I don't want her to mess up the peaceful atmosphere of this place," I suggest.

He takes my hand and when we reach the foyer, there's a woman throwing daggers at me. Her blue eyes are darkened with fury.

"So, this is why you want me out?" she snaps without even greeting us. "You are leaving *your child* homeless because you decided to play family again?"

"Lower your tone or I'll have Demetri escort you out of the building," Nate warns her.

She huffs and punches him with a very low blow, "Who knows, that kid might not be yours either."

He glares at her.

"You have five minutes to explain your presence, Bronwyn," he says calmly. "I recommend you use them wisely. One more shot at Nyx or the baby and you're out."

"That is my house," she claims. "Our son was born in that house and now you just expect me to leave. You gifted it to me."

She glares at me and throws her poison, "He's going to set you up nicely until he's bored of you and starts traveling," she complains. "You are no different. One day you'll live in this palace and the next he'll shove you to Brooklyn. Do you know when was the last time he saw his son?"

"When he had to find out that you lied to him and get his cheek swabbed hoping that the baby he called his wasn't going to be taken away from him," I answer.

She looks at me, frozen, and then at Nate.

"Listen," I continue. "I'm sure the notice came unexpected, but if you need more time, your lawyer can request an extension. This isn't about my baby or me. Not at all. This is about Nate and you moving on with your lives. This situation is...unhealthy."

Fucked up is more like it, but I am trying to sound classy and professional.

She points at my belly and yells, "He's going to leave you, and your kid will never have a father. No one will love him."

"I might fuck up in a lot of ways as a father," Nate says with a calm voice. His thumb caresses the tattoo on my wrist. "But our baby will always know how much I love her. She might fear me when she breaks curfew, but she'll never doubt that we adore her and will do anything for her."

Words are being said, but my mind is frozen as it keeps analyzing what Nate just said. He loves my baby.

Our baby.

"Callum...he skips child support," she complains.

"You can get a lawyer to help you with that," I suggest.

"Well, my lawyer will be busy fighting for the house," she presses.

"Actually," I stop her, ready to bullshit her with my words. "I wouldn't do that because then you'll piss *me* off, and I'll be demanding you to pay for the five years you lived in that house—rent-free. Not sure how good you are at math, but we're talking about a property that can lease as low as five thousand dollars and as high as... well, I'm sure you know how much you can charge. That times seventy-two, plus the interest accumulated for all the years you missed paying rent..."

"Who are you?"

"I could be many things, like an advocate for your child seeking child support from his *real* father, or your worst nightmare if you try to screw with Nate."

"We could work things out," she begs Nate. "You said you'd love me. Forever."

He turns to look at me and says, "You can see her, can't you?"

"She's not your type," she presses. "This woman looks like she can recite the Constitution if I provoke her."

He grins, "And in seven languages."

I glance at her. She's wearing a pair of shoes that Persy just posted on her blog. They cost more than a thousand dollars. They are almost brand new, and I doubt there's a knock off style out yet.

"We're going to have our P.I. investigate your son's father to see how much we can get for child support," I throw a little fib. "I can get you a good lawyer to—"

"That's not necessary," she interrupts me. "I can figure that out for myself."

"Leasing out a property that doesn't belong to you is illegal," I throw another fact. "Just food for thought in case we feel like visiting you soon and we find out that it's being occupied by another family."

"Time for you to go," Nate prompts her. "I'll walk you downstairs."

He presses a kiss on top of my head and whispers. "I'll be right back."

I stare at him suspiciously as he steps into the elevator with *her.*

THIRTY-SEVEN

Nate

"SO, YOU LIVE WITH HER?" she asks.

"This has to end, Bronwyn," I request. "You need to stop mailing me pictures, handmade crafts, and updates. You made your choice. You're exploiting *your* kid, for what?"

"You never looked at me the way you look at her," she argues, her voice even sounds like an accusation. "When you found out I was pregnant, you proposed to me, but you never asked me to live with you. Mom is the one who said I should move in with you. It never came from you."

"My feelings for Nyx are not of your concern. My feelings for you were *never* your concern," I say, firmly. "Maybe I made a mistake by letting you come into our house. You upset her and probably my baby."

"You're going to have a baby," she mumbles. "It's like I thought you'd never get past what we had. I had the option available, and now..."

"But you never did," I claim. "The moment you played with me, you lost my trust."

"But you love me," she insists, the purr in her voice is fucking annoying. When did I find that enticing?

"No, I *loved* you once, and that died long ago."

And it was nothing compared to what I feel for Nyx. I don't tell her that because what is the point of even sharing what I haven't shared with the woman I love.

I held onto that memory because it's easier to pretend that something is there than create a new opportunity.

Until, unexpectedly, Nyx walked into my life.

"What about Wyatt?"

"I'm still mad at you for the shit you pulled. It's still painful, but I understand he's not mine to take care of," I clarify. "Marcia has orders to stop any packages coming from you and return them."

"This can't be the end?" she insists as the elevator reaches the lobby and the doors slide open.

"No, the end was years ago. Now I have to ask, why not break up with me when you fell in love with Callum?"

"I cared for you," she answers. "I cared for both of you."

"Did you ever love either one of us?"

"I loved the attention you gave me. No one has ever been so attentive, and our dates were always in places that I could only dream of going to...you were thrilling."

Sounds like you had a fun toy until you got bored. Thank you for at least being honest. I keep that thought to myself. Fatigue suddenly hits me, like the kind that takes over when I work for days without sleep. I'm done. I have time to finally recover.

"I wish I had done everything differently," she states.

"This is your chance to do it. Be the best mom Wyatt deserves.

244 • CLAUDIA BURGOA

Push the father to support him if what you said upstairs is, in fact, the truth. If not, try being honest. I'm fucking tired of your lies."

She opens her mouth, closes it, then finally asks, "If I had handled it differently?"

"What do you mean?"

"If I had told you I wasn't sure about who the father was?"

She really thinks that I would've been fine with her cheating.

"We'll never know, Bronwyn." I show her my wrist. "Life is a choice."

"You're a great guy. I hope she knows it."

WHEN I COME UPSTAIRS, Nyx is staring at me. Her lip quivers.

"You okay?"

She chews on her lip and nods, but fuck if my heart isn't breaking because I know this face. "What's going on?"

"You said you love her?"

"What?" I ask, confused.

She puts a hand on her baby bump and says, "You said you love *our baby*. You called her yours."

"Of course, I do. I adore our little blueberry demon." And damn fucking Bronwyn for ruining everything. This is a conversation for later. "No matter what happens between us, I hope you let me be a part of her life."

Her lip trembles faster.

"You're going to cry, aren't you?"

She chews on her lip and nods.

I smile and take her in my arms. "Come here. Thank you for whatever happened earlier. I could've taken her, but your legal retort was pretty hot."

"If Edward would just sign the papers or tell me what it is that he plans," she mumbles against my shirt. "I feel like that's what keeps us from...talking."

The results of the paternity test came back a couple of weeks ago. He's not excluded from being the biological father of the blueberry demon. There was never any doubt. Now, he's refusing to relinquish his rights until he is sure that he doesn't want the kid. The fucker is playing mind games with Nyx. And there's nothing we can do to force him to sign. Unless my P.I. finds some dirty secret that can give us the advantage, we might have to wait until the baby is born to fight him for custody.

"So, this is the plan," I tell her. "We have the sonogram on Monday, then leave for Colorado right after. We're spending the week with your family. We can pencil in a long, adult conversation for one of those days."

She frowns and looks up at me, "I have work to do."

"Remember I told you to take the week off and that we'd be going home for the week of the twenty-ninth?"

"Persy's birthday," she mumbles.

"We'll be there, okay?" I assure her, not giving away what is happening this upcoming Tuesday.

Ford is proposing to Persy. He wants us to be close by to celebrate with them. He knows Persy would want Nyx to be there.

"Then we'll have an adult conversation," she concludes.

"Exactly!"

THE WEEKEND GOES BY FAST, and on Monday, Nyx and I are wired up about the baby. I'm grateful that Marcia got us the seven A.M. spot. That way, we don't have to wait long, plus we can leave for Colorado right after. It is exactly seven twenty-two when we find out that Nyx is having a baby girl.

"She's perfect," I say staring at the pictures. "Can you see her smile?"

"Don't be ridiculous," she corrects me. "She's sleeping because, as we know, she loves to keep me up puking all night."

Nyx stares at her belly and says, "They said it'd stop at twelve weeks. You're almost at seventeen. This is a borderline tantrum, young lady."

I laugh and place a hand on her bump. "Don't upset my girl."

She looks at me with adoration. "She needs a name."

"We have time," I wave her off as we arrive at the airport.

"No, we don't. My parents are going to shove a bunch of lists at me, and then I'll be too confused to make an educated decision."

As we board the plane, I lift her chin and kiss her lips. "I'll make sure to keep you grounded. Though as a reminder, you're pretty strong at using the word no and ignoring them. Don't rush something as important as a name, okay?"

"Where's Brock?" she asks looking around.

"D is running behind. Don't worry. We won't take off without them, okay?"

THIRTY-EIGHT

Nyx

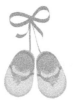

WHEN I BOARD the plane to Colorado, I don't know what to expect. I imagine Nate will be going to his penthouse and I'll be staying at my parents. Persy and Ford are moving into their new house this weekend.

However, almost six hours later, I find myself in front of my house. The one that, according to the documents I signed last month, was sold to a management company.

"What are we doing here?"

"Well, Ford and Persy have a mess at their places since they are packing," he explains. "I doubt you want to be at your parents'. If we stay at a hotel—"

"Cut the crap, Chadwick," I protest. "Did you buy my house?"

"My management company did."

"Same dog, different trick," I protest. "This is unacceptable."

"You haven't chosen a house. We need a place to stay," he concludes.

"We can stay at my parents'," I remind him.

He laughs hard. "And find them fucking in the middle of the hallway? Nope. I like them, but not that much."

I stare at him, and even though I want to be upset, I'm not. For the first time, I can see myself with someone. Nathaniel Chadwick. He doesn't care that I'm weird sometimes. He doesn't mind my family—they are a handful. He is okay with my lists and my plans and even finds them endearing and brilliant. He loves my baby—also calls her ours. He likes to take care of me, and I don't mind letting him. Actually, I love it.

Starting a fight because he makes rash decisions isn't worth it. I'll probably give him a hard time later. Not today.

"What are you thinking?" he asks.

That I might love you and I want you to kiss me without restraining yourself as you do every night before I fall asleep in your arms. I want your spark to ignite me. To burn me so deep that your soul will be seared into mine. I want us to absorb each other. For you to love me recklessly. To kiss with the intention of never letting you go.

"Saturday feels too far away," I confess.

"Yet, we're going to have to wait," he says. "Ford needs me to help him install some stuff in the new house. I also want you to check out a couple of properties that are close by."

"Are you planning on moving to Colorado?"

He scratches the back of his neck. "For the next couple of years, I can't do it full time, babe. I need you to think about that little piece of information. All I can offer is bringing you to your family often. Moving the entire company is impossible."

I adore my family, but I wouldn't care where I live as long as I'm with him. The thought surprises me and yet, fills me with so much hope. The hope that maybe this is exactly where I belong, with him.

"Part of our adult conversation?" I ask.

He nods. "I have to run to Ford's. Your car is in the garage. The furniture is back the way D found it. We have a lot to sort out, but I hope that you want to solve this *with me*."

I feel like he dumped the pieces of a puzzle on a table and wants me to assemble them or just forget about the puzzle—and him. To move on with my life and leave him behind.

Is he scared that this isn't permanent?

"Hey, can I ask you something?" he asks, and doesn't wait for a response. "Would you take me if I didn't have a penny to my name?"

"That sounds like a question for Friday," I answer, but he's actually responding to my silent question. "You're trying to figure out if I'm going to choose my family over you, aren't you?"

I stare at him, barely breathing.

"No, I don't want you to choose. I just want to know what you need, because I don't want you to leave me." His voice is almost cracking.

"First of all, I need you to trust me that I am not with you because you can just buy a house within a day. I don't care about your checkbook. I can make it on my own. If you lose everything today, we will start together from the ground up working side by side to build our future," I clarify. "Also, you have to trust that when I decide to say, 'I'm in,' I won't leave you. I'm me. Not your mother, Bronwyn, or any other woman. I need to figure out what is going to happen with Edward before I can make a decision about my future."

He nods. "Just to recap, I stopped loving Bronwyn years ago. What I feel for you is a trillion times bigger than what I felt for her. You have all the time in the world. However...I need you to keep me in the loop."

We kiss briefly before he leaves, and I make my way into the house with Brock by my side.

As Nate mentioned, nothing has changed. Except, the place doesn't feel like mine anymore. There are flowers all around, just the way we have them at his place. It's something I recommended a couple of months back, mentioning that they'd bring happiness into his home.

Taking a deep breath, I call Edward.

"I told you I need time," he snaps when he answers the phone.

"This isn't a game, Edward," I say. "Meet me at my house in thirty minutes."

"I thought you were in New York, being Pierce's bitch," he says in a snarky tone.

"Listen, you either control your language or we're going to have a problem," I warn him. "The only thing I'm requesting is for you to relinquish the parental rights of a child you obviously don't care about."

"I care so much that I'm working with a family lawyer to ensure that you come back to this state where I can make sure my kid is safe," he threatens me. "I am ready to fight for full custody of my son."

"It's a girl," I announce without mentioning that he can't file for custody until the baby is born.

"What the fuck?" he growls. "There are no girls in my family. We all are boys. You need to get a real test. Just know that from now on, things will be done my way. You'll go to the doctor I assign and stay in the state so I can see to my kid."

"You need to lower your voice," I demand. "You want to do this the hard way. I'm ready for it. Just know that when this is over and done with, there'll be a restraining order against you. You won't be able to approach us."

He hangs up on me, and I email Pierce right away.

I SPEND the rest of the week with my family. Ford proposes to Persy on Tuesday. We celebrate her birthday on Thursday. My parents are excited because I have my house back. I don't have the heart to tell them that it's Nate's and not mine. That I haven't decided what I'm going to do with my future because the last few months with Nate have been the best months of my life.

Yet, I don't know what we're doing because Edward might be trying to do something stupid. I've worked for the Bryants. I know what they are capable of doing, and they have connections.

By Friday, I'm emotionally exhausted. I want to stop time because I have an adult conversation scheduled. I'm dreading it, and not because I don't want Nate and me to exchange the words that we've been harboring from one another.

I feel like I'm going to say, "Well, I love you, but...I'm in the middle of a legal battle."

Pierce reminded me of something I've been thinking about since my bitter call with Edward. His family knows a lot of family judges, and with a good bribe, they can keep me in Colorado until the baby is born. In theory, the fetus can't be treated like a child for the purpose of a custody battle. However, there's a document I provided that reads *the probability of paternity is 99.9999%.*

My mind keeps running scenarios about my girl's future all night, and around five in the morning, I get out of bed. I prepare myself some tea and turn on my computer, trying to find a good family lawyer in case I need one. I keep flipping back to the cases I worked on while working for Bryant, LLC. This feels like karma. All the mothers and fathers who relinquish the custody of their children because of me are claiming revenge. This is how I pay for the wrongdoing. I place a hand on my belly and send a prayer that my fears are unfounded.

"You're awake," Nate comes out of his bedroom and looks at the time on the microwave. "Wait. You slept through the night?

I frown and nod. "Yeah, I—did you notice all day yesterday I—"

"You didn't get sick at all," he confirms and smiles. Then he takes me in his arms and hugs me tight while twirling me around.

"Are you trying to make me sick?"

"No, I'm happy for you. However, I don't have an excuse to sneak into your bed," he confesses and sets me down.

He rests his forehead on mine and encircles his arms around my waist. "Are you ready to tell me what's bothering you?"

I nod, and tell him everything, including the fact that I might get served with an order that won't allow me to leave the state. He kisses my lips and says, "I won't let that happen."

Cupping his face, I sprinkle a few kisses along his jaw before I untangle myself from his grasp.

"They play dirty," I inform him. "We—Pierce and I—have heard the rumors that their firm buys judges. Edward and his brother once confirmed it while they were drunk. I think that's why Pierce focused on the part of the firm where he didn't have to deal with his family as much."

Nate runs a hand through his hair and asks. "How do I help?"

"I don't know," I whisper. "But that adult discussion has to be tabled until I am in a good place."

"Can he actually force you to stay in the state?" he asks. "Is that even legal?"

I shake my head and start researching in case there's a precedent.

That's when I find a case that happened a few years back. A famous Olympic skier who fought for custody of the fetus. He lived in California; his ex moved to New York.

In theory, I have worked and lived in New York since August. Aldridge Enterprises and Merkel have been paying me. They have both the Seattle and New York addresses as my residence.

The best way to take away the power the Bryants have is by leaving today and not coming back until the custody of the baby is squared up in a court where they are looking out for the welfare of the baby and not because the Bryants are paying them to take away my kid.

Moving my laptop toward Nate I say, "Read this. I think I might have the answer."

Nyx: *Remember the custody case of the skier and the former marine?*

Pierce: *It's six in the fucking morning. I am busy feeding the animals.*

Nyx: *I might have the answer to my problem. I'm texting you a link with the case. New York has precedent about a dad trying to use a fetus to fight for custody.*

Nyx: Said dad is from California. They fucked up pretty bad therefore there's something that will make it pretty clear for them to deny Edward's request. I should be safe if I fly back there.

I drum my fingers against the counter while I wait for Pierce to text back. Nate's eyes scan the screen. His frown deepens.

"What a tool," he complains, pushing the laptop slightly. Then he places a hand on my belly and rubs it. "First, he wants her to terminate the pregnancy, and then he wants to claim the child while in utero...which isn't different from what Edward is doing. He doesn't want our blueberry demon. He just wants to fuck with you."

"In theory, I could sue him for threatening my rights to move and make a living," I say, relaxing even more as I see a light at the end of the tunnel.

He shakes his head and kisses my nose. "So, you think that since the New York system learned their lesson it'll be safe to move there for the remainder of the pregnancy."

I nod.

"Let me handle the details," he says, and I don't pay much attention to him because Pierce finally texts me back.

Pierce: I remember this case. I agree with you. It'll be best if you leave. You could move to New York or Seattle. I can defend you in either place. Neither one will demand you to go back to Colorado. If you need a plane, I'll have one soon. Leave now.

Nyx: You think they're going to do something, don't you?

Pierce: They'll try. Don't let them. The sooner you leave Colorado the better.

"Babe, I'm going to walk Brock," Nate announces. When I look up, I realize he changed his pajama bottoms. He's wearing a pair of shorts, a sweatshirt, and tennis shoes. When did he change? "The plane should be ready to depart soon. I just texted Ford in case Persy wants to see you before we leave."

"You don't have to go. I know you and Ford have a lot to do tomorrow since it's officially moving day," I object.

"Our blueberry demon is more important than the move. He'll understand. Demetri, your dad, and Eros can help him," he argues, and walks toward me, brushing away the strands of hair covering my face. "Remember, you're not alone. *We* are in this together."

"I'm sorry, I feel like I'm complicating your life," I say, trying to remind myself that it's okay to let others help me.

He rubs my belly, places a kiss on it and then looks at me saying, "You two are worth it. So what if we have to stay put in New York? It doesn't matter where we live. Home is just a place within us. For me, it's become wherever you are. I can't guarantee that this is going to be easy, but I'll be by your side, and I'll make sure that he doesn't take away our baby."

"I wish..."

"Me too," he says, giving me a kiss. It's longer than a peck but not too long that I lose myself inside him. "Get ready."

"By the way," I say before he leaves. "We can go to Seattle instead. It's about choosing one of them, and we just go to the other place once a month."

He nods and leaves with Brock.

I place a hand on my belly and whisper, "It'll be fine. No one is taking you away from us."

THIRTY-NINE

Nate

WE CHOOSE SEATTLE. Nyx said she'd be okay moving to either place. Though she's honest with me, I know she favors the house by the lake better than the penthouse. We live within an hour from her figuring out the best way to avoid a messy, yet illegal, custody battle.

To no surprise, Edward files for custody of the unborn baby. Since Nyx lives in Seattle, he files a second petition in the state of Washington demanding her to go back to Colorado.

Thankfully, Pierce is able to have the case dismissed in the state of Washington because the child isn't born yet. He also sues Edward for endangering Nyx and the fetus because he tried to run roughshod over her rights.

Pierce's suggestion that we don't go to Colorado until the baby is born is now a prerogative. He knows they are waiting for Nyx to be served with an order from a judge to stay. It's illegal, but Edward Bryant's family has several judges in their pockets.

Nyx assures me that she's fine, but I can feel the tension weighing her down. Her family comes to spend Thanksgiving with us. During dinner, Persy and Ford announce that they are planning on getting married at the end of the year, in the Maldives. They want something simple and family only.

I'm happy for my brother, but their news sits like lead at the bottom of my stomach. A month ago, I was about to tell the woman I love that I wanted to explore the possibilities of an us. I wish I could just propose to Nyx and say, fuck it Edward. We haven't even sat down to talk about us. I can't, and they are getting fucking married.

I hate the days when she retreats into her own world and ignores everyone—even me. My only consolation is that there are evenings when all we do is sit by the fire holding each other.

It's understandable. She's terrified of losing the baby. I am too. This wouldn't be the first time I lose a child, and it's killing me that I can't even say that out loud because I'm literally nobody. Just her roommate. I can't be more because what if they use our relationship against her. She's preparing for the fight of her life, and I know that we're there for her, but also that I can't be too close because they can use me as ammunition.

I'm so fucking paranoid that I gifted her a phone with a Seattle number that we can use to communicate, just in case they subpoena her phone log and her texts. After dinner, we set up the seven-foot-tall tree we bought while we were shopping in New York. She thought it'd look perfect right next to the staircase. Her family helps decorate the tree.

"How is she doing?" Persy asks once Nyx goes to bed around nine. "She's been too quiet."

I blink and let out a loud breath. Quiet is an understatement. "She's vocal when she's on the phone with Pierce discussing a new approach to the custody."

"It's going to be okay," she reassures me.

Raking my hair with my fingers I let out a breath. "See, that's the problem. You can't know until we have a judge reiterate that it's going to be okay. That he won't take her away. It's so fucking painful to lose your kid. This...we can't lose *her*."

Persy smiles at me. "You really love them."

I nod and don't tell her all my fears because again, who the fuck am I to worry. But what if Nyx shuts the door between us because that's what's best for the baby. I'd lose both of them, and then what's going to happen with me?

"You have no idea," I claim. "They are my life."

Ford squeezes my shoulder. "We have the resources, Nate. You'll hire whoever we need to keep that baby safe with her family."

"Maybe you should talk to Nyx," Persy suggests. "Sometimes she needs space but others...you have to drag her out of her head, or she'll drive herself crazy. Look, I totally understand that you're trying to respect her, but how do you guys want her to remember her pregnancy?"

I could say something stupid like, we're not together or this isn't my baby. Except, I love this baby as if she's mine, and Nyx has become my entire life. Persy is onto something. I gave Nyx four weeks to use her logic and come up with at least thirty solutions to the custody battle that won't start until our baby is born.

"See you tomorrow morning," I say, marching back into the house.

Eros is in the living room reading. He stares at me and says, "You owe me an explanation."

"I don't have time," I announce without stopping to hear his nonsense.

"Nyx seemed happy with you, until she's not," he states.

I halt. "What does that mean?"

"Listen, I told you to stay away but forwent the warning when I realized she was finally being more herself and less like the tight ass woman she became when she started working for that firm. But today...fuck, it's like dealing with a sad zombie."

He's right. Now I feel like a failure for letting this go too far.

"Good night, Eros." I wave at him and head upstairs.

Instead of going to her room, I go to mine first to change my clothes. That's when I find her on my bed. She wears one of my sweaters and Brock rests his head on her bump. I shut the door, put on a pair of pajama bottoms, and join her, pulling her body against mine.

"What's happening?" I whisper.

She shakes her head.

"I get it," I mumble. "The idea of losing her is frightening. You want to be ready to make sure he doesn't take her away but...we can't stop living while we're waiting for the worst of the storm to arrive. We can still sing, dance, and get ready for her. Celebrate our baby."

She turns around and snuggles herself closer to me. Her head rests against my chest.

"I miss this," she says. "Spending the night in your arms."

"Me too," I confess.

I want to tell her to listen to my heart. To listen to the many ways I love her.

"This fight is mine too, Nyx. He's not going to take her away from us," I say it out loud. "I understand how your mind works. You like to do things alone, but you're with me. If there's something I do well, it is protecting those I love."

Placing a hand on her belly, I say, "I need you to trust me. To let me back inside because being just a spectator doesn't help either one of us. We're in this together, right?"

She chuckles, and then I hear her sob.

"Nyx, talk to me," I beg.

"What can I say? Today I was thinking maybe I should just go back to Colorado, buy a house and leave this little fantasy. You'd be better suited with a woman like Persy. Just think about it. She's fun, carefree, and doesn't have baggage."

"Don't you think it's time to blow out the candles on the cake for your pity party and end it?" I ask and smile when I feel the blueberry demon kick against my hand. "See, she wants you to stop too."

"I'm happy. Your baggage is precious, and I can't wait to meet her. I don't need a carefree person who does stuff without thinking. I have enough of that with myself. I need someone who grounds me. You have flaws and I embrace them because they are part of who you are," I assure her.

She lifts her gaze and looks at me. "How could you say that?"

"You're the careful to my reckless. Those times when I want to be impulsive, you stop me because you're a sensible person. This is why things work so well between us," I explain, kissing her neck. I nibble on her earlobe, making her shiver. "You're a planner. I like to do things on the go. If it was up to me, we'd be in Vegas, eloping."

She laughs. "Really, in front of Elvis?"

"Wherever you want to do it," I say, planting tender kisses all over her beautiful face. "You've been in your own little world for so long. Today I feel like you shut the window you had open just for me. What happened?"

She shakes her head.

"Nyx, please," I mumble against the base of her sternum and run my lips all the way to her jaw. "What upset you?"

"I should be happy for my sister, but...envy overtook me. She's always been in some sort of relationship. I never cared about it, but after all the wrongs she found... she found him. The perfect guy who does everything for her and adores her. They are getting married, and because I was too busy planning my future, I'm alone and terrified that I might lose my baby and...what if you and I never happen?"

She's not saying this because she wants someone like my brother. What she wants is the security of having a steady relationship and a guy to hold her all the time. Maybe it's not just her who retreated during these past four weeks. I might have distanced myself. Between her need to have some space, my trip to Boston, and the few issues we had with production, I've been neglecting her.

This stops today.

"So, you're complaining because you get the shitty Chadwick?"

"What?" she squeaks and snort laughs. "No. I wish things

between us could work, but in reality, at the end of this, I don't get any Chadwick. I...you. We can't."

"Let's make a deal," I offer. "Starting tomorrow we forget about everything we can't fix. You let me focus on swooning you for the next five months. We concentrate our energy on this little one who needs a name, a nursery, and love."

"Just like that?" she asks, skeptical.

"It's pretty simple," I conclude, brushing my thumb along her bottom lip. "Choose being happy. I'll take care of everything. It's not easy to let go, but let me carry your worries and take care of my girls. Can you please trust me?"

She nods. "How do you make everything less daunting, or is it more manageable?"

"It's a gift," I tell her, kissing her eyelids. "Let's get some sleep. We're spending the weekend with your family. It's going to be hectic."

"Thank you," she whispers.

I wait until she falls asleep before I mumble, "I love you, more than you can ever imagine."

FORTY

Nyx

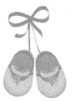

NOVEMBER WASN'T A PITY-FEST, as Persy likes to call that period. It wasn't nesting either, like Mom likes to believe. I was in a place where I felt like I couldn't see beyond the next minute. It's silly to say that I was scared of time, but every minute that passes is a minute closer to facing Edward and the nasty team of lawyers who are supporting his insane claim for custody.

A father who loves a kid would want to work something out with the mother of her child to guarantee her happiness. Fighting just for the sake of winning is spiteful. Persy and Ford have assured me that I can count on all of their assets. Nate though, he will surrender his entire fortune to keep her with us.

As promised, I stop retreating inside my head and let Nate take charge. This month hasn't been a fairy tale, but it's certainly close to it. However, this swooning business is something he's been doing all along. There's so much about him that I love. My favorite part about him is how much he loves my baby.

She adores him back because every time she hears his voice, she's kicking a storm. I can't wait to meet her and to hold her, but I'm pretty sure she's going to be the happiest in his arms. Time with him passes pretty fast, and before I can say Merry Christmas, we are already celebrating the New Year and waving at Persy and Ford who are going to Bora Bora for their honeymoon.

Seriously, wasn't the two-week stay in the Maldives enough?

Nate got us a two-bedroom suite because we're still in the *just friends* stage of our relationship. It's hard for some to understand, but with Edward trying to find an excuse to label me as an unfit mother, we want to keep this pretty PG, even when we share a few kisses that threaten to become only for mature audiences.

It's getting harder and harder to stop them. My hormones keep me horny all day long, but I don't act upon my lust. Someone should hand me a trophy, a medal, or some award. I should be part of the Guinness World Records for the most self-controlled hormonal woman living with a hot as fuck male.

"Have you ever imagined spending New Year's Eve like this?" I ask Nate as we watch the fireworks from the veranda of the suite on a swinging cabana.

Like almost every night, my head rests on top of his chest, his hands are on top of my bump, and we are watching the sky. This time there's more than constellations. It's an entire show celebrating that the new year is about to start.

"With a beautiful woman in paradise?"

"As if," I roll my eyes.

"You know what I think is ironic?" he asks.

"That my sister went on a honeymoon to another resort?"

"I don't see the irony in that. That's nonsense. Unless...they wanted to get rid of us," he laughs. "Then that's plain genius."

"You want to get rid of me?"

"No, but if this was our honeymoon, I wouldn't want to have your entire family around," he says, kissing my shoulder.

"So, what's the irony then?" I ask, shivering.

"That we're on a romantic getaway, and I'm still subscribing to your friend zone propaganda," he says. "To answer your previous question, no, I never imagined spending this night like this."

"What does that mean?"

"I wish I could say, 'my wife and my baby' but I don't have anything..." his fingers twirl my hair. His slow exhale carries longing and probably frustration. "Still, I'm happy with the company."

"A part of me thinks that we should have the talk. The one where I thank you for everything you've done and I move into an apartment," I turn my body to face him. His beautiful eyes are a bit darker than usual. "This roommate arrangement cramps your style."

"What does the other part think?"

I shake my head.

"Listen to whatever part that tells you to stay with me," he pulls me closer to him and kisses my forehead. "Being with you is all that matters to me."

He moves his head slightly. His mouth captures mine. This isn't a chaste kiss. It's Nate devouring me. I should stop him. Remind myself why we can't act on our feelings. But it's impossible to use my head when the man is nibbling my bottom lip. Sliding his tongue inside my mouth, tangling with mine, and making love to it the same way I want him to make love to me.

My hand goes to his head. My fingers comb through his thick hair.

His mouth moves to my neck, or maybe I'm pushing his head down, wanting his mouth all over my body, placing wet, hot kisses.

I've never wanted anything more than this...

I want...him.

"We have to stop," he says between shallow breaths. "I want this more than you can imagine, but not while things are too complicated."

He kisses my nose. "When this happens, it's because we can be committed to each other. Because once I have you, I won't be able to pretend that I don't need you—that I can't live without you by my side."

I'm frustrated with him, with myself, with the entire situation. Before I can get truly upset, the baby kicks, reminding me that there's someone who is our number one priority.

This could be a great moment to say, "Your life would be easier without us." I just don't have the heart to let him go anymore, because he owns my heart.

He kisses my cheek and goes inside the suite. When he comes outside, he hands me a gift.

"Christmas was a week ago," I joke, staring at the small present laying on my palm.

He rolls his eyes. "You have to get used to the fact that I like to shower you with presents."

My heart is all mushy because of this man. He keeps sending me flowers, bringing me ice cream, or just gifting me little things because he thought of me.

Meticulously, I unwrap the box and inside is a gold chain with a rattle charm in the shape of a heart that has a tiny blue stone that is almost the shade of his eyes. I frown and look at him.

"Well, the baby rattle is obvious, and the other is...me," he shrugs. "I want you to have something that symbolizes the three of us. Maybe someday we'll add to it when we have more kids. If you want more, that is."

I want to remind him that we shouldn't be having these kinds of discussions where we teeter around the edge of our feelings, that we have to keep everything inside. Pretending that I don't adore this man is becoming more and more difficult.

"This...you and me—"

He places his index finger on my mouth and shakes his head. "No, I can't hear anything remotely nice or I'll break my promise, and that might fuck the future of our baby."

He tilts his head toward the bedroom. "Come on. Time for bed."

"You're sending me to my room, aren't you?"

"I'm not a saint, and I'm running in self-control fumes," he confirms, giving me a chaste kiss on the lips.

My hands curl around his biceps. I stop him because I'm not ready to let him go just yet. He looks down at me and I realize that I've never wanted anyone, or anything, more than I want this and us. It's nearly painful, but he's right. It'd be a billion times worse if we lose our baby. It's weird to go from never stopping to realizing that there's more in life than work and a career.

To finally be in love with someone. To finally enjoy the sunrise, the sunset, and life without worrying about reaching for the goals I keep raising.

"Sweet dreams, beautiful," he whispers as he bends down to kiss my cheek and then leaves.

FORTY-ONE

Nate

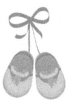

THROUGHOUT JANUARY, Ford is in Seattle most of the time. We're launching a new product in February. Persy comes along, and other than Simone, her cat, and Brock learning to get along, the visit is pleasant. Unfortunately, the next month I have to be in New York most of the time—and Ford too.

Leaving Nyx in Seattle doesn't sit well, but she can't fly during her third trimester. I call her at least twice a day, and we text all day long. I hate that I am home only on the weekends, but I'm making sure that when our blueberry is born, I can be in Seattle one hundred percent of the time.

One night, while we're on FaceTime, she says, "You must be tired of dealing with all this."

"Of not being with you every day?" I ask. "Yes."

"No, of having to fly every week and..." she shakes her head. "Do you miss Brock?"

"Not as much as I miss you, and before you offer to let me take him, I have to remind you that he chose to stay with you."

She smiles. "I think he chose to stay with the blueberry demon."

"Seven more weeks to go before we meet her," I remind her, trying to keep our conversation upbeat. "Are we going to choose a name soon?"

"I was thinking of Verity," she suggests.

"No," I answer. "Verity...is it going to be Verity Brassard, no middle name?"

It's on the tip of my tongue to ask her if she would allow her to be Baby Chadwick. I want her to be mine too.

"What's up with that frown?"

She shakes her head.

"Nyx?"

She's playing with pendant I gave her on New Year's Day. It's become a habit of hers to play with it when she's anxious.

"Is it wrong to want her to be Chadwick...but then I panic when the answer is that she will most likely have to be a Bryant too," she mumbles, and I wish I was there with her.

"We promised we wouldn't think about it."

Her eyes look up at me and they start watering. "I can't lose her."

"We're not losing her, Nyx," I assure her, but fuck if this isn't killing me because I don't even know if I'm just lying to myself.

All I know is that I can't lose another kid. And I can't stand thinking what's going to happen to Nyx if we do. "But she'll stop talking to you if you continue picking shitty names for her. Now, if you allow her to be a Chadwick, I'd be honored."

"What was your grandma's name?" she whispers, and fuck if she's not losing her strength today.

"Gladys, and as much as I love her, I won't let you name our baby that."

She smiles.

"What?"

"I really wish you were..." her voice trails.

Her dad. She doesn't finish the sentence.

"If you allow me, I'll be the best Dad she'll ever have," I promise.

Fucking Edward. If Pierce hadn't stopped me, I would've been at his office breaking every bone in his body. The guy is a fucking weasel. We could drag his ass to jail. I have to be careful and patient. In the meantime, he's breaking Nyx. Not because she can't fight, but because he's using the baby to get to her.

Around midnight, she falls asleep. I keep the phone on because that's the only way I can be with her.

THE WEEKS GO by too fast and not fast enough.

On her thirty-sixth week, I am officially working from home. The doctor says the baby can be born any day starting the thirty-eighth week, but with the blueberry demon, one can't be sure. She does whatever she wants.

Edward's lawyer requested the judge make Nyx surrender the baby when she's born. Fortunately, the judge shut him down, telling him that if he wants to see his child he has to travel to Washington. If he wants visitations, he needs to have a place here. Also, he can't have her visit him at his address when she's dependent on her mother. We start to panic when he arrives at my house, demanding to see the baby —who hasn't been born. He is buying a property in the area, plus his lawyer is submitting new documentation that would try to prove Nyx isn't suited to raise the baby.

"Thirty-eight weeks, two days and I have to be at an emergency hearing," Nyx complains staring at her swollen belly.

On a Monday morning we are in a conference room with the

family judge, Edward, his lawyer, who happens to be Sarah Bryant, Pierce, who represents Nyx, and Nyx too.

"Pierce, I wasn't told you'd be here," Sarah glares at him.

"I want to make sure this doesn't go on for much longer, Mother," he answers and then looks at Edward. "I hope this was worth the effort."

"It is, Son," she assures him.

"That's his mother?" I ask, almost wanting to slice the tension between them with a knife. "Talk about family drama."

Nyx sighs. "You have no idea."

A couple of people enter the room at Pierce's request and then he asks us to leave.

"I need to stay," Nyx insists.

"Trust me." Pierce waves his hand toward the door. "I rather you just get good news once I'm done with them."

We walk out and stand outside the room.

"What do you think is happening in there?" I ask.

"Honestly, I don't know. Pierce has been having a lot of issues with his family, and shutting down their firm is one of his goals. Now, we're in a different state so I don't know what he is trying to do."

"The baby isn't born yet. Can they even claim custody?"

She shakes her head. "I don't know what proof they have against me," she answers, her hands are trembling. "But they are good at tampering with evidence—"

"Hey, we need to calm down," I say. "Deep breaths."

She does some breathing exercises while rubbing her back.

"Are you okay? You keep touching your lower back."

"I've been having these weird cramps since last night," she announces.

"Contractions?" I ask.

"No. Haven't you watched movies and TV? Women yell when they have contractions. I'm having these small spasms and my lower back bothers me when it happens."

She makes that sound again, the one that she's been making since breakfast and then touches her back. I time her, and there's just a minute between each episode.

"You're having the baby," I declare.

"No, I'd know," she insists.

"Humor me, please," I beg her.

"There's no pain, my water hasn't broken, and it's not time," she swears.

"Just let a doctor confirm that I'm wrong," I beg her.

"I need to know what's happening in there. This baby can't be born until I know he can't take her away from me."

"He won't, I swear, but let's go."

"What if they snatch her from my side."

"Can you trust me?" I beg her.

I'm not sure what I'm promising because other than kidnapping the baby and hiding somewhere in the Caribbean, there's not much I can do according to the fucking legal system.

FORTY-TWO

Nate

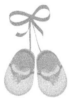

MY HEART POUNDS FASTER the closer we get to the hospital. I've heard those funny stories where the husband has to stop and help the wife deliver the baby. Every time I hear that shallow moan Nyx makes, I push the gas pedal.

We arrive at the hospital within twenty-five minutes. I text Ford as we head to the maternity ward. Nyx's family is in town. They're staying at an Airbnb close to downtown. I'm not sure if I need them, but I know Nyx wants them close by. I've done this before, going to the delivery room. But this feels different. When the doctor says she's almost ten centimeters dilated and we just arrived in time, I almost say I told you so, but instead, I say, "We're about to meet her."

"You won't let anyone take her, will you?"

"Nope. I'll be right by her side," I swear.

She's connected to several monitors. One of them measures her contractions. They have to break her water. The doctor explains that not every pregnancy or delivery is the same. Women are different. The average is what everyone hears, twenty-four hours of pain, water breaking dramatically, and the mother screaming bloody murder. Some are just serene, like Nyx's.

When she has the next contraction, the doctor says, "Okay, they are now spaced pretty close to each other. I think it's time to push. Are you ready?"

"Yes, you are," I whisper, kissing her temple.

I'm holding her, watching the doctor as she's coaching Nyx to push and breathe.

"The head is out," the doctor announces, and I take a look at the squishy little face. With a second push comes the rest of the baby, and I'm asked to cut the umbilical cord.

I don't think twice. I just do it with the tool they hand me and take the most beautiful girl in my arms. She cries, but when I say, "You're safe, my little love," she sniffs, and I swear looks at me as if she knows exactly who I am.

"Let's meet Mama," I tell her, handing her to Nyx who is sobbing.

"I love you, pumpkin," she whispers. "I'm Mom."

I kiss her forehead and then brush her lips. "You did amazing."

The nurse takes the baby to clean her and another one puts bracelets on Nyx and myself. I watch our little girl closely. While they take them to their room, Ford texts me.

Ford: *Security is on the premises. We're on our way.*

Until I have a signed order by the judge, Edward won't get close to my baby girl. He might have donated his sperm, but he has nothing to do with her. The only reason he's been fighting Nyx is just to fuck with her.

I grab the little pink bundle from the plastic crib and hand it to Nyx. "We still don't have a name."

"Livia?" she asks and shakes her head.

"Mairi?" I suggest.

"Nivia?" Nyx counteracts and scrunches her nose.

"Nova," I offer.

"I was thinking Wylder. It goes with Chadwick," she says.

"Leave Wylder for our boy," I respond.

She chews on her lip. "We..."

"We will talk when the storm ends. I can feel that's about to be over," I say calmly. "We've been through a lot, but we survived, haven't we?"

She nods. I brush her hair and kiss her lips. "You're the most beautiful woman in the world."

"Flattery won't get you far with me, Mr. Chadwick."

"Good, because I never want to be far away from you," I assure her.

Persy and Eros are the first to arrive. Edna and Octavio were on their way to Orca island and won't be able to get back to Seattle for a couple of hours.

"She's so beautiful," Persy whimpers. "I want one."

"You make cute kids, Andromeda," Eros declares, smiling at my baby. Then he looks at me and asks, "What's happening with the asshole?"

I shrug. "We had to leave the *emergency hearing* since the little one decided it was time to arrive."

"I told you she was a Monday baby," Nyx protests. "She's never going to let me sleep."

"Do we have a name yet?" Persy asks curiously.

Pierce enters the room and looks at Nyx shaking his head. "She's just like you. She couldn't wait for a couple more hours, could she?"

Nyx shrugs.

"What happened?" I ask, because I need to make sure that this is the happiest day of Nyx's life.

He smiles and hands Nyx a folder, glancing at my baby who is now with Eros. "Edward relinquished his parental rights."

"What happened to him?" I ask, wanting to know if he's going to come back. I know that those papers assure me that he can't do anything, but what if he still wants to fuck with us?

"Well, my cousin is going to spend a few years in jail. Fraud, embezzlement, bribing judges...the list is long. They are transferring him to Colorado. Mom lost her license. The rest will happen at home where the prosecution is ready to take down a few judges and law firms."

"Just like that?" Nyx asks.

He nods. "We've been investigating them. I happened to find the last piece of the puzzle last week. This was going to be handled differently, but...they chose the hard way."

"So, what now?" she asks.

"You're officially on maternity leave," he states. "I'm heading back home because I can only use so many days away from the hell hole before I get everyone in trouble. You three are about to start something new and wonderful. Enjoy it."

He leaves and Nyx glances at our little girl. "Can I have her back?" she requests.

I take her from Eros, place her in her arms, and kiss them both.

"What are you thinking?" I ask, hoping she found the name.

"New," she repeats.

"You're not calling her New," Eros protests. "That's worse than Apple, Blue, or Bear."

"Nova Gladys Brassard-Chadwick," she says the name while looking at her. We know that the last name won't happen until I officially adopt her, but I hope we can file for that soon.

"I think it fits her," I say, staring at the most beautiful baby I've ever seen.

My baby.

"Nova?" Persy asks.

"That's new in Latin. It also means brightness," Nyx mentions, looking at our baby with so much love she's about to burst like a supernova.

"You're calling her after Grandma?" Ford asks when he enters the room. He looks at the baby and smiles. "She's adorable. I think Gladys would have adored her first great-grandchild."

"I want one," Persy tells him.

"We can try to grab one from the other rooms or wait until we make one. Your choice," he answers and gets closer to the bed extending his arms. "May I? I just washed my hands. I swear."

When he takes the baby in his arms, he looks at me and says, "You did good, kid. Little Nova is safe with her family."

IT'S AROUND six when we're finally alone, but a last visitor arrives.

"Hey, can I come in?" The female voice is a lot similar to Persy and Nyx's but with a little squeak to it.

When I look up, I see Callie, Nyx's baby sister. She's been gone for almost a year. Ford and I have been keeping an eye on her. We visited Boston last November to convince her to attend Persy's wedding. She refused, but we hoped that she'd visit when Nova arrived. Ford called her after I texted him. We had everything set up for the trip in case she agreed.

Nyx looks up and smiles. "Callie."

"I heard you were having someone new to boss around and I thought, hmm, it'd be a good idea to warn her about you," Callie answers and smiles. "You're a mom."

"Come on in," I prompt her and get closer to her, showing her Nova. "Nova, meet your Aunt Callie."

"She's so tiny," Callie whispers. "Beautiful, like her mom."

"How are you?" Nyx asks.

"I'm fine," she answers. "I'm sure you know since these guys happened to find me easily."

"We just wanted to make sure that you're okay," I announce. "For your family's sake. I know it's hard to understand, but they worry about you."

"It's all good, I promise. I just have to do my thing," she claims. "Don't take it personally. Well, it was a little personal, but now that

I've been doing things on my own, I understand that I needed to step away from you guys to appreciate you."

"Mom and Dad would love to see you," Nyx says, giving her a sad smile. "If you're not ready, at least send them a text."

Callie nods. "I promise that I'll contact you guys more often. I'm staying for a couple of days. I'll try to visit again before I leave if that's okay with you."

"Always," she answers.

Once Callie is gone, Nyx thanks me.

"There's nothing to thank me for," I claim. "I only want to see you happy. Listen, I know you can make your own future and that you don't need me to fix your life. But being here, making things happen for you, that is what makes me happy."

I take a deep breath and say it because I have been swallowing the words for months. "I love you. I not just love you, but every night I fall in love with you even more. No matter if I'm next to you or if I'm on the other side of the phone, just talking with you reminds me how amazing you are and how I enjoy your presence. How I can't live without you. These have been the best thirty-five weeks of my life."

I take her hand and trace the words we tattooed a few months ago and say, "I choose you to be my life. You and Nova. I promise to love the fuck out of you. To love you fully without conditions. I don't know how tomorrow will look, what will happen in a week, or what the world is going to look like in ten years. All I know is that whatever happens, I can take it as long as you two are in my life."

"Can I tell you a secret?" Nyx whispers.

I nod.

"Come closer," she whispers again.

"What's the secret?"

"I think I started falling in love with you since the first time we met," she confesses. "But that's not the real secret."

"What is it?"

"You've been the one keeping me sane for the past thirty-some weeks. I felt as if some outside force kept picking me apart and destroying the life I had structured so carefully. While I mended myself into something different, there you were. I don't know where I'd be without your voice, your heartbeat, and your hugs. I think that's all I need to survive," she says. "I am okay if we don't know our destination as long as we're holding hands along the way."

She kisses Nova's head and then me. "I didn't expect you, but you guys are what I've been missing all along."

It's true what they say, the right life is never the one that we planned. My life is here—with my girls.

Epilogue

Nate

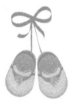

NYX and the baby stay in the hospital for one day. Even though Nova has her nursery, when they come home, Nyx and the baby stay in the master bedroom. It's big enough to fit a changing table, the bassinet, and a rocking chair. I'm staying in one of the other bedrooms temporarily. At least until we can get a few more hours of sleep and talk about our situation.

The Brassards stay in town for a month in the rental. Since having a newborn is overwhelming, her family limits their visits to only two people at a time. I had no idea how thoughtful they were until they came up with this plan. Octavio and Edna weren't kidding when they said they'd retire as soon as the baby was born.

They did, and now they are free to travel again and come to visit Nova anytime they want to—when they aren't doing research on their next book. That's their new plan, writing books while visiting places they couldn't while their children were young. Not that they limit themselves that much.

Once Nova is old enough, I want to start traveling with my girls. My girls. I can't wait to adopt Nova, or for Nyx to be my wife. But I am waiting for just the right moment to propose. For now, we're just focused on the baby who needs a lot of attention.

Nyx and I fall into a routine where I wake up at night to change Nova's diaper, Nyx feeds her, and then I pat her back as I soothe her to sleep. That time I spend with my baby girl is precious.

Our baby is now seven weeks old. This little demon likes to wake up several times during the night and sleep throughout the day. We're not surprised at all. While I'm rocking and singing to her, I notice Nyx watching me. She stands by the door holding a glass of water.

"Like what you see?"

"Love who I see," she corrects me, setting the glass on top of the dresser. "Both of you."

"We love you back," I respond, looking down at the already sleeping baby. Praying that she stays like that for at least a couple of hours.

"I never thought I could love so much," she continues. "I...I was afraid that you wouldn't care for her and now... Looking at you two together makes me want to have more babies with you."

"Marry me," I ask.

"Still making those plans to propose, Mr. Chadwick?" She grins because I keep asking about her dream proposal.

I want to make it special. There's a ring in the nightstand drawer waiting for her, but I can't find just the right moment.

"Obviously," I answer as I set our sleepy girl on her bassinet, ensuring that she's safe.

"I think you've told me that you can't plan the best moments of your life," she argues, and fuck. She is right.

"Well, this time is different," I say, reaching for the box that's been tucked in for too long. Then I walk to where she stands.

"Different?" she asks as I bend on one knee and smile at her.

"Well, I decided to stop asking you because clearly you don't have a preference. And the best moment won't be while we're in an air balloon or on top or the Eiffel tower. It'll be when you say 'yes.' So, this time, I am not only asking you to marry me. I am handing you my heart, for always. This is a promise that I'll love you for eternity if you accept to be mine. I swear that I'll hold you when things seem to be crumbling around you. I compromise on having sex only twice a day during weekdays. Weekends...well, that is a different story."

She smiles. "God, you're proposing, and we haven't even..."

"That should tell you how much I love you, Nyx. I'm a patient man, also demanding," I say and I'm not sure if it's a promise, a warning, or just a fact. "We've done everything backwards, and it has worked for us. I would love for you to be my wife, but if you—"

"I love you more than you can imagine. Of course, I'd love to be your wife," she agrees.

Standing up, I cup her delicate face between my hands and brush her lips with mine.

"I'm going to kiss you," I warn her. "This time I'm not going to censor myself. This is going to be better than the first kiss we shared. But it'll feel like the last we'll ever have. It'll feel as if I'm trying to fill my lungs with the oxygen your blood carries. As if I'm trying to fuse us."

"Please," she whispers.

As we kiss, I let our souls entwine. The gentleness of the kiss only lasts for a few beats before her wild side takes over. She's a cyclone. She's the most powerful storm.

This kiss is full of fire that spreads through us. I lift Nyx and carry her to the bed where I set her down. The night light we have for Nova's routine lets me see her features. She's breathtakingly gorgeous, and in this moment, I realize that I want more than just make her mine. I want to surrender myself to her.

I move closer, settling myself on top of her. Our eyes meet, our noses almost touch, and I can feel her warm breath against mine.

"I love you, Nate," she whispers.

Instead of mirroring her words, I kiss her.

Slowly.

Tenderly.

Lovingly.

I want for us to savor every second of this first time. Like a slow dance under the moonlight. My mouth moves down to her neck as I strip her from the oversized t-shirt she's wearing. I love that she wears my clothes when she goes to bed. I love that she's about to be mine. Most of all, I love that she loves me back.

My hands slide under the waistband of her boxers and push the fabric down. This is finally it, and I'm not even sure where to start because there are so many things that I want to do to her. This is when everything that's happened in my life before differs from this moment. Because all I can focus on is being inside her. Finally become one with her.

If I have any doubt about what I should do, Nyx erases it when she says, "I need you. No foreplay, no games. Just you."

I quickly reach for the condoms I have in my nightstand, open one of them, and roll it on.

Placing my hands on each side of her face, we lock gazes. I want to see her as I slide my way inside her.

"Nate," she whispers as I thrust slowly pushing myself deep, deep almost reaching her soul.

This, what we're doing tonight, isn't just sex. It's loving all of her for the first time. Allowing ourselves to finally accept that we have become the beginning and the end of each other. Finally accepting that perhaps we hadn't loved anyone fully because we were waiting for each other.

I don't miss jumping from a plane or searching for my next fill of adrenaline. My life is finally fulfilled by this woman and our beautiful baby.

She might think that I was here for her, but since I met her, her wind blew me to a place where I could find peace, set the pieces of my heart back together, and discover who I belong to.

She is worth every sleepless night. Every tear, heartache, and scrape we endure together. Because after everything, I found my happiness, and I found them.

FIFTEEN MONTHS LATER...

"It's hot as hell. I'm willingly wearing a suit. I swear, this better be good," Eros complains.

"His weddings suck," Ford mumbles. "During the last one, the bride said the wrong name."

"Thank you for keeping this real, you useless assholes," I grunt. "Now shut up and smile."

I adore Nyx, but this wedding in Costa Rica, where it feels like a hundred degrees, wasn't one of her best decisions. She wanted to celebrate the first milestone of Eros' company too. Plus, this is one of her favorite places in the world. Was it necessary? Not really. We've been married for a year. After I proposed to her, we went down to Baker's Creek so Pierce could marry us—Nyx's family was there too. And I also filed for adoption so Nova could be officially mine.

This ceremony is to fulfill a wish that Nyx didn't know she had until Persy's wedding, and I'm happy to make it happen.

When the music starts, I look to the end of the aisle. Holding a small basket and dropping petals is Nova. More like she's just holding the basket and smiling at me. Next to her is Brock. Of course, the one guiding them is Demetri, who holds Nova's hand. Even though she's been walking for a couple of months, she still needs a little help sometimes.

Demetri deserves some honorable mention. He does anything and everything for Nova. Like everyone who meets my little princess, she has him wrapped around her little finger. When Nyx was trying to figure out how to make this work, D volunteered to help.

As Nova approaches, I squat and open my arms. She comes waddling toward me.

"Daddy!"

"You did wonderful, sweetheart," I assure her.

She hugs my neck and gives me a sloppy kiss. The music changes tempo and the maids of honor walk in a line. Then, I spot her, Nyx. She is walking with Octavio, laughing until she spots me, and her gaze is filled with love.

"Mama" Nova points at her.

"Let's wait until she reaches us," I tell her, and she nods and waits patiently.

When Nyx arrives, she hugs Nova and kisses me. "Go with Grandpa, baby."

"Papa Tabo," she says, going with my father-in-law.

"You look beautiful," I whisper, kissing the back of her neck.

"You don't look that bad, handsome," she answers.

"Ready?"

"With you by my side, always," she says, giving me a small kiss before the ceremony begins. "I love you, my wicked man."

Dear Reader,

Thank you so much for picking up a copy of Didn't Expect You. I am so grateful to have you as my reader and if you are new to me, I hope this is the beginning of our journey together.

This book wasn't part of my 2020 schedule but the Brassard sisters (Persy and Nyx) were a great way to push away the stress that this year has created. I needed to have fun, think light romantic, and possible.

Writing this Single-Mom-to-be meets wicked playboy was a lot of fun for me. It has a mix of humor, angst, and a few real-life details. A couple of friend's had babies with minimum pain (I envy them a little). While a really good friend of mine had an experience similar to Nyx's. She has a beautiful ten-year-old daughter, and a wonderful family now.

When I sit down to pen these stories, I'm inspired by the strong women I've met who overcome the obstacles that are thrown their way. I'm truly thankful to have met them and that they let me stich a few pieces of their life into the tapestry of my stories.

If you haven't read Persy and Ford's story and would like to follow their journey, you can grab a copy of Wrong Text, Right Love.

Now, for those who have asked about Eros, his story releases early next year.

Love Like Her is a romantic comedy I've been meaning to write for a couple of years but hadn't found the right characters until now.

One last thing, if you loved Didn't Expect You as much as I do, please leave a review on your favorite retailer and on Bookbub. Also, please spread the word about it among your friends.

Sending all my love,
Claudia xoxo

Acknowledgments

There are two things that are super hard for me when I write a book, making sure that I don't forget anyone because it's always important to be grateful to our people. The second thing is blurbs. Which brings me to thank you to Megan Linski for always helping me with titles and blurbs.

She always helps me find just the right one for my books. Also, Heather Roberts who polishes them once they are ready.

Hang Le, my longtime cover artist. She's amazing at making my books look beautiful.

Darlene, Karen, Melissa, Patricia, and Yolanda for always responding to my incoherent questions. Their feedback is important just like their friendship.

To all my readers, I'm so grateful for you. Thank you so much for your love, your kindness, and your support. It's because of you that I can continue doing what I do.

It's never enough to say thank you to my BFFL Kristi. She's been walking with me through this journey for almost five years and I'm thankful for always stepping onto any role. She's my person.

My amazing ARC team, girls you are an essential part of my

team. Thank you for always being there for me. My Bookstagrammers, you rock!

To my Chicas! Thank you so much for your continuous support and for being there for me every day!

Thank you to all the bloggers who help me spread the word about my books. Thank you never cuts it just right, but I hope it's enough.

Thank you to my husband, my children and my family for supporting me in this journey.

Most importantly, thank you to God because he's the one who allows me to be here and who gifts me the time, the creativity, and the tools to do what I love. Thank you for all the blessings in my life.

Thank you for everything.

All my love,

Claudia xoxo

About the Author

Claudia is an award-winning, *USA Today* bestselling author. She writes alluring, thrilling stories about complicated women and the men who take their breath away. She lives in Denver, Colorado with her husband and her youngest two children. She has a sweet Bichon, Macey, who thinks she's the ruler of the house. She's only partially right. When Claudia is not writing, you can find her reading, knitting, or just hanging out with her family. At night, she likes to binge-watch shows with her equally geeky husband.

To find more about Claudia:
www.claudiayburgoa.com
Sign up for her newsletter: News Letter

CPSIA information can be obtained
at www.ICGtesting.com
Printed in the USA
LVHW050355210621
690710LV00010B/1244